keeper

of the

bees

Also by Meg Kassel

BLACK BIRD OF THE GALLOWS
CLEANER OF BONES

keeper

of the

bees

MEG KASSEL

Entangled Publishing, LLC
2614 South Timberline Road
Suite 105, PMB 159
Fort Collins, CO 80525
rights@entangledpublishing.com

Entangled Teen is an imprint of Entangled Publishing, LLC.

Visit our website at www.entangledpublishing.com.

Edited by Liz Pelletier
Cover design by Deranged Doctor Design
Interior design by Toni Kerr
Cover images by
luchioly/shutterstock
EMstudio/shutterstock
Yellow Stocking/shutterstock
NottomanV1/shutterstock
kritiya/depositphotos

ISBN 978-1-64063-408-4
Ebook ISBN 978-1-64063-406-0

Manufactured in the United States of America

First Edition September 2018

10 9 8 7 6 5 4 3 2 1

an imprint of Entangled Publishing LLC

For Pete, who I'd marry again.

Dresden

the
target

I can't tell you how many cities, towns, villages I have passed through. I stopped caring about their names long ago.

I *can* tell you that this town is flat and dusty and utterly uninteresting. It's somewhere in the Midwest, surrounded by miles of farmland. It's a mystery why people live here, although most of the places I visit are worse. Not that it matters.

This town is marked.

Harbingers of death have chosen to settle here for a time, which means in less than a month a good number of residents will be dead, and I will have moved on.

The park I walk through is thickly wooded, divided by winding footpaths. The trees offer shade from the blazing summer sun, but no one is here. They are all indoors, bodies by their air-conditioner vents, eyes on their televisions, and minds on absolutely nothing at all. I suppose I am fortunate that I don't feel the heat.

Or the cold. Or anything. Yes. So terribly fortunate.

I keep a slow pace, waiting for the sense, the *knowing* that a dark, unsettled person is nearby. Inside my chest, a hive of bees roils, restless with their long confinement. *Soon*, I think to them. *Very soon*. The bees can read my emotions well. They should, considering how long we've been bound together. We've grown ancient, the bees and I—unchanging relics of an era long erased from history.

Finally, I sense it, a prickling on the skin and a sharpening of my senses. A familiar surge of anticipation quickens my breath. There is a person nearby who interests my bees. I can feel my target as a human can feel the rain on their face. I walk faster. The bees hum louder. They pile into my sinuses, clog my throat. I pull in a great, sharp breath, sending them tumbling back into my chest.

Control yourselves! my thoughts snarl, not that the bees understand the exact words. Not that they would care if they could.

I find myself in a well-tended, perfectly square clearing. It's a playground, complete with slides, swings, and a colorful jungle gym. It's deserted except for a teenage girl. Pale hair hangs around her face, unbrushed. She sways idly in a swing, wearing jean shorts and a flimsy top. Her bare feet scratch up the dusty ground. She holds an animated conversation with her kneecaps.

I lean against one of the few trees lining this parched square of earth and watch her. She's different from the people my bees usually prefer, who are full of hatred and savagery and wrath. Their anger hits me like needles, blades. Sharp tacks driven deep.

This girl, however, does not have a dark mind. She looks to be around seventeen. Not much younger than I was, when I was human. Her energy is light, effervescent, and feels like bubbles popping all over my skin. She is as harmless as a broken doll. It's too bad for her that I encountered her now, when I am burning from the inside with the need to release my bees.

I don't have time to find another target.

She is alone. This would matter if I had the sort of face someone might try to describe to authorities, but I'm the closest thing to invisible. A shadow. An impression of a young man that the typical human mind turns away from before features can be registered. "Just a guy" is how I'm usually described. It's one of the brilliant details of the curse I'm saddled with. The curse of the beekeeper ensures that my face is rarely actually *seen*. It's certainly not a face anyone would *want* to see.

One determined bee crawls up my throat and into my nose. He sits in my left nostril, waiting to be released. Brazen little bastard. Fine, I'll let that one go, then.

The young woman stops swinging. Her head tilts up, and her gaze locks on me. She spots me, finally.

I pause, bee hanging on my nostril like a buzzing nose ring.

Wait. I inhale sharply, dragging the bee back inside my nose. It buzzes a noisy objection but holds still.

The young woman cocks her head to the side and stares at me. What she sees is anyone's guess. It could be the bland, nondescript countenance caught on photos, or the grotesque, shifting array of features that even I can't endure the sight of. More than likely, she's seeing something entirely of her own imagination.

Her mind works on a unique frequency, after all. I wouldn't have been drawn to her, otherwise.

She points at me. Her light blue eyes are incredulous. Her mouth, a circle of awe.

My chest constricts with the knowledge that she is *seeing* me. *Me.* My horrific face. And she's not screaming. She bursts into laughter, and I start with surprise. It's a high, fractured sound. Poor girl. She'll feel the bee sting but won't realize her last shreds of sanity are gone until she's fallen over the edge. And maybe not even then.

She *sees* me. How unusual. It's a spark of something interesting in my unvarying, monotone life. I push off from the tree and walk toward her.

I'm curious. How close can I get before she screams?

She continues to stare at me, even when I stop right in front of her. Pale eyes gaze up, fearless, fascinated.

I watch her reach into her pocket and pull out a plastic baggie with tiny balls inside. She extracts one and pops it in her mouth. Drugs, I assume. For reasons unknown, I'm pinched with disappointment. But then, she crunches the thing between her teeth, and the air between us bursts with the bright smell of pepper. Another surprise.

Her eyes water. She blinks rapidly, then frowns. "You're still here?"

"Apparently. Why are you chewing peppercorns?"

The girl shrugs. "I see things that aren't there. Pepper makes them go away long enough so I can tell what's real and what's not." She gives me an accusatory look. "*Most* of the time."

Fascinating or not, I should walk away. Now. "So you don't think I'm real?"

"How can you be?" She spits the chewed-up bits of peppercorn on the ground. "Your face changes like a kaleidoscope. Dr. Roberts would tell me that's not really real." She leans forward conspiratorially. "But you know what? Sometimes I think Dr. Roberts isn't real. Last week at our session, he had a forked tongue and he kept flicking it at me." She demonstrates with her first two fingers. "He wasn't happy when I pointed it out."

Good Lord, maybe stinging this girl will be a kindness. "In this case, your Dr. Roberts would be incorrect."

Her eyes go wide. "You're real?"

"I'm afraid so."

She smiles, shakes her head. "Of course you'd say that. No one wants to be someone else's delusion." She points at my face again. "Does it hurt when it changes like that?"

An odd question. "Yes, but not terribly."

"Can you make it stop?" she asks. "Can't you just pick one face?"

"No and no." For the life of me, I don't understand why I'm still standing here. Am I so desperate for conversation?

She cocks her head. "Which of those faces is yours?"

"None of them," I say with a twinge of…regret, maybe. An unnameable something, vicious and long repressed, twists my stomach. I angle my face, giving her a full view of my horrible features. Bees roar in my throat. I'm sure she can hear them. I'm taunting her, pushing. Trying to make her recoil in fear like she should. "They're the faces of all the people I've killed."

She raises one eyebrow, seemingly unimpressed. "Are you planning to kill *me?*"

I am a monster. A beast. Lying about it would be pointless. "Yes."

2

Essie

my pretty delusions

Oh, I like this boy. I *do*. I like his long bones and ragged voice and how he smells like fresh honey. I like his pretty, pretty face, with all those slowly shifting features. It's like poetry, like a thousand people are crammed inside him, each taking turns pushing through.

I like him despite what he said about him killing me.

Perhaps we can work on that. Or not. It hardly matters, because despite his claims, he's not-not-*not* real. I'm full of cracks right now, so I see things all over the place that aren't real. I know I'm on my way to an episode when hallucinations talk to me, and *most* of them want to kill me. They never do, though.

The boy emits a whirring hum, kind of like a blender. The sound comes from his chest. Is he even aware of it? I look up and give him my best smile. The one showing all my teeth. "My name is Essie. Essie Roane."

The eyebrows shift from bushy red to thick brown and draw fiercely together. "Why would you tell me that?"

"You should know the name of a person, if you want to kill them," I say. "But you *don't* want to hurt me, do you, silly boy?" I laugh, sending lovely pink bubbles floating out of my mouth. His gaze does not drop to the bubbles, and I fiercely remind myself that I'm the only one who sees them. I fish out another peppercorn, crunch it between my teeth. It's godawful, but the bubbles disappear. The boy with the shifting face remains.

A sad smile pulls at his lips. "You really are out of your mind."

"Oh yes." I nod emphatically. "No one ever lets me forget that."

"I'm Dresden," he says with a sigh. "You should know the name of a person, if they intend to kill you."

My heart races. I like his name, too. "Dresden like the German city?"

"No, not at all like the city."

"Oh. Okay anyway. You're terribly pretty, Dresden. I could stare at you all day long."

He blinks rapidly, then lets out a sound that is either choking or a laugh. I can't tell which. "You think I'm... *pretty?*" he asks.

"Of *course.*" Irritation sharpens my voice. "All those lovely faces, coming and going like slow waves of an ocean—not that I've *seen* the ocean in person." Or ever will. Concordia is my home, and I can't imagine I'll ever journey far from it. St. Louis is an hour by car, and the farthest I've traveled. "I wish you were real. Dr. Roberts tells me every week how the things that don't look like they belong in this world are *not* real. You definitely do not look like you belong in this world."

His faces darken. "I *don't* belong in this world."

A bee appears between his lips, just briefly, before he moves a hand over his mouth and takes a step back. He smooths a hand over his throat. When he looks at me again, he looks regretful. "It's the bees." He says it through closed teeth. "They want to hurt you. They're screaming to be released."

I look down, unreasonably flattered. "Thank you for holding them back."

"I won't be able to forever."

I reach for his hand, but he snatches his arm away. I try another smile, not so big this time. "There's no such thing as forever."

"Believe me, there is." He turns toward the path, tugging his baseball cap low over his face. "It was a pleasure, Essie," he says, surprising me with a formal bow. Then he walks quickly away and seems to disappear down the path. Gone. Just like that.

I launch out of the swing to follow but stop when I hear Aunt Bel calling my name. She's jogging up the path toward me, panting like a puppy.

"Es-Essie," she puffs. She stops, leans against a tree, and draws in deep breaths.

I hurry to her side, fan her cherry-red face with my hands. "Why are you running? Are you being chased by an animal?"

"No, of...course not." Her gaze moves to the path opposite her, the way Dresden left. "Who...who was that boy?"

I stagger back a pace. "What boy?" There's no way. He's not real.

Impatience flashes in her eyes. "That *boy*," she repeats. "I saw you talking to him. I didn't get a good look at his face, but he didn't remind me of anyone from town." Her eyes narrow to slits. "Did he try any funny business with you? Or try to sell you drugs?"

"No, he didn't. I thought…" My voice fades off. My skin goes clammy, despite the day's heat.

"You thought what?" my aunt asks.

"I thought he wasn't real."

"Oh, my sweet lamb." She huffs out a great breath and pulls me against her great, baby-powder-scented bosom. "My poor dear. Of course you'd think that. I saw him, though, so he must be real." A firm arm curls around my waist. She casts a hooded glance backward, then guides me from the playground. "Let's get you home. I shouldn't have left you alone to run my errands when I know you're not feeling right," she chastises herself. "You're a pretty girl, you know. You're going to attract boys who may not know of your condition. Some people are not good people."

My heart races. I can't stop blinking my eyes. *Aunt Bel saw Dresden.* So either Aunt Bel is seeing things too, or *he* is real. I don't think she is seeing things, which means he *is* real.

But he did things real people *can't* do.

Or maybe *Dresden* is real, but our conversation *wasn't.* Maybe he was asking me for something ordinary and innocent, like directions, and I was asking him whether or not he was there to kill me.

Confusion warps my mind like hot plastic. Sweat breaks out on my palms. I look down. The sweat turns black and oozes from the lines in my palm like streaming black ink. *No, no, no!* My breath hitches as the black stuff flows down the front of me and Aunt Bel. I whimper and tuck my fists under my armpits. We're leaving sloppy black footprints on the path.

Not real, not real, not real. I squeeze my eyes shut, but black stuff still flows down my sides, making my shorts stick to my legs. I can't unclench my fists to reach for my peppercorns. The differences between reality and the products of my inventive mind fall around me like a rain of tinkling glass. My vision narrows down to a distant point, then grays out entirely. I begin to hum a discordant, comforting tune and lean into Aunt Bel's softness.

"It's not him, it's the bees," I whisper urgently into Aunt Bel's ear. She's got to *understand.* "The bees are the ones who want to hurt me, not him. *Not him.*"

She shudders and pulls me closer. "It's okay, dear," she replies gently. "We'll get you home. Soon enough you'll be right as rain."

She says that often—that I'll be "right as rain," but I never am. I never will be.

Dresden

walmart

I leave Essie and head to the outskirts of town. I can move very quickly when motivated. I'm currently very motivated.

The bees are roiling in my head and chest with such vigor, it feels like they're burrowing through my innards. I don't blame them for their fury. I should have stung that girl. I don't know why I didn't. I *should* have, because now I'm sweating—I can't remember the last time my body perspired—and worse, I'm shaking like an addict. My limbs are heavy with fatigue. I'm tired. So miserably tired. I need to sting someone. Soon. The bees will take over if I don't.

They might even go back for the girl, Essie.

I wait until I'm far away in a secluded field to turn into my traveling self. It's a brief, snapping pain, then a feeling like the wind. Like I'm everywhere at once. My body breaks apart, transforms into thousands of tiny honey bees, and joins with the hive in residence under my rib cage. Together, we make one massive swarm. My thoughts are the collective. My intentions are no longer separate from the hive. It's not easy to explain, this merging. The bees and I are one. My consciousness still calls the shots, but *I* become *we*.

I can't imagine how terrifying it must look when I do this.

We speed out of the town, flying miles and miles alongside a highway to a small cluster of box stores and strip malls, and knot up near the rear loading area of a Walmart, where I'm likely to find a lot of people concentrated in a relatively small space. More people makes it more likely that I'll find a target for my bees. I find a secluded spot between two trucks and return to my human form. I'm wearing the same ball cap, gray shorts, and T-shirt I had on in the park. I don't get to choose my clothes, which are as generic as you can get. Garments appear on my body like another layer of skin, like camouflage. Their purpose is to make me to blend in. It's another thing the curse does for me. Another thing I stopped caring about.

I stroll into Walmart, head down, trembling hands tucked deep in pockets. I'm as average as average can be, and, as usual, no one looks at me. Not one person. The cameras see a person who doesn't look like anybody, just the shadowed, blurry face of a guy as generic as the clothes on his body. I know this because I've been in those stores with the cameras and monitors right where you walk in. The first time I entered one, I stood there marveling at my image for an inordinate amount of time. It was pleasant, seeing this bland mask the curse invented for the camera. Far more pleasant than my real reflection, which reveals the horrible truth of what I am.

It only takes until the frozen foods section before my senses pick up a target. It's a man, middle aged with a stoop that makes him look older than he is. He must have come here from his job, as the tie around his neck is tugged open. The energy he gives off is dark and saturated with an old, repressed hatred that's seeped into every bit of him. Maybe he was made this way by someone. Maybe he was just born with bad wiring. Either way, he's mine.

I don't hesitate this time. I open my mouth and release the bee waiting behind my teeth. It flies low and straight to the man, landing on the cuff of his pants. The man opens a freezer case and pulls out a handful of individually wrapped burritos.

I'm walking past him when the bee stings. The man curses, scrabbles for his ankle. Burritos scatter to the floor.

Relief is instant. My joints unclench. The bees ease their frantic beating. I'm not done, though. I need another target to fully appease the bees. I find one in electronics—a woman. She's shopping with a man and a beady-eyed teenage boy. The man snarls something at the woman, and the boy laughs. It's a cruel sound. The woman glances away. Something dark and calculated hangs in the whites of her eyes. Pent-up hatred, probably aimed more at herself than anyone else. I release a bee and watch it wind a meandering path to the woman. She may kill the man and the boy. She may just kill herself.

I feign interest in a DVD sale bin until the bee stings. It punctures the flesh of her wrist, but she barely reacts. She lazily brushes the dying bee to the floor and shuffles on behind her man and the boy. Soon, two more people's features will grace my horror show of a face.

At last, the bees rest. Strength seeps back into my limbs like a slow drip. The queen bee at the center of the hive, nestled below my breast bone, goes still and contented. For now, I let out a long breath and head for the exit.

I walk through the parking lot to the garden center. There are fewer cars there, on account of it being August and gardening being pretty much finished for the year. I lean against a pallet of mulch and gaze up at the sky. There isn't a cloud in sight. It's crystal-clear blue. The sun washes over my face, the exposed skin of my arms. I stare into the sun until its whiteness blocks out the blue. I think briefly of the people I stung today, but not with sentiment. The woman was awash in violent thoughts. She would have snapped without my sting. All I did was speed it along. The man has a little time left in him. He may last until the disaster destined to hit this community.

A threesome of crows alights on the edge of the store. The plastic mulch bags crinkle as a second body rests against them.

I don't look. I know who it is. "Hello, Michael."

I'm here, ultimately, because I followed this harbinger of death here. He and his kind have the talent of sensing where a terrible event is going to take place. All beekeepers follow them, and I am no exception. We feed off of fear, while harbingers feed on energy given off by the dying. It's all very symbiotic. All very horrible.

If any of us could find a way to *not* do this anymore, we would. We would happily die.

The harbinger of death squints at the sky, then looks away, rubbing his eyes. "How does that *not* destroy your eyes?"

"I'm a difficult thing to destroy."

"Hmm." He runs absent fingers over a puckered scar that runs from his elbow up his arm. If you could see it, you'd know it covers most of his back. Under his shirt, Michael is a mess—burns, bullet, and knife scars. But that's the way it goes for a harbinger. They get hurt like any human. I don't pity them, though. Their curse is still quite generous. They're not horrific to look at, like beekeepers are. *They* aren't compelled to send psychosis-inducing bees to sting people. *They* weren't tasked with the job of creating chaos.

"So, who'd you sting in there?"

I jerk my chin toward the tie-wearing man limping through the parking lot. "That one. He's got time. And there's a woman, but she'll go quick. A day. Maybe two."

Michael glances at the crows, then nods toward the man I indicated, who is fumbling with his keys and mumbling to himself. One of the crows swoops down and perches on the lamp closest to the man. It will follow him home and keep tabs on him.

"Will they take out others, do you think?" He can ask me this, because we're friends.

It's the only reason I answer. "It's likely."

Michael nods in his annoyingly good-natured way. "Okay. Thank you."

"Don't thank me." I say it more harshly than he deserves. "Don't ever thank me for it."

"I'm not thanking you for stinging people, dumbass. You know that." Michael rakes back his long hair. "You're on edge, even after releasing bees. What's going on with you?"

"Nothing."

He raises one tawny eyebrow. "I saw you with that girl."

His words slam into me. They're like a judgment, a conviction, even though it's absurd to think that way. Beekeepers don't answer to harbingers, and in fact my and Michael's friendship is a very rare thing. The only one between our two kinds that I know of.

It started on a whim during the Napoleonic Wars, some two hundred years ago. I'd been following Michael's group for only a few years when I found him lying on a Prussian battlefield, holding together his sliced-open abdomen with his hands. He was dying, of course, and I wanted to see what happened to a harbinger's body when it expired. I knew it transformed back into a crow, and after a few years the harbinger would once again be able to change between human and crow forms at will, but I'd never actually witnessed one of them die. So I sat in the blood-soaked field and talked with him until he passed.

It took longer than I'd anticipated. I ended up talking more than I should have, apparently, because after Michael regenerated, he declared us friends and has not ceased talking to me since. I denied the title of friend for nearly a century. In truth, I wasn't very pleasant to him, but Michael never relented. Eventually, I did. I'm still not very pleasant to him, but I'm a beekeeper. We're not very pleasant to anybody.

I was, however, unnaturally pleasant to that girl today, and I'm not happy that Michael witnessed it. "Your point?"

He shrugs. "She's pretty. Don't tell me you didn't notice."

"I didn't." *Truth*. "I don't notice those things."

Michael makes a scoffing noise. "Yeah, sure. You can't

tell me her looks didn't impact your choice to not send a bee to her."

"They didn't. The only thing I see about people is whether or not I can send a bee to them."

His light brown eyes brighten with interest. "Then why did you spare her?"

"She could see my true face."

"Really?" He turns to me, head cocked. "How did she react?"

My mouth curves at the memory. "She said I was pretty."

He laughs. "Well you can't sting *that* one, can you?"

My smile drops. "I certainly can. She chews peppercorns to sort out hallucinations from reality."

Michael shrugs. "So avoid her."

"Unlikely. This is very small town."

"How do you feel about stinging the one girl in the world who thinks your mug is pretty?" And this is why I hate Michael sometimes. His questions are unrelenting.

"This is not therapy, Michael." Bees whirl around my head, sensing that I'm unsettled. "We have an arrangement—I tell you who I sting so you can take their energy when they kill or die, and you let me follow your group to the disasters you sense. I don't need advice from a scavenger."

"This girl must have really twisted your panties." He clasps a hand over his chest, feigning hurt feelings. "You called me a scavenger, Dresden." He's fine. I know when I've hurt his feelings.

"You *are* a scavenger."

"What if I called you a hive mouth?"

I sigh and look back into the sun. I've done altogether

too much talking today. "Call me whatever you want, just don't tell me who to sting."

"All I'm saying is, it's clear your instincts are telling you not to sting her. Maybe you should listen to them. Especially if she can see your true face. That's very unusual." Michael scratches his slightly stubbled chin and nods toward someone crossing the parking lot. "Is that the woman? The one with the flowered skirt?"

"No." I shift my feet, feeling twitchy. "Why shouldn't I sting her? You're here because this town is going to be devastated. Which means the girl is likely going to die anyway."

"People survive disasters. Besides…" Michael pauses. He scans the parking lot, and his voice drops, as if he's concerned about being overheard. "There's talk that change is in the air."

Good Lord, here we go. Harbingers are such gossips. "What do your rumors have to do with me stinging that girl?"

His eyes flicker, crow like. For an instant his eyes go black, before fading to their normal pale gold. "Not *rumors*. Talk is the curses are changing. Possibly even weakening. That there may be ways to crack them. And if your gut is telling you something about that girl, think about trusting it."

I press my fingers to my own eyes. "Let's leave my gut out of this." I jab a finger toward the exit doors, right at a woman in black jeans. "That's the woman I stung."

Another crow alights from the wall, follows her.

Michael rolls his eyes. "You could be a bit more subtle."

"You could be a bit less idealistic." I point to my face. "See this? The curse is not changing. It isn't weakening."

"Fine. Do what you want." Michael throws up his hands. "I thought it might give you hope."

I am so far beyond hope, I don't even know the meaning of the word. At least harbingers can eventually find death. Granted, they have to be pecked to death by their own kind. Even then, their curse just gets dumped into some new, unfortunate, dying person. Still, there is an escape for them. There is nothing for me.

My queen senses my unease. She crawls around my lungs, restless. "I've been around a lot longer than you, my friend," I say quietly.

Michael eyes me, then nods. "Yes, you have. But I'll tell you, something's in the air. Something's...sour."

"Maybe it's your T-shirt."

He laughs.

The third and final crow on the roof swoops off and caws loudly at us.

"That's my cue." Michael ducks between the pallets of mulch, pretending to tie a shoe. "You reminded me save my clothes for me, will you, Dresden? I'm tired of abandoning perfectly good outfits every time I change."

"I'll drop them off at the motel you're staying at." I look away, knowing what's coming next.

The smell of smelting metal hits my nose, then a large, puffed crow stands in a puddle of clothing. Michael, in his bird form, blinks up at me with red-black eyes. The crow caws once and jumps up, into flight. I watch him disappear behind Walmart, then I slowly pick up the harbinger's clothing. "Nothing changes, you foolish scavenger."

But I wish it would.

4

Essie

the snake doctor

Dr. Roberts always sits too close. I can smell his cinnamon gum. His stinky aftershave.

"Miss Roane, please look at me." The voice is smooth as butter, cool as frost. "You know we aren't going to get anywhere if you refuse to speak to me."

I shift my gaze from the clock on the wall to Dr. Roberts, sitting in the chair opposite me. His tongue is forked again, unfortunately. I can't eat a peppercorn because I learned that trick from Grandma Edie and Dr. Roberts disapproves of Grandma Edie. Probably because she's not *his* patient.

"I'm not 'refusing,'" I say. "I just have nothing to say today."

"How can that be? You had quite an episode in the park two days ago." He glances at my file sitting open on the table next to him. "It started when a stranger approached you while your aunt was running an errand and you didn't know if he was real or imagined?"

It's not a question. He shouldn't say it like one.

And I *still* don't know how much of Dresden was real. Part of him obviously was, but my feelings about the encounter are so unsettled, I haven't allowed myself to think about it much.

"I'm fine now." I *am* fine. Once an episode passes, I get a stretch of time when my mind is calm. At least, I'm able to sort out reality from the visions, which are milder. Nevertheless, the amount of antipsychotics circulating through my body makes me feel like a hollowed-out tree.

He scoots forward another little bit, bumping his knee against mine. "If you are having difficulty recognizing a person as a real thing, then it's safe to say you are *not* fine."

I press back into the chair. "It was a mistake, clearly. The boy was…strange-looking."

Very strange-looking.

He removes and replaces his glasses for the twenty-third time during our session. He must not know what to do with his hands. "There are lots of strange-looking people in the world. It's a problem if you are unable to identify them as *people*."

Telling him about Dresden is not even a remote option. But I'd like to see Dr. Roberts take a look at Dresden and tell me he knows *for sure* what he's looking at.

"I'll do better next time."

Dr. Roberts flicks out his long, snake-like tongue. Ugh, it's so close. His eyes look hooded, too. I hope he doesn't grow fangs. "Estelle—*Essie*—it's not about doing better. It's about *being* better. It's about functioning in the world. I don't think you're able to do that right now."

Uh-oh. Here we go again.

"You father is concerned about you. He agrees Stanton

House might be the best place for you right now."

Stanton House. The institution where plenty of members of the Wickerton family line—my family—are sent when they become too much for their families to handle. The place was originally built in the early 1900s because my family produced too many people *not right in the head*, and not enough sane ones to care for them. Although it's a fine enough place—not some cold institution, but a home with a well-trained staff—many of my relatives have withered away and died in Stanton House for lack of another option. This is where my father wants to send me.

I meet Dr. Roberts's gaze directly and force a smile. "I like living with my Aunt Bel."

"What if your aunt can't take care of you?" he counters. "She already has your grandmother to care for."

My heart skips a few beats, starts to race. Does my aunt want me committed? Have I become too much for her? "I'd like to stay with Aunt Bel," I say firmly.

Dr. Roberts leans back, shakes his head. He makes a note in the file. "I don't agree," he says stiffly. "As you know, your condition defies diagnosis at this time. The things you see are far too detailed to be considered classic hallucinations, and medication does little to help. Despite your condition being atypical, your family history of paranoid schizophrenia makes me believe you need a more controlled environment." But that's all he says about it. All he *can* say about it.

My gut unclenches. Aunt Bel hasn't turned me out, then. She's co-guardian with my father, so they can't send me to Stanton unless she signs off on it, or I do something to hurt myself or someone else, which hasn't happened.

Turning eighteen next year is *not* going to emancipate me. I will probably always need a guardian.

No mystery where it came from, either. My father's side has a colorful history going back to my great-great-grandma Opal Wickerton. She cut off her toes, believing demons were living between them, and ended up hanging herself from her clothesline.

About half of all her descendants wound up with mental disorders to one extent or another. I had a great-aunt who told such accurate predictions of people's death dates, no one in town would go near her, and an uncle who took to carving Bible passages into his skin. My great-grandmother drowned herself in Pember's Lake by tying her entire set of cast-iron skillets to her limbs, so it's little mystery why I'm sitting in a psychiatrist's office and take a rainbow of pills every day.

I look pointedly at the clock. "Are we finished?"

Dr. Roberts slides glasses onto his nose and peers at me over them. His pupils are thin black slits. "For today, yes." The *s* is drawn out in a long hiss. Like a snake.

God. Maybe I do belong at Stanton House.

I get up and head for the door. "Have a nice… afternoon," I manage before slipping into the hallway.

Aunt Bel rises from the waiting room chair. She packs her crocheting into her massive purse and smiles. "How'd it go?"

"Fine."

Her brows draw together. "*Not* fine."

I jerk one shoulder and hold the door open for her. "He's talking about Stanton House again. Says Dad wants me to go there."

"Your father has no idea what's best for you. The man

can't even take care of himself." Aunt Bel's mouth hardens. "He may dictate that you attend weekly sessions with that man, er *doctor*, but I'm still your co-guardian. You won't be sent to Stanton House while I live and breathe."

My breath hitches. "But you won't live *forever*, Aunt Bel. I'll wind up there eventually, won't I?"

Her hand curls around mine and squeezes. "Let's not worry about 'eventually.' That's a long time from now." She digs her keys from her handbag. "Anything could happen in the meantime."

Essie

the farmstead fair

Three days later, Aunt Bel rounds up me and Grandma Edie, and we all go to the Farmstead Festival. It's a big deal in Concordia, drawing out *everyone*. Aunt Bel is a fan, for reasons I can't fathom. I'd rather stay home. I bet Grandma Edie would, too, but neither of us are in the habit of telling Aunt Bel no. She asks so little of us, so we go.

A breeze carries the scent of animals and diesel, sugar and grease. The town green has been transformed. Rows of crafters and artisans, and some junk sellers, have set up their tents. The sounds are many: the rickety-rack of amusement rides on metal tracks; the roar of fans in animal enclosures to keep smells out and draw cool air in; people talking, babies crying, children wheedling for another crack at winning a toy. All of it creates a cacophony of noise that makes my hands sweat and my temples throb.

I'm standing in the middle of this, waiting for Aunt

Bel to finish smelling every soy candle in a packed booth. One of my hands holds Grandma Edie's, while the other pins down the skirt of my cotton sundress against the breeze. I should have worn shorts.

People walk by. They have no idea about the medication I take, or the opinions of my psychiatrist, or the fact that my senses are overwhelmed in a place like this. I look like a nice teenage girl at the fair with her grandma.

A group of teen girls pass by, bent toward each other, giggling at something. It's been years since I'd attended school. One ugly "episode" that scared some parents and teachers ended my public-school experience. Now, Aunt Bel homeschools me with the help of tutors. I look away from the girls with a pang of longing. For friends. For a sense of belonging. For that underrated state of ordinary.

Grandma Edie sighs and squints at her daughter, my Aunt Bel, wedged in the press of the soy candle booth. "Don't know why she bothers smelling them all. She's going to buy the apple one."

I nod. "She always buys the apple one."

We're both having a decent day so far. Neither of us wishes to cause problems at the fair for Aunt Bel, but it's hard.

"Too much movement here." Grandma Edie's voice is tense. "Too much noise." She's right. Everywhere we move through the fair, the sounds change. Near the bandstand, the brass band playing an old Bruce Springsteen hit, while different music pumps out of the Ferris wheel. Noise doesn't do good things for either of us. It seems the Wickerton affliction has diluted over four generations, but really, you'd think there wouldn't *be* four generations. I glance down at Grandma Edie, who stands half a head shorter than me. At eighty-nine, she's still shockingly lovely, with long silver hair and the bone structure of a Disney princess. Apparently, her beauty was enough to make poor late Grandpa Walt see past her…eccentricities. Neither of them struggles with the Wickerton curse, though it's debatable with my father.

Bad luck for me that it skipped a generation. A few of my other aunts and uncles and cousins weren't so lucky, either.

Grandma Edie lets go of my hand to fish a peppercorn from her purse. She crunches on it, and I breathe in the pepper. It's become a comforting smell to me.

She lets out a long breath. "Something strange going on here this year."

"What do you mean?" I ask, because I kind of feel the same way.

Grandma Edie waves a thin hand, encompassing the fair. "There are people here who aren't people. Pretenders. Creatures hiding behind human faces. Do you see them, too?" I can hear the plea in her voice—the great desire for what she sees to be validated. I'm not the best judge, but I agree with her.

I gently squeeze her hand. "I saw one earlier this week. He had a thousand faces and smelled like honey."

Grandma Edie's head snaps up to look at me. Her eyes flash, sharp as glass. "You saw *him?*"

"Him who?" I blink down at her. "I saw a strange boy, but I'm not sure how much of him was real."

"Why didn't you tell me this earlier?" She draws in a sharp breath. "Essie, did the bees sting you?"

I go still with surprise. *I didn't mention any bees.* "No. He said they wanted to, but he didn't let them."

"You *talked* to the bee-man?" Her hand grips mine like a vise. "What did he say? Tell me exactly what transpired."

I give her the rundown of my conversation with Dresden, more to placate her than anything else. I tell her what I can remember, ending with Aunt Bel's arrival and my subsequent unravelling.

"He told you his name. Sweet Lord." My grandmother's mouth slackens. "He told you his name and he didn't allow his bees to sting you."

"He *did* say he was going to kill me, though he seemed sad about it. But I *really* don't think that was a real conversation."

Grandma Edie's pale blue eyes water up and lose focus. "Oh, my sweet Essie, I'm quite certain it was a *very* real conversation. It is a miracle he didn't send a bee to you, but he isn't likely to be merciful again. Pray you never see him again. Pray he's gone far, far from this place."

"But—"

Her grip on my hand turns crushing. "Those bees will send you into a madness you cannot come out of, my dear. You won't survive it. And he *won't* be sad about it."

A ripple of panic threads down my spine, followed by the thought—holy crap, maybe she's serious. "Grandma Edie, what do you know about the bee-man?" I asked this question too late. My grandmother tips her face to the ground and rocks back and forth, singing a little song in a language I can't identify.

Aunt Bel returns with a poured candle in a jar. "I got

apple-scented," she announces. Her face falls when she notices Grandma Edie. "What happened?"

"She said there was a lot of noise." Not a lie, but not the exact truth.

Everything about Aunt Bel droops. "I suppose we can go home."

I bite my lip. "The parade is starting soon. Why don't we get some food and go back to our spot? It's near the house, and if she doesn't come out of it, we're close enough to take her home."

Aunt Bel brightens. "Excellent idea, Essie." She says it with genuine delight, and I know how much she's enjoying the fair.

I take one of Grandma Edie's arms, and Aunt Bel takes the other. Together, we slowly weave through the crowded fair to Main Street, where our chairs have been set up roadside since yesterday afternoon.

We settle into our seats with blooming onions and roasted soybeans and a massive bag of kettle corn, but Grandma Edie does not come out of it. If anything, she gets more agitated, and as the crowds thicken along the parade route, she starts to scratch at her wrist—her nervous spot—where a raised, lumpy scar exists from years and years of so much scratching.

"Okay," Aunt Bel announces. "We've got to get Mom back. She's not having it today."

"Get her settled in and come back," I say around a mouthful of popcorn. "I'll keep your seat."

She hesitates. "Are you sure? What if someone approaches you? After what happened last time I left you—"

I hold up a hand. "I'll be fine."

I know she wants to see the parade. In all her life, Aunt Bel has never missed Concordia's Farmstead Fair Parade.

She looks conflicted for a moment, but relents, clasping Grandma Edie close. "I'll be right back. Stay right in that seat, please."

I wave her off with a hunk of fried onion. "Yup. Go. I'll be *fine*."

6

Dresden

the
farmstead fair

Fairs and festivals are favorite places for killers like me. Everyone outside, not paying attention to anything but what they're eating and where the port-a-potties are. All this festivity for no apparent reason. Here, I am more invisible than usual, and a few bees is not an unusual sight.

I've stung two people. Both men. One of them got a little violent right on the spot, punching the side of a food truck. The other barely noticed. My bees are quiet in my chest. Their queen rests, so *I* get to rest.

The crowds along the main road are thickening. The parade is starting soon. I work my way through them. There's no point in lingering here. I can be out of here before the floats roll in. Maybe I can view a movie at the local theater. I do enjoy the pleasant distraction, and the matinee will be mostly empty today.

My stride falters as the sensation of effervescence shivers over my skin. It's familiar in a way that's appealing and repellant. The instant I remember where I felt this way before, I stop dead in my tracks. My gaze moves with laser focus over the crowds—searching, scanning for the one person I'd been hoping to never see again.

It's *her*. Across the street. Sitting in a folding chair. Eating from a takeout box on her lap. She's wearing a soft, cream-colored dress. The bees perk up. My legs move without my making a conscious choice about it. The first floats of the parade are slowly tracking down the street. A marching band breaks into their rendition of "Eye of the Tiger." I cut through the crowds and cross the street ahead of the parade. She looks up. Her gaze shifts, locks on me.

There is no fuzzy teasing in her eyes this time. Her fingers pause midair in the process of delivering food to her mouth—a mouth that is currently as round as her eyes. There's fear in the stark white of her face. She knows I'm not a delusion. I told her I was going to hurt her. Now, she believes it.

I approach her slowly. *Settle down!* I firmly think to the bees, and surprisingly, they do. Only because they're satiated. A dampness coats my palms. My belly quivers. I'm…nervous.

The girl—Essie—stays in her seat, staring up at me, as I stop next to her. I have to nudge some people aside to gain a spot in the tightly packed crowd. I'm acutely aware of how close I am to her. About a foot of space separates me from her chair. It's far too close for either of our comfort.

The bees buzz an erratic pattern in my throat and mouth. They're confused. Frankly, so am I. There is no logical reason for me to be here, *nervous*, struggling to come up with something non-threatening to say to a human girl. A *target*, no less.

"Hello Essie." I dip my head. "Are you afraid of me now?" Good God. Nearly a millennium's existence with humans and I open with the most inappropriate line ever.

She frowns up at me. "That depends on your intentions."

Intentions? I close my eyes and try to figure out what they are. I'm surprised to realize my only wish is to have a conversation. With *her*.

"I do not intend to harm you." I say it softly, with all the sincerity my harsh, bee-droning voice allows. "Not right now, anyway."

Her eyes widen. Is she angry or frightened? I can't tell.

"So maybe *later?*" she asks in a hissed whisper.

"Maybe." *Damn.* "I don't know. I'd rather not ever, to be honest." My faces are changing rapidly now. I must look frightful. I turn to the street in case she starts panicking. The parade is almost upon us. The band is now butchering an old U2 song. From the corner of my eye, I see Essie fumble for a napkin, wipe her fingers on it, and close the lid of her takeout container.

I've ruined her appetite, apparently.

"What do you *want*, Dresden?" Her voice trembles. "Excuse me. I mean, why are you here?"

She's trying not to be rude. Sweet, but unnecessary. "I don't know," I say again, truthfully. I can hear the bafflement underlying my words. "I saw you and wanted to say hello."

Her mouth is surprised. "Really?"

I smile, just with my lips. I don't dare open my mouth, not with bees pinging off the backs of my teeth. "Really."

She smiles back, and it's not polite or forced. It's just a smile. For *me*.

"Okay." She says it just like that, and I'm rendered speechless. Her simple acceptance is more than I expected. Certainly more than a doomed creature like me deserves.

A woman shoulders through the crowd to join the man standing next to me. I move over, and the distance between myself and Essie reduces to nothing. I gaze down at the top of her head. A crooked part runs through the center of her hair. The strands are lit golden by the afternoon light. I feel a strange peace from standing next to this girl. She bends down, places her food container on the ground. The ridge of her spine presses a curving line of bumps through the thin fabric of her dress. *So fragile.* She sits up and smiles at me again, and I get a little lost in it. In all those white teeth.

She points at my mouth and giggles. "Oh, I like that mouth, right there. Can you keep that one on?"

I blink down at her, then realize I had forgotten how my face is a mess of changing features. For a few precious moments, I was just here with her. Not a monster. Not a killer. Just a boy enjoying the company of a girl.

"I can't control the faces." I turn back to the parade. A pickup truck creeps up the street, pulling a giant soybean float. Three girls with green-painted faces wave from holes cut in the sides.

"I didn't mean to upset you." She leans toward me and says quietly, "I still think you're pretty, by the way."

I swallow hard, sending about a dozen bees to the back of my throat. Twice she's said this, and both times I've been rendered speechless. Not by the compliment, such that it is, but by her easy acceptance. It twists my gut in a way that hurts. I don't dislike it.

"I know now that you're real," she says. "But how

come no one is staring at you? Am I the only one who can see…" She circles a finger toward my face. "All *them*."

Everything about this interaction is so bizarre, I just stare at her for a moment. If she's not squeamish talking about my legion of interchangeable features, I won't be. No reason why I can't answer a few simple questions about myself. "Most human minds turn away from my face. They don't see it. You do, for some reason."

"Is it because of my condition?"

A smile curves my lips. She is much more self-possessed today than last I saw her, but I suspect it takes some effort to maintain that appearance. "What condition is that?" I ask because I'm curious how she perceives her own uniqueness. One thing I have decided: Essie is unique in a very interesting way.

"The Wickerton curse." She tilts her head and taps the side of it. "Runs in my family."

There's a bitter snap to her words, and she doesn't explain further. "A curse?"

She lifts one slender shoulder, lets it drop. "That's what they called it way back when. No one knows what to call it now. The Wickertons can't be diagnosed."

So she calls her condition a curse, as I do, like it's something that could be lifted, with the right words, with some magic. A mistake on both our parts.

"I've been around many, many people," I reply mildly. "None have noticed my true face. Most don't notice me at all."

"So I'm special." Her eyes gleam with genuine pleasure.

I hold her gaze and say the most sincere thing I've uttered in ages. "You are."

"My grandmother thinks you're dangerous."

Her grandmother? I hold back questions: *What does your grandmother know about me? How does she know what I am?* also, *You told your grandmother about me?*

"I am dangerous."

"Not to me." She says it with such confidence, I have to look away. I say nothing, because I can't guarantee that. I may not leave here without changing her into something dangerous. The bees still identify her as a target.

Her fingers flick through the air, reaching for something unseen to all but her. "If it makes you feel better, no one notices me, either," she says, ignoring my non-response. "Or, if they do, it's because I make them nervous. I've never hurt anyone." She says it fervently, as if she needs to convince me, of all people, of her harmlessness.

"I know." I know it better than she does, as the darkness of a soul is something I'm acutely tuned to, and hers is all light. I still wonder why the bees want her. I still wonder if they will have her. It would be awful, what their sting would do to her. My hands clench at the thought of it.

Without warning, a figure abruptly appears to my left. It's Michael, with a wake of annoyed people glaring at him for pushing through. He's sweaty, and his eyes are more birdlike than they should be.

"Dresden." He's breathless. His T-shirt is inside-out.

Essie gapes up at him. Maybe she's surprised someone other than her is talking to me. Maybe she finds him appealing. I suppose he'd be considered handsome by today's standards. I prefer the former possibility.

"Who are you?" Essie asks Michael, but he ignores her and grips my shoulder.

"We have problems," he says.

"*What* problems?" I ask sharply.

His hooded eyes turn slowly to the crowd across the street, where I had been before I'd spied Essie. My gaze follows, falling on a tall, thin man. Every bee inside me drops to the bottom of their cavity inside my body. I cannot move. I cannot think through sharp flashes of a rarely utilized response called *panic*.

A wide-brimmed hat shadows a face nearly as disturbing to look upon as my own. Sounds are swallowed by a roaring in my head. There is nothing in this world that frightens me. Nothing, except this: the Strawman.

Only a few of these creatures roam the world. No one knows what they do or what they are, but the word evil comes to mind. A beekeeper may draw out and intensify the evil in a person's soul, but a single touch from the hand of a Strawman can turn a pacifist into a raging killer. They have awful power over harbingers and beekeepers, too. Although Strawmen rarely meddle with beekeepers, if this one touched me, I'd lose supremacy over my bees. They would rule me. The last shreds of my humanity would be lost to the swarm.

Essie would be theirs.

The thought startles a gasp from me—not because I've realized this, but because I've realized that it would bother me. I would *like* to leave this place without destroying Essie's life. Without wearing her features on my face.

The Strawman raises a slow hand toward us, and the ground drops out from under me. I hiss out an expletive in the old language. A word lost to the ravages of time.

According to Michael, the last visit from a Strawman was in response to a harbinger saving a human woman from a fire, which resulted in the harbinger being struck unable to ever fully transform into a human again. He lived for over a decade, either in crow form or in a mutated meld of the two, until he was granted the *mortouri* ritual by his group and was mercifully pecked to death.

"What's he doing here?" Michael asks in a horrified whisper.

"I don't know." And yet I have a very bad feeling that I do. My thoughts spin faster than I can manage, but one blots out all others: he's here because of me.

Essie starts to rise from her seat. I place one hand on her shoulder and hold her down.

She makes a noise of surprise. "What are you doing, Dresden?"

"I'm sorry, I need to go." I snatch my hand away on a wave of light-headedness. What am I doing? Speaking to her—*touching* her—puts her in danger. I may as well paint a target on her back. I turn and muscle through the crowd with Michael right behind me.

We stop behind a convenience store, near the trash bins. Michael paces furiously. "What the *hell* is a Strawman doing here, Dres?" He runs shaking hands through his hair. "Why now? I haven't done anything. No one in my group has broken any rules."

"Maybe you're right." I run my hands over my face, currently sporting a large nose and wrinkly brow. "Maybe the curses are changing and he's here to—"

"What?" he snaps. "It's too much to hope he's here to end us. They *only* ever make things worse."

True. Oh, so true. Beekeepers may draw up violent impulses in those already given to darkness, but Strawmen make people *evil*. Like, Norman Bates evil. And they have the unpleasant ability to tinker with our curses, never for the better.

"It's the girl, isn't it?"

I close my eyes. "I don't know. Maybe."

He curses viciously. "I only told you not to sting her, not to make her your girlfriend."

Fury shivers under my skin, an emotion as forgotten as joy. "You don't tell me to do *anything*, harbinger." I say it quietly, coldly, shocked by the snarl in it. I pull in a deep, fortifying breath. "And that's a disgusting suggestion, considering what I am. You—"

I don't finish my thought. With a crackling snap and the scent of decaying flesh, the Strawman stands before us. All seven feet of him command our attention. He exudes a weariness that I relate to on a bone-deep level, but also a power and control that roots my feet to the ground.

Michael lets out a strangled gasp. I've encountered these creatures before, but Michael hasn't. Strawmen are pure mystery, weighed down by secrets. Some say they are wraiths—the blighted shells of ancient sorcerers, and the very ones responsible for turning us into monsters in the first place. It would explain how they are so tightly connected to us and the curses which control us. I'm inclined to believe this is who they are, but I see no resemblance to my original torturers in their appearance.

I take in the black thread stitching shut his eyelids, lips. His skin is dry, cracked leather. The smell of decay and fresh-cut hay fills the air. The Strawman lifts a hand toward Michael and flicks it lightly in his direction.

The harbinger launches backward as if an invisible bomb detonated in front of him. He collapses with a cry of pain. Black smoke explodes from him, twisting around his straining body like vaporous chains. This is a forced transformation, and Michael fights it. Nevertheless, he hits the wall as a crow. Disoriented, flopping, the bird struggles with one wing bent at a bad angle. I take a step toward him, but he collects himself and awkwardly takes to the air. He looks stiff, but holds himself aloft, quickly disappearing behind the trees.

My mouth opens, and bees gush forth like blood from an artery. They form distressed knots between myself and the Strawman who, despite his sewn-shut eyes, is looking straight at me. There's ice in my belly, creeping down my limbs. "Why did you do that to him?"

As if puzzled by the question, he cocks his head to the side. The movement carries the sound of dry, snapping straw, giving his kind their name. He doesn't reply, even though I know he can. It's said that a Strawman's words, when they choose to impart them, are never straightforward. Like an oracle, they could be interpreted endless ways.

"What do you want?" I take a step back despite my leaden feet. "Why are you here?"

He raises that hand again, and my eyes go wide, but he only points at me.

"You're here because of me?" I ask.

Yes, replies a voice that does not sound through the air, but only inside my head. It is old and touched with the accent of the old language. *And no.*

My heart no longer works quite like a human's — none of my organs do — but it sets up a hard, fast beat. "Because of her?" He knows it's Essie. I won't soil her name by speaking it to him.

He nods once.

"Because I didn't sting her?" I'm shouting now, beyond

caring if anyone's near and listening. "Because I chose to spare one innocent girl?"

Spare one to sacrifice many. You have an unusual sense of justice, beekeeper. Or perhaps you are operating under a different influence altogether. She isn't afraid of you, is she?

I shake my head, aware that I'm showing my hand. "I target those who are already touched with evil." My vision grays at the edges. "The bees are mistaken."

He makes a rough noise, like sandpaper on wood, that I belatedly recognize as a laugh.

The bees are never wrong.

My belly clenches. It's as I feared, then.

I am here to right a wrong. And to see that you do the same.

You have this one chance, beekeeper.

"A chance for what?"

He's done with my questions. In a flash of light, the Strawman disappears, leaving only the pungent whiff of rot and a charred black circle on the pavement where he stood. The bees return quietly to my chest, and my gaze turns to Michael's discarded pile of clothes. They're blackened and smoldering slightly from his struggle against the Strawman's transformation of him. I won't be retrieving them this time, not that Michael would want them back. I'll check on him later, but now, I need to get away from here. Someone could walk by. Someone could be watching.

I burst into bees and fly as far as I can bear. I fly over fields of corn and soybeans. I cross highways and rivers and parking lots that are crumbling, baked from the sun. I fly until I simply can't any longer. Until going farther will get me in trouble with my bees. As it is, they are nervous.

They're behaving dangerously and strangely, holding themselves slightly separate from me in our collective swarm. It's not good. I don't need them rebelling on me now.

I crash to the ground in a dried-out creek bed and plummet into my human form. Dirt and rocks grind into my skin, but I don't care. Can't feel it anyway. Damage has to be considerable for me to feel pain. I'm just relieved to be alone and many miles from that blighted town.

Essie. The girl who thinks I'm pretty, even though I am a hideous creature whose real face is long since swallowed up by my victims. No, not *my* victims—the curse's victims, but what's the difference? People are dead because of me. So many thousands of people. It doesn't matter that I never wanted to sting any of them.

I sit on the rocky creek bottom and drop my head on my knees.

Think, Dresden. *Think.*

The Strawman is here because of me—and *not*, according to his non-answer. The full motives of those beings can't be known. This one has proved incapable of forthright talk. As it is, *I am here to right a wrong. And to see that you do the same* is miraculously straightforward for one of them. I wish he would have spelled out exactly what he wanted me to do, but there's only one clear interpretation.

I've been a beekeeper for many hundreds of years, following harbingers for most of that. Not since the beginning, when I was still rebelling against what I had been turned into, have I hesitated to sting a human who called to my bees. Not until now. Not until Essie. But *why?* My fingers knot into my hair, pull. Something wells within me. *Emotion.*

She, and my reaction to her, are the reasons why the Strawman is here. I deviated. I refused the dictates of my curse, and since these creatures are so connected to the curses, they sense ripples in them. They *do* appear when someone is foolish enough to push against what they are.

This curse-weakening "talk" Michael referred to may have stirred them, but I had a moment of…weakness, curiosity, *something*, and now a Strawman is in Essie's town.

I expel a great breath, and hundreds of bees flow from my mouth. They fly in a leisurely figure eight a few feet above me. The bees serve me, as I serve them, but we both serve the magic that binds us, which rules us.

There's only one thing I can do to end this—to send the Strawman away and prevent something more terrible than whatever terrible fate awaits this town.

I must right my wrong. I must be the monster I am and sting Essie.

7

Essie

terrible things

There is a crow sitting in the tree outside my window this morning when I wake up. I can see the dark shape of it through the curtain which billows in the breeze. The bird stands there like it's waiting for something. I'm pretty sure it's real.

I tug off the covers and crawl to the end of the bed, yank back the curtain. It flutters its wings but doesn't fly off. Instead, it cocks its head and peers at me with curious, dark red eyes. Well, that's not normal. I squint through the screen, but sure enough, they're red.

Okay, so maybe it's not real, but it's too early for peppercorns.

"I don't need this." The crow just blinks at me with what I swear looks like amusement. A different day, I might have grabbed my sketchbook and drawn this bird. It's a rare treat for a subject to sit so close and so nicely. The details are exquisite. "Go away," I say. "Be someone else's hallucination."

The crow tips its head back and lets out a gravelly caw.

I *really* don't need this. I turn away, pull the curtains closed. My bedroom darkens. I sit on the edge of my bed and scrape my fingernails on the sheet. I'm so weary of questioning everything I see, of fighting to appear average and ordinary enough to not disturb people.

My mind turns to Dresden. I lie back down on my bed and cross my hands over my chest like a corpse. Aunt Bel doesn't understand why it's such a relaxing pose. She thinks it's morbid, but she should try it. It might relax her, too, and make her stop smoking cigarettes.

But even in my calming—*morbid*—pose, I can't stop thinking of the boy with the faces. I think he is real. At least, part of him is real. That guy who he left the parade with looked as regular as can be, and I don't think I made him up. He appeared freaked out by something. So did Dresden.

I didn't see anything unusual. I sure felt something, though. Something I will never forget, because it's a thing I have very little experience with: relief. When Dresden's hand touched my shoulder, it was like a hand unclenched from my mind. My mind felt clear, free. I can't explain or verify it as real. I don't *care* if it was real. I would like to feel it again.

But those faces…they don't make sense. But in a way, they make *perfect* sense. If ordinary people can't see them, then the reason I can see them is because I'm so very *not* ordinary. Maybe he and I are not ordinary in a way that's the same. But then there's Grandma Edie's warning about the "bee-man." I can't dismiss her warning. She's not ordinary, either, and I have a strong feeling that she was completely lucid when she told me he was to be feared.

Still, I want to see him again. And I am afraid to see him again.

I sit up and roll bad-night's-sleep stiffness from my shoulders. It's a cooler morning. Comfortable, for the first time in weeks. I pull on capri leggings under my oversize sleep shirt and head downstairs for breakfast. In the doorway, I glance back. The crow is gone from the tree, but I catch the sound of a caw.

Aunt Bel sits at the kitchen table, frowning at the newspaper. I lean down and kiss her pink cheek. She leans into me, and my heart melts like wax.

I pull away and begin getting my breakfast. Cereal. Orange juice. My pills. "What are you frowning over, Auntie?" I ask her as I shake Raisin Bran into a bowl.

"Terrible things." She taps one finger on the page she's reading. "Truly, terrible things. I want you to make extra certain the doors are locked. Double check after your grandmother."

"Why?" I pour some milk. "What's going on?"

"There was a murder last night at the college campus." She winces and bites her lip, and I know she's regretting what she just told me. Worried about triggering an episode. Worried, worried, worried.

I shake pills from the dispenser marked *S*, for Sunday, into my palm and bring my breakfast to the table.

"Can I see?" I draw the newspaper over. She doesn't object. The college murder is the big story, not because murders never happen in Concordia, Missouri, but because of the nature of the killing. I recoil in my seat as I read. No one saw a thing. No one heard a scream. No one had a clue that an unnamed twenty-year-old man was strangled with a rope then gutted in the campus apartments yesterday. While half the town was at the parade, a young man was being killed. It's gruesome, even knowing the police have withheld most of the details.

I pass the paper back to my aunt, who lights a cigarette and pulls out the "Food" section.

My cereal is soggy. I eat it anyway, because there isn't enough milk for a new bowl. I pick up each pill and send them down my throat on a wave of orange juice.

Grandma Edie marches into the kitchen. Her hair is slicked back into a severe bun. She wears a gold hoop in one ear and a fat crystal stud in the other. Her gaze slices to the newspaper, then to me.

"See?" she says. "I *told* you the bee-man was here to cause problems."

Aunt Bel sighs. "Mom, there's no bee-man."

"I was speaking to the girl, there." Grandma Edie nods to me, face glowing with righteousness. "She knows what I'm talking about."

When Grandma Edie turns away, I give Aunt Bel a little shrug. It's cowardly and dishonest, because I know *exactly* what my grandmother is talking about, but I'm not going to talk to Aunt Bel about Dresden. For more reasons than I can count.

I get up. "I'm going for a walk."

Grandma Edie narrows her eyes but says nothing. I don't meet her gaze. Somehow, I feel like I'm betraying her.

Aunt Bel's coffee cup freezes between her lips. Then lowers. "No, you're not. Did you not just read the news?"

"It's Sunday morning. There's a 5K race happening right now in the park, I'm seeing cars on the street, and the Briggses just walked by on their way to town. The world isn't grinding to a halt because of that." I point to the paper. "It's a nice morning and I feel really good. I'd like to go for a walk before it gets hot. Please, let me go."

"I'll think about it."

I bring my dishes to the sink. Rinse and stack them in the dishwasher. Aunt Bel watches me from the corner of her eye. She knows I wouldn't do any of that if I were on the verge of an episode. I wouldn't even think about it.

"You know, you have a few cousins at that college. Just saying." She slurps her coffee, then lets out a gusty sigh. "Fine. I can't keep you inside this house your whole life. Otherwise, I'm no better than your father, who wants you locked up in that Stanton House." She waves a hand. "Go for a walk. But take your phone. And change into regular clothes first. The neighbors will start calling if they see you roaming the streets in a Hello Kitty nightgown."

I chuckle, then seal my mouth shut. Oh, those stupid bubbles. Just once, I'd like to laugh and *not* see them floating out of my mouth. "Will do, Auntie. Thanks."

I go upstairs to change into a long blue T-shirt and leave the leggings on. I gather my hair into a smooth ponytail and tuck it inside a blue baseball cap. I add running shoes and stick my phone in my waistband. The mirror reveals an ordinary-looking girl. Someone who looks like they could be in the 5K. Maybe I will jog a little.

Aunt Bel snags me on the way out. "Stay to the main streets where you're visible—*not* the park," she calls after me. "I don't want you going anywhere isolated with a murderer out there."

"Okay. I won't be long." The screen door bangs shut behind me. I start out at a brisk, purposeful walk. I am totally going to the park, but I'll stay out of the wooded, isolated parts.

I rub my hands together with a surge of anticipation. My eyes are looking, looking.

Looking for *him*.

But he is nowhere to be found. Perhaps he doesn't wish to be found. It's stupid to think he'd appear just because I want him to. He has better things to do than hang around with me. Hopefully, better things than stinging people with those bees of his. I sit on a bench and draw circles in the dust with my sneakers. I'm next to the running trail, so a few people jog or power-walk by, but no one notices me. Of course, not everyone would. It's a big town, as Midwest ones go. We have a college and everything.

"Dresden," I say to the dust circles. "I hope you're okay. I'd like to talk to you, but I get it if you don't want to talk to me. I just…" I'm better if I can say what I'm thinking. Holding back words makes them fester in my mind like pus filled abscesses. *Disgusting*. But I surely look strange right now, talking to the ground. I'm not, though—strange, that is—because I'd hold back the words if there were people around right now, and there aren't.

I'm completely alone. Alone, alone, alone.

8

Dresden

irrevocable
choices

I have stung three people today.

Three people: An office supply delivery man. A transient. A businessman at the golf course with a gang of associates. Their energy was vile, like acid to the skin, the businessman being the worst. He was all name-brand veneer over a boiling mess of rage. For whatever reason—hard-wiring, biological instincts, who-knows-what—men exist closer to the edge of violence than women. Not always.

The woman in Walmart was a mess. But it's the violence, and the fear that comes with it and after it, that I want—no, *need*. If it was merely a want, I wouldn't sting anyone. I was not always like this. I was an eighteen-year-old man with a life once.

I'm sitting in a tree, about twenty feet up, Essie almost directly below me on a park bench, talking to her shoes. Once again, her mental energy hits me like effervescence to the skin. Bubbles carried on the wind,

MEG KASSEL 51

popping erratically. I wish she hadn't been the one my bees had targeted after a long journey. If I hadn't felt so desperate to release bees that day, they wouldn't have noticed her. If I had walked a different route through this town, I would have found a better target. Not this gentle, kind young woman.

I'm going to sting Essie. I *am*.

Just. Not. Quite. Yet.

This girl *is* harmless. She won't hurt anyone but herself. Even after the cursed bee venom breaks down the rest of her mind, hers will be a miserable death. It will be slow and excruciating because she lacks the tools or the skills or the desire to end herself with economy. The mental image of this sends bile to the back of my tongue. I simply can't stand the thought of it.

I listen hard, but I can't make out what she's saying. My hearing is no better than an ordinary human's. She shakes her head and pushes dirt into a pile between her feet. She holds a baseball cap in her hands. Blond hair spills over her back like a smooth sheaf of wheat. Poetry? *Please*, no. I shut my eyes and mouth, not that I need to worry. The bees are not clamoring through my sinuses, buzzing for release. They are still. They've settled deep in my chest, and I don't know if they're sending me a message or if they're regrouping for a big, unpleasant mutiny.

I wouldn't blame them if they *did* mutiny. My behavior is not in line with what they've grown to expect. We're both stuck with this curse, and I am making it worse for them. But it has been a very long time since I have had an opinion about stinging someone. Since I have encountered a person that I *should* sting but would like not to.

I was not always like this. I would like to tell her that. I would like her to see what I used to look like. I was handsome, apparently. Handsome enough to turn the head of a queen. Handsome enough to inspire that queen to rip me from my home, from those I loved, and imprison me with the rest of her ill-fated harem of boys and men. To doom me for the rest of time.

I would like to *not* sting Essie.

My fingers clench around the smooth branch I'm perched on. I feel like a harbinger, lurking up in a tree. Michael would say…no. It doesn't matter. I haven't spoken to him since yesterday. The harbingers weren't in the motel they're staying at when I came by. They are still here, though. I've seen the crows. They're watching, wondering what game I'm playing.

But this is no game.

I close my eyes and unclench my jaw just enough to release a bee. It falls from my lips with a whispered line of swear words directed at myself. I've been a monster for a long time, but stinging this girl takes my self-hatred to a new, loathsome depth. I'm forfeiting my last few shreds of humanity as a sacrifice to the Strawman, and for what? So I can remain the creature I am instead of becoming something *worse?* Is there anything worse?

Before I can call it back, the bee zig-zags through the branches, makes a meandering line for her. My hands clench the branch so hard, my fingers dent the wood. Every fiber of my being screams to jump down, snatch the bee out of the air. To save her.

Essie's head snaps up with a surprised look on her face, like someone just called out. Maybe she heard the buzzing. The bee is not attempting to sting her with any urgency, but weaving around, as if choosing an ideal spot of skin. Essie, however, is not so hesitant. With speed and accuracy that astonishes me, she whips off her hat and bats the bee from the air. The bee tumbles to the ground, where she smashes her sneaker into it. The entire sequence takes about two seconds. Essie glances around her, then slouches against the bench with a sigh.

I blink down at her in confusion, elation. That wasn't supposed to happen. Bees don't miss. *Bees don't get it wrong like that.*

Not without a reason.

The hive knots low in my belly. They aren't reacting to her right *now*. In fact, they don't want to go anywhere near her. *Strange.* And problematic. It took all my will to send that one bee to her. I can't comprehend sending another. I simply *can't.*

My thoughts are jumbled, but I replay my brief conversation with the Strawman again. Maybe I misinterpreted his words or misheard. Who knows what he was trying to tell me? He never said sparing Essie was *wrong.* He said the bees weren't wrong. Perhaps they're not wrong right now.

It could be there's some other wrong I need to correct. Lord knows, I've committed a great many wrongs. I don't consider sparing Essie one of them, although he did affirm that this atonement I must make had something to do with her. But maybe stinging her isn't the answer. So I have no idea what *else* to do, but I can take this a day at a time, see how it goes.

The notion that I may not have to sting her after all makes my every muscle go slack with relief. My body's reaction makes my bees rumble in one rolling wave, then go quiet again. I feel light, buoyant, but also a little unsteady.

I gaze back down at her. She's fallen quiet. Her head turns to a pair of lady joggers springing by on neon sneakers. They don't look at Essie, and her body relaxes again when they are gone. She lets out a gusty sigh and gets up.

Her movement is a study in disappointment. An errant thought creeps in my head — an absurd hope that she was hoping to see me. I brush it away. Impossible. She won't mistake me for an interesting hallucination again, and I haven't forgotten her first glimpse of me at the parade. I saw the fear lick over her features before I assured her I wouldn't hurt her. I will do my best to keep my word on that, and the best way to do so is to keep my distance. Just because I am endeavoring to not sting her does not mean I should attempt a friendship with her.

Essie starts a brisk pace back up the path she arrived by. My primary options are three: Stay here. Go somewhere else. Follow her.

Against better judgment, I follow her. It's almost a compulsion, but I change into a swarm of bees and stay up in the tree branches, out of sight. I will track her safely back to her home, then avoid her completely until it's time to leave this godforsaken town. That day can't come soon enough.

With the scattered, omnipresent consciousness of the bees, I see her from many angles at once. From above, the side. I send a part of me to well in front of her, so I can see her face. Her mouth is unhappy. She wrinkles her nose and tugs at the ends of her ponytail, hard.

All of a sudden, her attention snags on something

in the woods to her left. She comes to an abrupt stop, eyes narrowed. She peers through the trees at something, craning her neck, squinting. I gather my bees on the edge of a tree and send a few out to see what's caught her interest.

There's a dead body in the woods. A woman, narrow and blond, in a short blue dress. The body lies facedown and half suspended on the bent and straining branches of low bushes. She looks to have been hastily abandoned.

There is blood, but not a great deal of it, coming from the cutting off of the woman's—

Essie! I remember her with a jolt. I am unmoved by sights like this, but Essie, with her unpredictable mind, is *not* the one who should discover this scene.

I send a few bees back to check on her, and panic disorganizes my buzzing swarm. She's *here* already, through the trees. She climbs around thick brush, only to reel backward in horror. Her hands fly to her gasping mouth. She turns, rushes blindly into the impenetrable bush, losing her blue hat to the snarls of a thorny bush.

I immediately draw all the bits of myself together and fly to the forest floor. I take my human form right in front of her, without thinking. Bees compress into arms and legs and head, and I'm standing before her. Her eyes widen to perfect circles of terror. Her mouth opens.

My hand claps over her mouth before she releases the scream. "Shush." My voice is a growl. Not reassuring. Not soothing. "Relax. You're safe."

The scream fades from her throat. I release my hand from her mouth and bend down to examine her. "Are you okay, Essie?"

"How did you…?" Her voice is squeezed, pitched high.

"You were just…" She shakes her head, and her terrified gaze begins to slide from me and back to the body, but I move to block her view.

"Don't look at that. Look at me. Right here." I point at my eyes, then remember I am no less scary to look at than the sight of the murdered woman behind me.

But Essie *does* look at me, and inexplicably, some of the terror eases from her eyes. My chest constricts, almost painfully, at the sudden knowledge that this girl finds looking at my face less scary than the harmless corpse behind me.

"Dresden." She's breathing too fast. Her face is too pale.

Dresden. My name was once incredibly long, full of the bouncing consonants and rich vowels that came with life on the Mediterranean Sea. Somewhere over the years, most of it went missing, along with much of the rest of me. Now *Dresden* is all that remains of it, and it feels woefully lacking. I want to give her more. I want to show her something of what I once was.

"Easy now," I say. "Calm down or you're going to pass out."

She seizes the front of my T-shirt. I freeze at the feel of her tense knuckles against my chest.

"Is he still here?" she asks.

"Who?"

"The-the…person who k-killed that poor woman?"

She doesn't think it's me. Even knowing that I'm neither human nor a proclaimed good guy, there isn't a shred of suspicion clouding her clear blue eyes. I look out at the forest, draw awareness to my skin, but the only unstable mind I detect is Essie's. Certainly not the slicing mania I would feel from a person capable of squeezing the life from another. "No," I say. "He's gone."

She looks up at me, lips slack and colorless. "Are you s-sure?"

"Yes. I'd sense him if he were nearby." I try to smile. Try not to think about what my face is doing right now. I hope the features on it at the moment are pleasant, at least. "You're safe," I say again.

She closes her eyes. Her breath hitches. Then she does the improbable and throws herself against me, wrapping her arms around my waist.

I am paralyzed. Motionless, breathless in my first embrace in a millennium. To be touched... My eyes close as I tremble from head to toe. The pain is glorious, excruciating.

"Thank you," she breathes against my chest. "You calm my mind. Why is that?"

"I don't know." Speech takes an unbearable effort. I'm overwhelmed in every single possible way—destroyed on a level she can't begin to comprehend. My arms hover, uncertain how to return her embrace and unsure if I should. Unable to push her away. I feel as though I will shatter if I move, but my arms slowly close around her. One of my hands falls on her hair, where her elastic has loosened. The thin band slips from her hair and falls into my hand. My fingers close around it.

There's a buzzing in my ears, but not from my bees. The swarm sits low behind my ribs, unsettled and unsure. They make no move to climb up my throat. Maybe they think we're about to die. It could happen. Right now, a lovely human girl is holding me. *Anything* is possible.

"Essie." Her name slips from my mouth. A prayer. An

offering. My very undoing.

She is shaking. "Is she still there?"

"Is who still where?"

"The woman. The d-dead woman."

My breath releases with a shudder. Essie is oblivious to the effect she has on me. She has no inkling of the wound she's sliced open. Of the beasts awakening inside me that howl and gnaw at my mind with maddening ferocity. And she mustn't know. The depth of my feelings at this moment is monstrous. "She's not going anywhere without help."

Essie leans back with a frown. But her arms stay around me. "Are you joking?"

"No." I swallow thickly. *Act normal!* "That woman is deceased, Essie. The life has left her body. She cannot touch you or harm you in any way." *Whoever did this to the woman is another story.*

Her frown stays, but it's no longer directed at me. It's a thinking frown. "Who is she?"

I don't know, of course. Essie clamps her lower lip between her teeth and peeks over my shoulder. I don't try to stop her this time. She can't see that much. The woman's face is tilted away, a good deal of her is obscured by the bushes, but Essie takes a long, quiet look. Her nostrils flare. Her nails dig hard into my waist. It's such a sweet pain I can scarcely breathe.

Then she closes her eyes and presses her forehead against my breastbone. I let out a quiet gasp. I'm not sure how much more of this I can take.

"Her toes," Essie squeaks. "They've been...cut off."

I don't say anything. I saw the toes. In bee form, I also saw the purple mark around the neck and the scraped-red hands that tried, briefly, to fend off whoever was squeezing her throat.

"M-my great-great-grandmother cut off her toes," Essie says. "All of 'em. Just like that."

I did *not* know this. "Are you certain?"

"Yes. Everyone knows about it. Opal Wickerton. The first one with the Wickerton family curse." Her breath warms my shirt and the skin beneath it. Can she hear the bees, boiling under my ribs? Can she feel the uneven rise and fall of my chest? If my heart beat normally, it would be pounding right now.

She raises her head, looks up at me. Her eyes are glassy. "Do you think there's a connection?"

Probably. "Probably not." My first lie.

She steps back and fumbles at her waist. "I have a phone. I need to call the police."

I cover her hand with my own. "No. You need to go home. Tell your parents."

"I live with my aunt." Her brow creases.

"Fine. Bring her here if you need to, but *you* shouldn't be the one to call the police."

"Why?"

She's really asking this question? I won't lie to her this time. "Because it's not a good idea. Get your aunt to report it."

Her face pinches. "They'll think I did it?"

I place one finger under her chin and tip her head up. "There will be a lot of questions. You'll need support." I pause, unsure for a moment if I am giving correct advice. Her aunt could be a horror on two legs. I've seen enough of humanity to know that people who require caregivers, like Essie, are the ones more often abused. "Is your aunt someone you trust?"

"Yes. Aunt Bel is wonderful." She swallows, making the muscles in her slender throat move. "She doesn't see me as a burden."

I let out a breath of relief. "If you are a burden, I am a nightmare."

"No, Dresden. You are a dream." She holds my gaze, blinks slowly. "Thank you. It's kind of amazing that you appeared like that. Were you following me?"

I drop my finger from her chin. "Yes."

"Why?"

I was talking myself out of killing you. "I saw you and wanted to make sure you got home safe."

"What's with the-the…bees?" She asks it hesitantly, as if unsure if she's crossing into forbidden territory.

I smile and feel a mustache tickle my upper lip. *Great.* "The bees are a story for another day."

"I'd like to hear it."

"It's a very unpleasant one."

She goes still. "The most interesting stories usually are."

Neither of us speaks. I don't know what's happening here, but she's gazing at me with, of all things, *affection*, and it's sending me into a dangerous state of euphoria. My head doesn't feel entirely attached to my neck. I can't read her mind, but in this moment, I am sure neither of us are thinking about the dead woman lying six feet away.

"Maybe someday," I say thickly. "It's time you get back."

"Okay." She tucks errant hair behind her ear and pauses. "I was looking for you, you know."

My heart gives an erratic bump, but I say nothing.

Emotion has a grip on my throat so tight, it's a fight for air, let alone words.

"Someone was murdered in the college dorms yesterday," she continues. "I wanted to ask you if you knew or heard anything about who did it."

"You didn't think it was me?" I rasped out.

"No, you were at the fair. Besides, you don't murder people, do you?"

What a question. Hard to answer. I think of myself as a murderer. Right now, however, I want her to think the best of me, so I choose the literal interpretation of her question. "No."

Because I don't use guns or knives or fists to take people's lives. I just release bees whose sting pushes the dark-minded over the edge and makes them do terrible things. It doesn't matter that it's not my choice.

I reach out and draw back the snarl of brush she climbed through. "I'll keep watch over you. No one will touch you," I say, then remember how very unpredictable her faculties are. "Are you okay on your own?"

"Yes. I—" She pulls in a deep, shaky breath. "Will I see you again, Dresden?"

My throat goes dry and raw and aching. "Do you want to?"

However she answers will be excruciating. There will be no recovering from this encounter. From the memory of her touch and her wide, trusting eyes. Good gods, from her embrace.

She nods.

I am doomed. "I'll find you later. I'll…" *What?* Knock on her door and ask her aunt if I can invite her to the movies? Not in this universe. "I will see you again, Essie.

I'm not sure when."

"I'll look for you," she says, finally releasing her hold on my T-shirt. "Be careful." And she's gone, disappearing into the woods, back toward the trail.

I catch a glimpse of blue fabric and golden hair streaming through the trees. The hair elastic is like a living, pulsing thing in my hand. I vow to keep it with me as I transform into bees. I stay high in the trees where she can't see me and examine every person within a thirty-foot radius of her with deadly intensity. I follow her until she opens the door and disappears into her house. God help anyone who tries to hurt her. I *would* become a murderer, then.

9

Essie

just
the toes

I don't think Aunt Bel believed me.

I told her about the body in a rambling rush while she stared at me, cigarette angled over the sink. She glanced at the tear in my leggings and the twig in my hair. With a sigh, she turned on the sink and drowned the cigarette in a stream of water.

"I sure hope you're imagining this," she said, looping her handbag over a shoulder.

I wished I was, too, but I'm 90 percent sure I'm not. Maybe 85 percent sure.

My tears start as soon as we enter the wooded part of the path. They extrude from my eyes like fist-sized water balloons, then burst and splatter water all over my clothes. I have to hold my sodden shirt out in front of me so it won't plaster to the front of my body. Otherwise, everybody would be staring at my wet T-shirt. The few people we pass are the last of the 5K racers. They straggle through, panting, but a couple do double takes at me, which makes me cry even harder.

We're close to the spot where the dead girl is, and my shaking and crying and shirt tugging apparently makes Aunt Bel stop and face me. She leans close. I can smell her nicotine breath, the aerosol hair spray she uses to keep her bouffant pouffed a solid six inches off the top of her head. "Essie. Stop doing that with your shirt."

"B-but there's water all over it."

"Look at me." She unrolls my clenched fingers, clasps them tight between her own. "There's no water on your shirt. You're just crying, is all. Your shirt is dry."

"I'm afraid."

"Afraid of what?"

"Of seeing her there again. Or of *not* seeing her there." The memory of it lies as fresh and vivid as the corpse herself. I remember the bright, metallic smell as unfamiliar but one that twisted my insides with primal fear. I remember all the colors. Sky blue of her dress next to the harsh white of her skin. The smears of red blood accenting everything from her hair to those innocent bushes she lay on. The stumps of her toes almost didn't look real. I thought at first that they weren't, but even my visions have never been so gory. Frightening sometimes, yes, but never gruesome.

Aunt Bel tugs my head down and rests her forehead against mine. "Whatever we find, we'll deal with it. Understand?"

I let out a ragged breath. "Yes."

She leans back. Fine lines dig around her eyes. "Now stop crying. And leave your shirt alone."

"Okay." It takes all my effort, but I manage to walk the rest of the way with a wet shirt plastered to my skin.

No one stares at my chest. *Because the shirt is dry*, I fiercely lecture myself. I'm finding it hard to hold on to that certainty right now.

I stop at the place where I spotted that patch of color in the woods. Aunt Bel glances at the tamped-down brush where a rough path leads into the thicket. "Here?"

My tongue feels like a rock in my mouth, so I nod.

She goes in first, and I follow, keeping my gaze on the back of her head. It's still in the air—that odd, metal scent from before. She comes to a stop, just where I knew she would, and lets out a sharp curse.

"Open your eyes, Essie," Aunt Bel says.

I hadn't realized I'd closed them. I open them.

The body is gone.

"But—" I start, but she raises a hand.

"You said you saw a body here?" she asks sharply. "A *whole* body?"

"Yes." My voice is thin, but it's not relief I'm feeling. A deeper dread slides under my skin.

The bushes and shrubs that had partly suspended the woman above the ground are crushed and blood smeared.

My aunt points. "See that down there on the ground?"

There's something on the ground, visible between the broken branches. It's a plastic baggie. The kind for sandwiches. There's something in it.

I lean forward and squint. "Are those..."

"Toes." My aunt rears back, hand flattened to her chest. "Sweet Lord in heaven, there's toes in that bag."

"It wasn't like this," I say. "All of her was here, *except* the toes."

Aunt Bel turns abruptly and herds me through the brush, back to the running path. Back on the pavement, her hands clamp around my upper arms. Her face is a mask of cold and hot and profound worry. "Essie, you look in my eyes and tell me the truth, now. Back at the house, did you tell me everything? Every single thing?"

My aunt's piercing gaze is almost as frightening as finding the dead woman. The water balloons threaten to come popping from my eyes again, but I force them back.

A half hour ago, I stood in these woods with Dresden, listening to him tell me to relax, that I was safe. I remember the feel of his buzzing, humming chest under my cheek and the shaky, uncertain way he held me. I draw in a deep breath and stretch my scattered mind to grab hold of the small, slippery parts that fit together. "I told you everything," I say firmly. "She was *here*. Face down. In a blue dress."

Aunt Bel's eyes soften, then her hands gentle. "Okay, baby. When the police get here, you tell them exactly what you told me. You didn't move anything, did you? Touch anything?"

"No." The only thing I touched was Dresden. *Look at me. Right here*, he'd said. And I did, but I can't tell my aunt about that.

"Thank God for that." She digs into her purse and pulls out her phone. Her hands shake as she calls 9-1-1.

An hour later, I'm with Aunt Bel in the police station. We're sitting on the guest side of a metal desk across from an unhappy-looking detective who I know from past encounters. And because she's a cousin, second or third or once removed. Something like that. I wouldn't know that if she hadn't told me on an earlier occasion, when she was picking me up from walking down the interstate in my aunt's bathrobe—*don't ask*.

I'm related to a lot of people in Concordia, where the Wickertons have resided since colonial times, but I couldn't tell you who they are. We don't do family gatherings or holiday parties or anything like that. About half are affected by the Wickerton curse, to one degree or another, and the rest are busy watching after the affected half. It's not a crew anyone wants brought all together. As a result, my sprawling family is a scattered bunch. The only place the Wickerton descendants congregate is in the Holy Trinity cemetery, where a sizable section of land is secured for our graves. Each generation produces fewer offspring than the one previous, on account of the Wickerton curse striking younger and younger.

A can of Coke sweats on the desk before me. I'm thirsty, but I don't drink it. There's a little stand-up name plaque with the name: Detective Annemarie Berk. I stare at it, offended on her behalf that they smashed her name together like that. It's Anne Marie, two words. She must have been promoted recently, because the last time I saw her, she wore a blue police uniform instead of this gray, ill-fitting suit, and she looked a good deal happier.

The heavy pile of papers teetering on the edge of her desk likely isn't helping her mood. Nor is my presence opposite her desk. I have no gripe with Detective Berk. As *Officer* Berk, she's returned a good number of our relatives to their respective residences after episodes, including Grandma Edie. Including myself, a few times. I don't remember a whole lot from those encounters, but when she was the one bringing me home, I never returned home with bruises on my arms.

Detective Berk's sleeves are rolled up to the elbows. On her left forearm is a mark the shape and size of a large hand. It's black and curls around her arm like a charred burn. She's an impressively large woman—tall and broad boned. Strong. She looks like a superhero in off-duty clothes. I want to ask her what happened to her arm, but I don't know if that would be rude.

"So Essie, you're telling me you were walking, alone, in the park this morning. You found a body—minus the toes—went immediately home, got your aunt. When the two of you arrived back at the scene, the body was gone but the toes were there."

"Yes," I say. "In a baggie."

"Right." She marks something down on a pad. "Why didn't you contact the police immediately? Why did you go home first?"

I glance over at Aunt Bel. Chin high, hands clasped over her enormous handbag, my aunt looks so solid, so formidable, she feels like a giant. She pats my knee and nods, slanting a look at the detective. "It's okay, my lamb. Detective Berk is a friend."

The definitive emphasis on *friend* draws a sigh from Detective Berk and a shuddery breath from me.

"I was afraid you'd all think I did it," I mumble.

"Why would you assume that?" asks Detective Berk.

What a silly question. I give her half an eye roll. "Because of my condition, obviously."

"Nothing obvious about this." Berk glances at her notes. "You have no history of violence, Essie. I'm not assuming you did this, based on what I know of you, but it's important you not hold back any information. I need to know everything you saw and did, so we can find who *did* do this."

Everything. Yeah, not a chance. "I told you everything."

Except for Dresden.

Berk folds her hands, places them on the desk. She sighs again. "Here's the thing, Essie. An officer interviewed some runners who passed the scene during the time frame you said you were with the body. He has a witness who claims she heard people talking in the woods. A female *and* a male voice."

My head goes dead blank. Ice. Stone. *Nothing.* "That wasn't me," I say flatly, hoping it passes for honest. "There was no one but me."

"There were a lot of people in the park today," Aunt Bel puts in. "Could have been anyone. Voices carry."

"They do." Detective Berk holds my gaze a moment too long. "Okay. If you're sure."

The one thing I'm sure of is I'm a crappy liar. I was already nervous, but now my heart is pounding so hard it's making the desk rattle. The Coke is about to fall on the floor. I snatch it off the desk and hold it tightly between my hands. I squeeze my eyes shut and try to calm my hammering heartbeat. *Quiet down!* Everyone's going to know I'm leaving something out. They're going to think I killed that woman and I'll go to jail forever. That would surely be worse than Stanton House.

"Essie, are you okay?" Detective Berk asks.

Some rank black goo is leaking from the name plaque, from the misspelled name, "Annemarie." It stinks like a sewer, and the glop is making a puddle on the floor near my feet. I jab a finger toward the offending plaque. "Why did they screw up your name?"

"What?" She blinks. "Oh, it was a misprint."

"They should fix it." I tuck my feet up on the chair. "That's not how you spell it."

Detective Berk's expression gentles. "I think that's enough for today."

"I agree." Aunt Bel stands up.

"Seriously, who do I have to talk to to get your name fixed on that thing?" I pinch my nostrils closed. "It smells like a backed-up toilet."

I can feel her staring at me. *Great.* I'm freaking her out. I tear my gaze from the oozing mess and stare at my lap.

"I'll take care of it, Essie," Detective Berk says with *that* smile, the one people give me when they're trying to placate me. They think I don't know what that look means. That I don't get how although their mouths say nice, reassuring things, the rest of their face is saying: "*I wish you would leave.*" And Dresden thinks *his* face is hard to look at. I'd prefer his slideshow of features to the sideways glances of polite distress I get from most people. I don't even blame them for it. I'm afraid of myself often enough.

Before we go home, Detective Berk makes me describe the dead woman in as much detail as I can. I do my best, describing things like height and weight and even the texture of her hair. The result is a generic description that reads nothing like my memory, but without seeing her face, the woman is like a department store mannequin. Featureless and anonymous.

Aunt Bel takes me to a sandwich shop for lunch. We sit across from each other, quietly munching subs and slurping sodas too big to finish. My aunt wipes her fingers on a napkin and eyes me. "Are you okay?" Her voice is quiet, but practical. She's not afraid I'm going to have an episode—she just wants a status report. I love that about her.

"I think so." I pick a tomato from my sub and put it

on my plate. "I'm really tired."

She nods. "We'll get you home and to bed. I want you to try to put this from your mind."

I roll my eyes. "That's not likely to happen."

"I know, I know." Her hands twitch toward her handbag containing her cigarettes. "I *knew* I should have made you stay home this morning. It won't happen again, you know. You're not going anywhere alone until this psychopath is found."

There is no arguing with this tone, but there is always a way to squeeze out of my aunt's edicts. "Okay."

In a practiced move, she slicks Moroccan Red lipstick over her lips. The result is a thin, scarlet line across her face. She raps her lipstick on the tabletop and shakes her head. "News of two murders is going to travel. We're going to have reporters from St. Louis coming out here, sniffing around. We're going to be on the goddamn nightly news again."

I take another bite of sub. "I won't talk to any reporters."

"You're damn right, you won't."

About a decade ago, Concordia had been on the news for a piece about the mental illness that made the town an unfortunate statistic. The Wickerton curse had been widely studied, to no real effect, but some TV producer had thought it would make an interesting segment on prime time and sent a crew out to question everyone who had anything to say about us.

I never saw it, but from what I heard, the piece wasn't exactly flattering to my family. The ratings, however, were excellent. I had even made it on the final cut, although I don't remember being filmed running around my school's playground. I was only just beginning to show signs of the condition. The following year was my last in public school. But regardless, that segment, depicting my family so badly, did damage in a community that already only tolerated us. As a result, there isn't a person of Wickerton descent—sane or not—who doesn't harbor tremendous hostility toward all news outlets, everywhere. *Forever.* What can I say? Half of us may see bubbles when we laugh, but we have our pride.

One thing keeping me focused and grounded is the prospect of seeing Dresden again. He'll know more about what's going on here. He may even have found out who killed that woman. But if I'm honest with myself, and I generally am, my desire to see him has nothing to do with the murder. I just like being around him. It wasn't just talk when I told him that his presence calms my mind. It's like all my twisted wires smooth out for a little while and I can just *be*. Of course, I'm aware that being around him can't cure me, and he's made it clear he's not going to be here long. But I like the way he looks at me, like I'm not a person to be feared or disturbed by or pitied. At least, if he *does* pity me, he hides it well.

I chew the last few bites of my sub and gaze outside the window. Aunt Bel checks Facebook on her phone. Downtown Concordia bustles on, unaware that a woman was murdered just a few miles away. I watch a guy in a suit turn to look at a pretty woman walking six tiny dogs. The dogs walk in two perfect straight lines beside her. I can't tell if the man is impressed by her or the dogs. Or both.

A figure farther down the sidewalk catches my eye. It's the tall man in the wide-brimmed hat that got Dresden all bugged out at the parade. People veer around the man, giving him a wide berth, but don't appear to *see* him. The man is silent and still. He is observing me. Something is wrong with his eyes, but he is too far away for me to make him out clearly. My heart thumps heavily, bumping against my ribs. My skin shivers with unease.

I don't want to be the object of that man's attention. I look away and take a deep pull of orange soda from my straw. There is something dark and lost and rancid about him that makes me feel filthy for just having his eyes on me. He may not be real. There's something wavering and insubstantial about his figure. As if he's working very hard to stand there. As if *being seen* is difficult for him.

When I look back, the man is gone, if he was there at all. Strange things are happening in Concordia these days, blurring the distinction between what is real and what are visions.

10

Dresden

the power of a girl

I am no longer the only beekeeper in town.

Another has recently arrived. I can sense him, smell him. Any other time, I wouldn't care. Beekeepers aren't territorial. Newcomers to an area can sting whoever they want.

But not this time.

The new beekeeper is in the parking lot behind the movie theater. I followed him here, and he knows it, which is why he's waiting for me to come out and say what's on my mind. What I'm doing is not conventional, and I have no idea what reaction I'll get. I step around the corner and immediately recognize the man leaning against a van, arms folded.

"Henrik." I say his name with neither relief or dread, because he sparks neither in me. I remember him from our imprisonment, long ago as human young men. Most of us had black hair and olive skin, but Henrik stood out with his light blond hair. He'd been a trader from the northern realms and his eyes, the color of a clear sky, had caught the attention of our captor.

I've crossed paths with Henrik enough times to know he isn't sadistic. He is also not *kind*, not that any of us are. Those who had been kind and good and loving as humans were the first ones to suffer mental breakdowns after the change. Henrik, if I recall correctly—which I may not—had kept to himself in our lavish prison, not mourning the loss of the life he'd been stolen from. Here, today, I don't need kindness. I just need cooperation.

He inclines his head. "Dresden."

"There is a Strawman in this town." I speak in the old tongue, which beekeepers reserve for the rare times we speak to each other.

Henrik takes this news with a sharp nod.

"Also, there is a girl under my protection. She is not to be stung." I sound like a self-inflated ass, braying in the wind. I have no right or wherewithal to protect anyone. I'm a shark warning another shark off a rotting whale carcass—*not* that I see Essie like that, but that's the problem, isn't it? I'm not seeing at least one of us as we truly are. But it's out there now, and Henrik is staring at me like wings have sprouted from my back.

"And how would I identify this girl you're protecting?" he asks reasonably. "Assuming my bees identify her as a target."

I am out of my depth. Henrik likely thinks I've lost my mind, and I can't make any assurances that I haven't. I pull a green hair elastic out of my pocket and hold it out to him.

Henrik looks from the elastic to me. A few of Essie's blond hairs twine around the thing, making her scent distinct. The fact that I have this is actually a big deal. There is no amusement on Henrik's face as he takes the elastic and holds it up to his nose. He closes his eyes and breathes deep.

"There is no fear on this." His voice is incredulous. He places the elastic back in my palm.

"No."

Henrik's nostrils flare. "Who is she to you?"

"She is…" The void that should be there for this question floods with a thousand descriptions, none of them right. Some of them frightening. "My friend."

Henrik's faces begin to change rapidly, the surest sign that he's unsettled. "Beekeepers don't have friends."

I won't argue that, although I suppose I could. "Nevertheless, I won't see her harmed."

"Is this why the Strawman is here? Because of *her?*"

I wince at that, and my bees sense it. They swarm out and surround my mouth like a hideous mask. I don't bother trying to contain them. "A Strawman's motives are never clear."

He opens his mouth, and bees empty from it like black and yellow buzzing vomit. "Look at me, brother," he says. "Look at me and see yourself. Now tell me how any human could care for you. For any of us."

For the first time in this conversation, I'm at peace with my reply. "It doesn't matter if she cares for me. I care for her." My fist closes around the hair elastic. "This girl is not to be touched. Please."

He looks at me for a long time, then nods. "Very well, Dresden. I will not sting her. And I will pass on your message, if I encounter any more of us."

"Thank you." My words come out with more relief

than I can afford to show.

"But if you have drawn the interest of a Strawman because of your…infatuation, your 'protection' will do her more harm than good. You should take the advice you just gave me and stay away from her."

He's right. I should know better than to get within two miles of her. I look away without replying.

Henrik shakes his head. "Fool." He bursts into a cloud of bees and disperses into the trees.

Yes, that I am.

It is night. Finally. I spent the afternoon watching the sun crawl toward the horizon with unreasonable impatience. All that waiting so I could be here, crouched in the elm tree outside her window like some lurker. Sheer white curtains fall in front of her window, but I can see the shape of her inside. Oversize pink T-shirt. Hair up in a bun with two pencils holding it in place. Long, beautiful neck. Bare feet. She's lying on her bed with a laptop, humming to a song playing through the computer's speakers.

Abruptly, she snaps her laptop shut and gets up. I watch her disappear from view, presumably to a desk to the side of the window, but suddenly she's at the window, jerking the curtains open, removing the screen. I go dead still in the tree as she sits on the sill, back against one side, one foot dangling outside. Her gaze is on the stars, not the tree. I am hidden for the moment, hopefully to remain that way. She's so close. Six feet away, maybe.

There's a slight breeze. It ruffles the tendrils of hair escaping her bun. Her nightshirt slides up her thighs, bunches around her hips. My throat goes dry, and my palms go clammy, and it takes me a moment to realize that what I'm feeling is attraction—not just the mental bit, but the physical element.

It's like a discovery—the memory of something so long forgotten, it's brand new again—and I'm not sure how to rid myself of it. Thoughts, images unfold along the lines I haven't had since I was a human man, so very long ago. They come unbidden—touching that smooth thigh, learning the texture of her skin, kissing her until we're made of breath and sighs. Feeling her touch…I close my eyes and recall her embrace in the woods. What an unexpected agony it had been to feel her pressed against me. But to be touched for desire rather than comfort—the thought is unendurable. And pointless. Whatever feelings Essie may have for me, attraction isn't one of them. My bees rumble a warning, but as usual these days, I ignore them.

"Dresden." Her soft voice drifts through the night air. It's the purest torment. A molten brand, searing my skin.

My belly contracts. My gaze snaps to her, breath held, but she's still only looking at the stars. There's a dreamy look on her face; a small smile playing on her lips. Long fingers slide along the ends of her hair. "Where are you?" she asks, so plaintive. So lonely. She doesn't expect an answer. She doesn't expect anything.

"I'm here." The words just come. I should want to take them back.

Her lips part on a tiny gasp, and she peers into the tree, searching for me. Henrik is right—I really am a fool, powerless to resist her. I push away from my spot against the trunk and emerge from the shadows.

Essie spots me. Her mouth breaks into a wide smile. I can't look away from it.

"It's you?" she whispers. "You're real?"

"Yes." My words come out sounding like a growl. "Very real."

She leans out a little more, and I thrust out a hand. "Be careful. Please don't fall."

She laughs, a little too loud for the quiet night. "I could say the same to you."

"It doesn't matter if I fall."

The dog next door starts barking. Essie looks to the street, narrows her eyes on the houses, a passing car. "You should come inside."

My stomach does a painful dip. "I don't think so."

"Oh, don't be dumb." She climbs back into her room and gestures me inside. "Come on. Before someone sees us."

I hesitate. Lurking outside her window is one thing. Going *in* is another. Essie's room is a forbidden kingdom. I don't belong in there. Or rather, it's the invitation that feels illicit. And there's the fact that my thoughts about this girl are not brotherly.

"Please, Dresden," she says. "It's not safe out there."

One day, I will say no to this girl and I will mean it. One day, I will walk away.

But not today.

11

Dresden

her
room

I change into bees as gently as I can, as she's so close, and aim my swarm for her open window. She steps back as I enter. Her face is alert but unafraid. I work to hasten the transformation back to my human shape. The sight of a huge bee swarm in someone's bedroom is a scary thing, but Essie stares in fascination as I re-form into the Dresden she knows. Her eyes are wide with wonder. Only a touch of uncertainty showing around the whites, revealing the sliver of her that wonders if what she's witnessing is real. My bees don't even react. Hopefully they've given up trying to get to her. I won't allow it, and besides, I've let them sting plenty. Too much, even. Their urges are satisfied, at least.

"I'm sorry about the entrance," I say. "I didn't know how else to—"

"It's fine. I've seen you do it before."

I try to keep my face in shadow. "I'm glad I didn't frighten you."

"I'm fine," she says again. "Were you out there long?"

"No," I lie, prideful creature that I am. "Just wanted to check on you. Are you distraught over...your discovery in the park?"

"You mean the dead woman we found? Yes and no." Her voice drops. "Did you know—when Aunt Bel and I returned, the body was *gone*. Did you know that?"

My eyes narrow. "I did not."

"All that was there was a plastic baggie containing her...toes. Detective Berk says they'll do everything they can to find the rest of her, and to find out who did it. It almost doesn't feel like it was real, you know?" She twirls the ends of her hair, then lets it spring back to straight.

"I wish it wasn't." I drag my gaze from her hair. "Real, that is."

"Me too. Poor Aunt Bel. She's so worried." She moves to the bed and sits on the edge, hands folded on her lap. It looks like it's taking effort for her to be still. "You don't have to hang out in the tree," she says. "Next time, just knock."

I smile faintly, not from amusement. "I don't think your aunt or grandmother would approve of me."

"Not on the door, silly." She rolls her eyes and waves her hands wildly in front of her face. She looks as if she's swatting bugs from the air—something only she can see. "On the window. I'll always let you in."

I close my eyes briefly. Does she have the slightest inkling how her words fill me with impossible thoughts? How she makes me want things I can never, ever have? Of course, she doesn't. Bees cluster in my throat, causing it to ache terribly. I shove my hands in my pockets and focus on a poster on the wall. It's a vintage movie poster from the mid-1980s and features a tease-haired goblin king, played by David Bowie, lording over his goblin subjects, surrounding the lovely girl trapped in his land. The film was called *Labyrinth*, and it was a good movie, despite the reviews it got at the time. I liked it. "Is it the movie you like, or Bowie?" I ask.

"Both." She looks at me in surprise. "You know who he is?"

"Of course. I enjoy going to the movies. It's a hobby, you could say." I move closer to the poster to put space between us. "Does that surprise you?"

"It does. You don't seem like you do many social things."

"There is nothing remotely social about watching a movie. No one notices me when I'm in a theater, anyway." I nod at the goblin king. "That was some hair, wasn't it?"

"And some pants," she says wistfully. "But that's not why—oh dear." Her face goes scarlet.

I can't help but laugh, and she does too. There's no denying Bowie's pants from the movie were spectacularly revealing, especially for a kids' movie.

"But seriously," she says, "I like Bowie because his music still smokes most of what's out there now."

"Can't argue with that," I murmur.

"…and he was odd, and talented, and dangerous, and he didn't care what anyone thought of him," she goes on, grinning. "And the movie…well, you don't ever know if the whole thing was real or Sarah's imagination, do you? I can relate to that." She pats the space next to her. On her bed. "Come sit with me."

I shouldn't, but my feet move before I've consented, and I'm seated next to her.

The power this girl has over me is terrifying.

She gives me a sideways look. "Can I show you something?"

My general policy would be to say no. But this is Essie. "Sure."

She slides off the bed and goes to the desk. That's when I notice the sketchbooks. A stack of black books, warped thick from paint and things glued inside. She chooses one and thumbs through it, brows furrowed. Somewhere in the middle, she picks it up and hands it to me. I take the book delicately in my hands and pull in a surprised breath. Goblins of her own design dance over the page. Hideous, misshapen creatures made beautiful by the hand of an artist.

"You drew these?" I ask stupidly.

She nods, going pink again. "They're some of the things I see," she says. "They're not all scary," she adds quickly.

I turn the pages with fingertips, careful not to smudge anything. The next page explodes in a vibrant watercolor of a dragon. As I keep going, I notice most of her pieces are fantasy or sci-fi based, with very few renderings from life. Then I come to a page of a simple pencil drawing of a man's face with a forked tongue and horns. There is a likeness here she's worked to achieve, and a tightness to this drawing that pricks my senses. "Who's this?" I ask.

She makes a face. "My psychiatrist, Dr. Roberts. I don't like him."

"Clearly. Is this how you see him?"

"Some days." She scratches her arm in an area that was already red and irritated looking. She opens her mouth, then closes it with a shrug.

"What?" I ask her. "Say it."

"He sits too close to me," she says. "And he wants me to live in Stanton House—it's a home for people like me and my family—but I don't want to. I really like living here, with my aunt." Her words tumble out in a rush. She bites her lip and glances away, as if she's ashamed to have an opinion about her circumstances. As if her life is a burden which must be thrust on someone.

I place a hand over her compulsively scratching fingers. They still instantly, and I pull my hand away. I don't want to get too used to touching her. "You should stay where you are happy," I say. "I can't imagine you are a burden to anyone."

She looks up at me, face solemn. "Thank you."

I take one last look at the drawing of Dr. Roberts's menacing face and forked tongue, then give her the sketchbook. She returns it to its spot on the shelf. I wait until she's sitting next to me to ask my next question, which seethes inside me. It takes great effort to not allow my voice to sound menacing. "When you said he sits too close to you, does he…touch you?" I growl out that last bit. If she says yes, I'll sting the bastard to death.

"No, he's just icky. But he's never…no. Nothing like that."

I relax my shoulders. "Why don't you get a different doctor, if he makes you uncomfortable? Can't your aunt find someone else?"

She hugs her arms around her middle. "We've tried, but my father has joint custody of me and insists on Dr. Roberts. Says he's the best around."

"And your mom?"

One corner of her mouth dips down, and I know this

is a question I shouldn't have asked. "She was an aid worker. She died of fever in a South American jungle when I was four."

I can feel my jaw going tight. This girl has no one except for an overwhelmed aunt, a dependent grandmother, and a potentially dangerous doctor. Her father isn't part of the day-to-day—just involved enough to make things difficult for her, and not enough to be even slightly useful. I can't do anything about her father, wherever he is, but I can, *and will*, take a closer look at this Dr. Roberts with the forked tongue. "I'm sorry."

She tilts her head, gazes up at me with those pale, water-blue eyes. "Can we talk about something different?" she asks. "Tell me something about yourself. Something I don't know."

"I wouldn't know where to start." I gaze over at her, at the pink still staining her cheeks. "You don't know anything about me."

Essie rolls her eyes. "Yes, I do, but whatever. I'll start. I was accepted to art school. A good one, in Rhode Island."

My brows go up in surprise. "That's wonderful."

"It is, isn't it?" She smiles, but her eyes are sad. "I'm not going, of course, but it was cool to be accepted. My grades are good, you know. When Aunt Bel can't teach me, she hires smart tutors."

"You're a very talented artist," I say. I don't ask her why she's not going for the same reason I shouldn't have asked about her mother.

"Thanks." Her smile wavers. "It's okay, you know? Even if I *could* go, we couldn't afford it. And my dad wouldn't help, but…" She shrugs. "But I'll always have that acceptance letter."

I nod gravely but say nothing this time. There's nothing I can add that would make her feel better, although I wish there was. A college curriculum has enough strain and anxiety to test the most mentally fortified.

"Now you," she prompts. "Tell me something about yourself that would surprise me."

"Surprise you?" I rub my chin and think. Most everything I could tell her about myself would surprise her. Terrify her. But there's one thing she might find interesting. Maybe. "A long time ago, before I was what I am now, I was married," I say, and am rewarded—or perhaps punished—with a look of pure shock.

"You were *married?*" Her easy gaze shifts to one of intense examination. "Shut up."

I smile at the abrupt shift in her scrutiny. "Okay."

"No, you're telling this story. All of it." She shifts closer. A dark flush works up her neck and into her cheeks. "Are you even old enough to be married? I can't tell your age by your face, obviously, but you seem young. What are you—seventeen? Eighteen?"

"I'm much older than that," I tell her. "But you are accurate, too—eighteen is when I stopped aging physically. People got married earlier than they do today. They usually didn't live as long, either." She stares at me expectantly, but I hesitate. "Do you really want to hear about this?"

"Yes! Spill." Her gaze flickers over me, brows arched. "Who *was* she?"

Her voice is tight with something when she asks this. I can't define it, but something about it fills me with a strange elation. There's an edge to her hesitancy, and I can't deny my heady pleasure at the way she's considering me right now—as someone who was desired, loved, once.

Worthy of love, capable of loving in return.

"She was a girl in my fishing village." Sadness pinches my chest. Like my own, I've forgotten her name, as well as a clear mental image of her. The details have eroded to a flash of smile, long, black hair, the general knowledge of lush, Mediterranean beauty. I have long since finished mourning the loss of my human life, but sometimes I mourn the loss of my memories of it. Still, it's hard to think about anyone other than Essie when I'm in the same space as her.

"We grew up together as children. Best friends," I say. "We always knew we would marry. We had only been together as man and wife for a few months when I...I was taken from my village."

Inwardly, I wince, because what comes next will be the story of how I became what I am. The story I have been dreading to tell, but also can't wait to share with her. "I was not always like this—" I circle a hand over my face, with a touch of relief. "I was a fisherman, working with my father and brothers on our boats. The seas were abundant, then. It was work I loved—work of the soul."

"What happened?" Essie asks softly. "Who took you?"

I lean back, focus on the ceiling rather than Essie's rapt face. "Many hundreds of years ago, the place I lived was ruled by a monarchy—a queen and, to a lesser extent, her king. She was great and powerful during her rule. There was peace, but she was also power obsessed, as many great leaders are.

"She...collected boys, men. Anyone who appealed to her, and apparently, I did. If she wanted you, her soldiers would seize you. It didn't matter if you were a father of ten, or a boy clutching his mother's skirts. She didn't care. We'd heard stories of mothers in the capital city disfiguring their handsome boys' faces, to keep them safe from the Queen's eye, but my family lived far from the capital. No one did this where I lived, as only a fraction of the rumors that came from the capital turned out to be true."

It's embarrassing, how badly I want to tell Essie this — how much I want her to imagine me as a man, rather than this creature I am now. "The Queen had never visited our village, it was so remote, until the one day she did, while on a grand tour of her lands. Her ship came into harbor the same time as ours was returning from a fishing expedition, and…" I pause for a moment with a shake of the head. This is the part I take pains to not think about. Not because it hurts, but because I remember how badly it used to. I can no longer summon any of the searing pain associated with those memories. The memories themselves are thin, as incomplete as my name. Like grainy snapshots from someone else's life. The emotions are fires that have long since cooled to ash.

"The next thing I knew, I was a prisoner in the Queen's private court. That was the end of my life as a free man." I shrug. "I never saw my wife or brothers again."

Essie lightly touches the back of my hand. I stifle the urge to turn mine over and feel her palm against mine.

"Did you fight? Did your family argue for your release?" she asks.

"Oh no," I say with a hard chuckle. "Those rulers were not challenged. Executions were swift and frequent. It was a different time. A far more dangerous time."

"So that was it?" Essie asked, astounded. "You could *never* go home?"

"Yes. She never released her prisoners."

"What did she want with you?"

I pause again, mulling over what to omit from this next part. It requires some delicacy. The Queen didn't take young men for decoration. She used us for her pleasure, which spanned quite a range of taste. Until that point in my life, I'd only known the enthusiastic, sometimes fumbling, but always joy-filled lovemaking of my wife. The world I was thrust into as part of the Queen's court was traumatizing, humiliating, degrading. There is no universe in which Essie needs to know what was done to me there.

"We served a variety of duties," I say carefully. "We were her personal servants."

"That's horrible," she whispers, thankfully not asking for more details. "Didn't the King object to his wife having a harem of boys at her disposal?"

My cheeks warm. Perhaps Essie is better at reading between the lines than I thought. "Yes, he did. He hated her, and vice versa, but the King wasn't the one wielding power."

She stares at me, puzzled for a moment. "Oh," she says. "He couldn't stand up to her."

"I suppose that's it, yes." I could almost laugh at the absurdity of discussing the personal habits of individuals who are so long dead, not even dust remains.

"Did you try to escape?"

I laugh. "No." I cock my head. It will be interesting to see how she digests this next thing I tell her. "There was magic, at that time. Sorcery, alchemy—whatever you want to call it. It was at the center of everything. People dedicated their lives to learning the secrets of the energy currents of the world. By the time the Queen took me, magic was reaching a tipping point. It had become a thing of hate, control, and oppression.

"There were new experiments starting, merging people with animals to create better soldiers, spies, messengers. Humans who turned into birds and who could scent impending death on the wind. Women with fish tails instead of legs to scout ahead of warships on the sea. Boys merged with bees whose sting could turn a whole army raging against itself, making it easy to defeat."

I roll my shoulders and cast a quick glance her way. "Is this too much?"

"No." She shifts closer. "It's…amazing to know that you lived in this world. That you lived in a place that sounds like something I'd see in a vision."

"Most people wouldn't believe me."

She raises one brow. "I am definitely *not* most people."

"No, you are not." She is a brilliant lily in a sea of grass. I clasp my hands together to keep them from reaching for her.

"Go on!" She bounces a little on the bed. "I want to hear how this ends."

"You can see how it ends," I say quietly, gesturing to my face.

Her brows knit. "How can you say that? This story is far from over."

I know she's not talking about the one I'm telling, but this one, here. Between us.

"The empire was crumbling," I continue, ignoring the *other* story for now. "The sorcerers needed 'volunteers' for their experiments, and when the Queen was off, the King had us rounded up and marched us off to the cellars. We were strapped down, sedated. What they did to us in that state, I don't recall, but I didn't leave the sorcerers' quarters a human being. The beekeepers had been created. I left with a belly full of bees and hungers so terrifying, I wanted to die. But I couldn't, of course. They made sure of that."

Essie closes her mouth, which had fallen open. I worry for a moment that I spoke too much. Frustratingly, her expression isn't revealing one bit of her thoughts.

"So all those men and boys—they were all turned into beekeepers? How many of you were there?"

"Thirty-five. We still walk this earth, centuries later, cursed forever."

"But what happened to all that magic?" she asks. "Some of it must still be here, right?"

"Well, shortly after we were created, the sorcerers and alchemists revolted. They went about destroying everything touched by magic. They aimed to purge the world of it for good. Mostly, they succeeded. All records of it were burned, so no one would find the secrets and could repeat the same mistakes they had. Millions died in this mass cleansing.

"They created several diseases over the years—the Great Plague being one of them—that targeted and killed those with magic flowing through their veins, and there were a lot of people affected by magic. When it was over, the world was thrown into the dark ages. People used primitive means to survive. Whole civilizations were reduced to rubble. Myself and those like me, as well as a few other types of creatures, could take other forms and escape. It was the biggest mistake we made. We should have died when we had the chance, because now there is no escape from this life."

I've gotten terribly morbid. I force out a chuckle. "So that's the story of how I was married once. Aren't you sorry you asked?"

"No." Essie's lips are white and the bottom one quivers a little. "What became of her? Of your wife?"

It shouldn't surprise me that Essie asks this, but it does. "I don't know. I never returned to my village after I became a beekeeper." I raise a hand, let it drop to the mattress between us. "I hope she led a good life and died peacefully."

"It's sad that you never got to talk to her again, to explain what happened to you."

"That would have been cruel." I gesture again to my face. "Can you imagine being married to this?"

She points at her temple without breaking eye contact with me. "Can you imagine being married to this?"

I gently pull away. "There's no comparison. I'm a monster."

"So am I," she says in a silky voice. "My monster lives inside my head. People are afraid of monsters, wherever they reside."

"People are fools."

She tilts her head. "Do you really think so? I look at what Aunt Bel goes through to take care of Grandma Edie and me and I think there's good reason to steer clear of people like us. I'm a lot of work."

"You're not."

"I am," she says. "I can't drive. I can't go to school or get a job. I'm on a lot of medicine, which is expensive and always changing because it never really works. And my condition is getting worse over time."

My hands clench at hearing her talk so matter-of-factly

about herself like that, like she's someone's albatross. Nothing more than a burden. I look at her, and I see magic.

"Okay, my turn," she says, waving her hands. "I bet you didn't know that I'm famous."

"You're right. I didn't know that."

"Well, I am. In the psychiatric world, everyone knows my family's name, and mine, specifically." She twirls a lock of hair around her finger. "They don't really know what's wrong with any of us. Nothing fits a diagnosis." She shrugs one shoulder, suddenly not so buoyant. "But my claim to fame is that the Wickerton curse struck me at the youngest age of anyone in my family, which is usually late teens to mid-twenties. I've had research papers written about me."

I scramble for a reply—something appropriate, whatever that is to her. Sympathy? Should I make a joke? "I'm sorry."

She looks at me, confused, and I want to kick myself for choosing the wrong response. I am out of practice with conversation.

"For what?" she asks. "You didn't make me this way." Her eyes widen, and she leans forward. "Did you? You didn't sting me as a baby, did you?"

"No, I did not," I say, and it's the truth, but her question clangs around in my head like loose silverware, refusing to settle. The words taste like acid on the back of my tongue. I back farther from her, sliding off the bed.

If I stay there much longer, with only a few inches separating us, I'm going to touch her again. It's best if I don't. She gets up, too, but with an inquisitive frown, closes the distance again. My hands start to shake. Suddenly, it's imperative for me to get out of here. Now. Before I do something stupid and declare my feelings for her. Her inevitable rejection would be far more painful than her innocent touch.

I step away, toward the window. "I'm glad you're doing well, after what happened this morning."

Her face pinches. "That *was* horrible."

It was nothing compared to the disaster headed for this town. The harbingers and I are here for one reason — to feed off death, fear, and pain. I hope I can save her then, when those things devour this community. We have a few rules, though no one's sure where they came from, but one of them is: no interference. Let the dying die. Let the suffering suffer. Feed off it, then leave. But there is no way I'm doing that with Essie. If it's within my power, she'll survive the coming event. To hell with the rules. The Strawman can come for me. I don't care.

"Stay back when I change, okay?" I say gruffly. "You shouldn't be too close to the bees."

"Wait." She reaches out, grabs my hand. I go still. Her hand is soft, her fingers long. Her palm presses to mine. The sensation is so intense it aches. It's hard to do this. I've gone without skin-to-skin contact for so long, I'd forgotten how amazing it feels.

After so long of feeling nothing, I'm feeling *everything*. A bottle uncapped. I'll never cram everything back inside and get it sealed up again.

Her thumb brushes mine, and my hand closes around hers. I want to shake her off, just so I can breathe again. But I go on standing there, letting her hold my hand. Letting a hurricane roar through my head, blood, heart.

"Will you come back?" she asks.

"Do you want me to?"

"Of course, I do," she replies.

"Why?" I ask, because it makes no sense that she would.

She smiles, looking perplexed. "I *like* you, Dresden."

It's a simple statement until you consider the many shades of the word "like." I don't know Essie's meaning of it in regards to me, but it almost certainly doesn't mirror my version of feelings for her.

My "like" is a beastly thing floating atop a millennium of deep and long and unbroken suffering. In all likelihood, Essie "likes" me in the most basic version of the word, the way she'd like a Labrador Retriever—uncomplicated and sweet. At least, I hope that's how she means it, because if her feelings are even a little more than that, it's a thing so unnatural the Earth may crack open and swallow us both.

"I like you, too," I say.

Her lips spread wide, and her mouth opens, giving me a view of her molars. Her smile is feral and desolate. To anyone else, this smile would be disturbing, but anyone else is anyone else.

"So, you'll come back?" she asks again.

"Yes."

"Good." She stares up at me, eyes blue as the sea, dark as an abyss. "One day, I'll see your real face."

This is too much. I close my eyes and lean away with a shudder. I can't do this, not with bees roiling in my chest and God-knows-what-horror sliding over my face.

"That face is gone." My voice is growly, and I don't think my expression is nice. Without another word, I turn and dive out of her bedroom window, giving over to the swarm the instant I've cleared the sill. I fly, tumbling over fields of soybeans and miles of roads, a chaotic mess of man and beast.

No matter how far I go, she's there: paper-thin glass spun into the shape of this girl.

A gleaming curve in the corner of my mind's eye.

Always. And, I fear, always forever.

12

Essie

the
white pills

I am a dull thing. The back of a spoon. A worn knob of a cane. All my edges sanded smooth by a rainbow of pills: Blue. Yellow. Green. White.

Okay, not exactly a rainbow.

The white one is new.

"Essie, tell me about how you felt, finding that girl in the woods."

I blink slowly at Dr. Roberts. The edges of him are a little fuzzy, but he's mostly normal looking today, except for the tongue which is still long and pink and forked at the end.

Something new: the smoldering carcass of a raccoon drapes over the top of his head. Smoke curls from it. The smell is like burned hair. Crispy paws and snout hang over his forehead, almost to his eyebrows. Bones protrude from the blackened flesh. The only way I know it's a raccoon is by the puffed, striped tail, which is untouched. Judging by how Dr. Roberts reacted to my comment about his tongue last time, I'm not going to mention the raccoon. He's still sitting closer than I'd like.

My gaze slides to the window, where some bees are lazily exploring the flowered window boxes outside. I notice bees everywhere now. They make me think of Dresden. I think about Dresden a lot, when my mind is clear enough for it. I started taking the white pill four days ago, and all it's done is strip away most of *me*. I haven't drawn in my sketchbook. Hours slide together in quiet waves. I've stared at the TV and slept.

Now I'm here in Dr. Roberts's office trying to answer his questions. What did he just ask me? Oh. He wants to hear about the dead lady.

"I was scared," I reply.

He leans in. His knee bumps mine. "Talk to me about that."

"About what?" I move my leg away as my stomach churns. The white pill makes me nauseous and keeps me that way, causing me to lack the energy or will to do anything. Today, my stomach is acutely unsettled. Alarmingly so. I glance to the door, where the bathroom is down the hall. There is a decent chance I won't make it through this session without throwing up.

Almost a week has passed since the night Dresden came to my room. Maybe a few days. Maybe a week. It's a memory that shines through the fog like a beacon. I think I did okay that night. I'm not sure why he hasn't come back.

"Tell me what you saw, how you felt about what you saw." Dr. Roberts positions his pen over his pad. He looks so eager. "Please be as detailed as you can."

"I don't want to talk about it." I wave a hand, and screw

good manners, I need some space. That raccoon carcass *stinks*. "Would you please lean back? You're too close."

Dr. Roberts has the nerve to look offended, but he leans back a few inches and adjusts his glasses. "I'm not trying to crowd you, Essie. I need to observe your reactions. Your father is very concerned about what you witnessed last week."

I snort out a laugh. "No, he isn't."

"Of course he is. He's your father."

Something inside me snaps. I'm the one who leans forward this time. The room swims a little at the quick movement. I wonder if this is what being drunk feels like. "My father is only concerned about where to find his next drink. He was horrible to me when I lived with him. When he visits, he says terrible things, calls me disgusting names. I don't know what face he shows you, but the one I see is a monster." I sit back abruptly, slamming my back against the tight leather chair. "So don't sit there and tell me that he cares about me. He doesn't."

The forked tongue flicks out, retracts.

My stomach heaves. Goddamn, those white pills. "And I don't like this new medication. It upsets my stomach."

He scribbles furiously on the pad. "Actually, I think they're working well. This is the most open you've been with me. I'd call today a mini breakthrough. We can begin working on this misperception you have about your father."

I roll my eyes because it's wiser than screaming at him. Aunt Bel tells me not to antagonize him. And besides, I used up all my energy speaking, which was apparently pointless.

My stomach clenches with acute nausea. Forget the

bathroom. "Do you have a trash can?"

He doesn't look up from his notes. "There's one next to my—"

I make a lunge for the can, but don't quite make it. I vomit the Apple Jacks I ate for breakfast. Some makes it into the trash can, but most sprays on his nice Berber carpet.

"I really don't like the white pills," I gasp, but I feel better already.

He gazes down at me with an expression I don't like. He looks as though he's trying to stifle a smile. "I'll prescribe you something to calm your stomach," he says, pulling out his prescription pad. "The white pills stay."

13

Dresden

falling

I don't care for Essie's psychiatrist.

I am in swarm form, clumped under the eaves of Dr. Roberts's office building on Main Street. A few bees are hanging out in the flowers, watching what's going on in there with Essie's appointment. I can't hear, of course, but the man's body is positioned all wrong. He hovers over her like a cat playing with a mouse. I get a few glimpses of his eyes through the window.

The way he looks at her is wrong. I've seen men look at a woman like this many times, when they want to do something with someone they know they shouldn't.

The energy he emits is dank and prickly. I'm well versed with this variety. He's not a good man, but not evil, either. He exists in a wavering gray space that's actually quite unstable. You would think not being evil would be a good thing, but true evil is a rare thing, indeed. Most so-called "evil" people are sick, damaged creatures, born with bad wiring in the head or ruined young by some other, equally sick person. I've encountered true evil only a few times in all my long years, and most who possess it prove incapable of hiding it.

Evil pulses from their pores, corrupts everything they touch, poisons the very air they breathe. These people rarely last long in society. They are dispatched by the populace, quickly and viciously, but leaving scars on those they touched long after their short, destructive lives are ended.

This man would not be here if he were *evil*. He maintains a place in society, a psychiatric practice, a residence. I am certain, however, that his feelings for Essie are not the simple doctor-patient variety. Essie should not be alone with him. He touches her now with bumps to the knee, casually crowding her space. He won't always be satisfied with being in her space, with little touches. One day, his restraint will fail him, unless he is removed from her life.

I wish I could hear what they are talking about in there.

Ordinarily, Dr. Roberts would be a person I would consider stinging, but only if there wasn't a stronger target around. I could never do it now. It would put Essie in even greater danger.

I wonder if he was stung by another beekeeper. I wouldn't know it, if he was. Our stings don't work like dogs marking a tree. It's possible to be unfortunate enough to be stung multiple times by different beekeepers. There's nothing I could do about it if he *was* stung. He has a shelf life, if that's the case, as he'll only be able to hide the venom's effects for so long. I'll keep a close eye on him, just in case. Perhaps the impending disaster the harbingers are predicting will take care of him. Perhaps I will ensure that it does.

A crow caws in the eave next to me, startling me into dislodging my swarm. The crow dips its head low and caws again, repeatedly. It must be Michael with something to tell me. I collect all my bees and roar away from town in an angry roil. None of the other beekeepers cease their activities to answer the call of a harbinger. Sometimes, maintaining a friendship is infinitely aggravating.

I take human form in a violent rush at the edge of the orchard, coming together in a jagged, disorganized clumping of bees.

Michael hunches in his crow form, head bent at a strange angle as he struggles to transform. This isn't right. I step forward in alarm, unsure how to help. Unsure if I *can*. Finally, a cloud of black fog billows from his crow's beak. It envelops him as usual, but the substance, which usually smells like smelting iron, instead carries the stench of stagnant water. The black stuff elongates, shapes itself into a man, but this one is much taller, thinner than Michael.

A wide straw hat emerges on the man's head, and a face forms. Clothing materializes—something harbingers do not get when they transform—but the garments are those of an old-fashioned farmer. It's the Strawman. I had no idea he could do this. The black fog, which usually pours back inside the harbinger's mouth, sinks heavily into the earth. The grass dies instantly, leaving a dead circle where the Strawman stands.

I'm afraid, and I'm so unaccustomed to fear that I want to attack him and flee simultaneously. The result is complete immobility. "Where's Michael?" I can't keep the wobble from my voice.

I don't know how a Strawman sees with those sewn-shut eyes, but he's looking right at me. Possibly through me. I shouldn't be surprised if some previous version of him *did* create me, after all.

Why?

The question sounds deep in my head. A rusty, ground-down voice not my own. It takes me a moment to remember this is how the Strawman speaks, as he did the same thing the day of the fair. And he's ignored my question, of course, and posited one of his own. Why should he bother with the inquiries of a lowly creature such as myself?

"Why, what?" I ask. There was a time, as a young man, when I was brought before a group of powerful sorcerers. I fell to my knees and begged for my life. A week ago, I would have said I'd never bow to anyone again. I can't say that anymore. I would do anything he asked, if it meant keeping Essie safe.

Why now, after all these long years? the Strawman asks.

For a second, I consider lying, denying. My first instinct is to protect Essie, keep her off the Strawman's radar, but she's already on it, and if he's speaking inside my head, he's likely seeing everything going on in there anyway. Honesty may be my smartest move. If I even have a move.

"Because now is *her*." It doesn't matter if Essie had been a hundred years ago or if her time wasn't for another five hundred years. It's about *her*. The Strawman knows this, so I don't know why he bothered bringing me out here to ask. "Don't hurt her."

The Strawman tilts his head. He raises a hand, and my body suddenly rises off the ground. I struggle against the sensation of constricting bands around my body. I attempt to change into bees, but I can't. Like what he did to Michael, he's controlling my ability to transform into my animal state. Bees expel from my mouth in an agitated cloud. Only the queen and her drones stay deep within.

The Strawman makes a fist, and the pressure increases. I can't pull in a breath. My bones bend like drawn longbows. I can almost hear them creaking under the strain.

If I do not harm the girl you adore, do not mistake it for kindness or generosity. I possess neither. I am neither. I am the darkener of minds and thief of light. I do not answer to you, beekeeper.

I nod. It's all I can do at the present. There's no air for breath. A single rib snaps in my back. I gasp at the surprise pain.

Perhaps pain was what he was waiting for, as he releases me immediately. I sink to the ground. The invisible bands around me disappear. Already, the pain is subsiding. The bone is knitting. The Strawman, for his part, stands slightly hunched over. His hands tremble before he locks them behind his back. Perhaps they are not quite so infallible after all.

"You said I was supposed to right a wrong," I say quietly. "But if you want me to kill her, I won't. You can break all of my bones. You can break everything, and I still won't."

There. It is said.

You are close, beekeeper. So close.

"Close to what?" I can't banish the anguish from my voice, my expression. "How can I protect her?"

Reach deep inside yourself. The answer is there.

Deep inside myself? And here we go with meaningless

riddles and nonsense that the Strawmen are known for. "Did you create a monster in this town?" I ask, risking another go with his crushing power.

You created the monster, beekeeper. I merely awoke it.

The Strawman bows his head. The black fog lifts from the dead circle of earth to envelop him again. The smell of it changes from swamp to the familiar, and much welcome, smells of a blacksmith's shop. A few moments later, Michael stands there, trembling and disoriented. The puckered mess of scars twisting over his torso is angry red and appears irritated. The black fog funnels into Michael's mouth, to be released the next time he transforms. He blinks at the poisoned earth beneath him, then up at me. "What am I doing here?"

I back up, rest against a gnarled peach tree. My knees aren't steady. My back still retains a slight ache. "The Strawman took over your body. He was just..."

"The *Strawman* was here?" Michael joins me in the shade of the tree. The sky is clear and blue. There is no breeze. "What do you mean, he 'took over my body'?"

How to explain something I don't even know the mechanics of? But more intriguingly, *why* did the Strawman do that? "What is the last thing you remember?"

He rubs his temples. "This morning, we took the death energy of a suicide just outside town. He was one of yours," Michael clarifies, because he thinks I'll ask. I wouldn't. Not today. "Older male, lived alone. Worked in a call center."

The harbingers feel an annoying need to acknowledge the dead by discussing them at length, but I do not. I will acknowledge them until the end of time by wearing the dead on my face.

"After that, I was..." Michael scratches the top of his

golden head. "Heading to the distribution center, where I found temporary work loading trucks. I was just walking down the highway. Next thing I knew, I was here." He looks down at himself, apparently just noticing that he is naked. "Damn. Lost my clothes again."

"Why would the Strawman need your body?" I murmur, more to myself than him. "He wanted me vulnerable, off balance. He succeeded in that. What better way than to take over the body of someone I—" I break off, roll away the words *care about*. "Someone I know." But the Strawman would know that his presence alone would throw me off balance. He would know that I *am* vulnerable in his presence. Unless that is no longer the case.

"Maybe they're weakening," Michael offers, mirroring my thoughts. "Maybe they're not as powerful as they used to be."

I can't argue with him. Each time I've seen the Strawman, he's exhibited great power, of course, but also an underlying fatigue. He holds it in the stooped curve of his body; in the deep heave of his chest. It is as if every expression of power comes at a price.

"Perhaps he needed your body because his own is starting to fail him." The words surprise me. "You'd recently taken in energy. You were charged up. The Strawman may have needed that. How do you feel, now?"

"I feel depleted. He drained me of what I'd taken this morning." He rubs his hands over his face. "What did he say to you? Of course, I understand if it's a private matter between the two of you." There's an edge to his words. A hint of distrust and suspicion that I don't like. I don't know how to assure him that I'm not in league with this creature, but I would like to.

Somehow, Michael's opinion has become important to me.

"He reminded me of his power," I say in measured tones. "He said I was 'close,' but didn't say what I was close to. He told me that I created the monster that is killing in this town, and he told me that the answer to keeping Essie safe was inside me and that I should reach deep for it."

"Reach inside yourself?" Michael frowns. "What the hell is *that* supposed to mean? The only thing inside you is a lot of bees."

"I know."

He shakes his head. "And I fail to see how you created a monster. We are monitoring every person you've stung, and none of them are—or were—involved in any psychotic business other than what usually accompanies your bees' sting. Your victims didn't murder that young woman everyone is talking about."

"I'd know it, if they did."

"Are you sure that was all the Strawman said to you?" Michael asks.

I straighten, eliciting a series of satisfying pops up my spine. "He reminded me, in dramatic fashion, that he doesn't answer to me."

He winces. "That mustn't have been pleasant."

"It was not," I say honestly. "Little has been pleasant since you birds set foot in this marked town. I feel as though I have fallen into a chasm I have no hope of emerging from."

I shake my head, annoyed with myself for saying that, and eager to steer the conversation elsewhere. "You know about that young woman Essie found in the park?" Nothing happens in a town occupied by harbingers of death that the crows don't know about. They are like the peeping toms of the supernatural world. "When your crow came to me today, I thought perhaps you came to tell me you knew who it was."

"Interestingly enough, we have no idea who committed that murder." He rubs his chin. "The killing did not call us, and whoever the murderer is, they don't carry the scent of death on them, which is odd. Most killers wear it for many years—some, for life. There are a few living here who bear that scent, but it's old. Nothing fresh, I'm sorry to say. If I learn anything, I will tell you, of course."

"Thank you."

Michael leans toward me, and I instinctively lean away. This has been happening often lately: people leaning toward me. It's unnerving. "You should know that more harbingers are coming. Not just because of the coming event, but because they're curious about what's happening with *you*. A beekeeper falling for a human girl—it's never happened." He gives me a long look, the way someone looks at a locked door. "Have you considered that maybe there's more to your connection than coincidence?"

I sigh, weary all of a sudden. "You're a superstitious, gossiping lot. There's no grand conspiracy here, Michael."

"My group and I aren't so sure," he says. "Harbingers are ruled by instincts, signs." His gaze slides away. "It says something that what's happening in this town is attracting so many of our kind. They think fate brought you here."

"Fate?" I barely contain a chuckle. "You scavengers can keep your talk of connections and destiny. I care about Essie, as unnatural as that is, and it's going to end one way: with her dying—preferably much later, rather than sooner—and me having to go on." My voice cracks on the last word. Bees dribble from my lips. "I can't bear the thought, but that's my *fate*, Michael. There is nothing grand or even noteworthy about it."

Michael cocks his birdlike gaze to the clear blue sky. "Actually, there's plenty grand and noteworthy about what's happening here, Dresden, but you are probably right," he says. "About how this will end with her, that is. Can you handle it, if she dies sooner, rather than later?"

He's asking me if I'll lose my mind if Essie doesn't survive our time here. It's a valid question. There are beekeepers roaming the Earth right now whose sanity evaporated long ago. A few have even lost the ability to speak, let alone use any good judgment. Their humanity is gone. Yet, *they* go on.

"I'll have no choice," I say. "I'll go on."

With all the monsters I've created.

With all the horrors I've breathed life into.

14

Essie

the rest
of it

On Friday morning, the body of the woman I found in the park turned up in Potter's Creek. What was left of her, anyhow. It hadn't rained for a while, and when it poured overnight, the higher water dislodged her from the spot she'd been left. The water carried her downstream to the McKannon farm, where Sylvia McKannon's dogs found her.

The only way I know this is because Detective Berk called Aunt Bel and me to the police station and told us about it. And the only reason she did *that* is because we knew the dead girl.

Detective Berk's name plaque is missing. Probably stuffed in a drawer because I made such a fuss about it during my last visit. I'd like to think it's gone because it's in the process of being replaced with one bearing the correct spelling of her name.

"The victim was a student at the college. She was twenty years old and lived in an off-campus apartment,"

Detective Berk tells us. "And a biology major."

Steam is coiling off the top of Aunt Bel's head. Literally, it is. It's like there's a pot of boiling water hidden inside her voluminous bun giving off steady puffs of water vapor. "You pulled me off a double shift at the hospital to tell us this poor girl's major?" she snaps.

"No." Detective Berk hands over a photograph. She smells strange today, like a glass of milk left out in the sun. "I'm telling you because this young woman tutored Essie. She'd been to your house."

I take in the pretty, smiling girl in a cable-knit cardigan. "Oh." My lungs empty. "It's Miss Leeds—Meredith."

"Meredith Leeds was your science tutor last year, wasn't she?" Detective Berk asks. "We have records of payment."

"Yes, I'm aware." Aunt Bel's eyes narrow. "And this is very, very sad news. But we could have established this with a simple phone call."

"Not the rest of it." Detective Berk slides over another photograph, to my aunt, this time. Not to me, but I can still see it clear enough. This photo is of Miss Leeds as the McKannons' dogs found her—skin gray and mottled, dress torn. Something blue is clutched between her fingers. She doesn't look anything like a person anymore, certainly not the bright, way-too-excited-about-science tutor who came over twice a week last year and wasn't upset about working with a girl who sometimes told her she was bleeding from the eyes. *She was*, I tell you.

I look away from the photo with a whimper. Aunt Bel flips the photo over with a hiss. "What is wrong with you, Anne Marie?"

"I know it's hard to look at." Detective Berk pushes the

photo back toward me. "I need you to take a close look at what she's holding. Here..." She turns the photo back over but takes several pieces of blank copy paper and blocks off the rest of the photo, framing out everything but what Meredith Leeds is holding. I never noticed before how large Detective Berk's hands are. "Do you recognize that, Essie?"

I lean forward and peer at the isolated part of the photo. It looks like she's holding... "Hey, that's my baseball cap," I say. "The one I wore to the park the day I found her."

"You confirm it's your hat, Essie?" Detective Berk asks.

"Well, yeah," I reply. "I lost it in the woods that day."

Aunt Bel draws in an audible breath. She clasps a hand around mine and squeezes hard. The steam puffing from her head turns thick and dark and takes on the odor of charcoal.

"There's a connection here, Ms. Roane," says Detective Berk to my aunt. "A connection between this crime and Essie that goes beyond her finding the body."

Aunt Bel's voice goes low and dangerous. "Do I need to call a lawyer?"

Detective Berk doesn't blink. "Only if you feel that's necessary."

My aunt pins her with a hard stare. "Is my lamb a *suspect?*"

"A few officers are looking into that witness's claim of hearing Essie and a man speaking in the woods the morning Miss Leeds's toes were found in the park. They think Essie is a possibility, considering."

"Of course. *Considering.*" Aunt Bel narrows her eyes.

The air clouds with smoky steam.

Detective Berk leans forward. "Look, I'm aware that Essie would have tremendous difficulty carrying a body this far. It's absurd to think she could manage such a thing, physically. Not without an accomplice. Plus, she's either with you and your mother, or a caretaker. And…" A small smile cracks her severe expression. "I don't believe it's in Essie's nature to harm anyone. But we must consider every possibility. My colleagues certainly will."

Aunt Bel's hand slaps on the desk. "My sweet lamb may see and hear things we can't, but she's never harmed anyone, not even when she's had reason to." She means my father. I had good reason to harm him, I suppose. Aunt Bel's hand eases its death grip on mine.

"Whether we like it or not, Essie is somehow involved in this crime." Detective Berk gathers up the photographs and tucks them back in the folder. "We don't know how yet."

"Am I being framed?" I ask. "Like on TV shows?"

"I don't know," Detective Berk replies. "That was your hat between Meredith Leeds's hands. And Miss Leeds was your tutor. And then there's the family connection. The toes were removed just like our Wickerton ancestor, something that's a well-known fact around here."

"You can't seriously—" Aunt Bel starts.

"We have to consider it," Detective Berk cuts in. "We'd like it if you ladies stayed local for a while, until this is all sorted out."

"Good heavens." Aunt Bel pats her collarbone. She looks me over, as if trying to imagine me hauling a body through the woods, then shakes her great, smoking head. "You can't be serious. The hat could have gotten in Miss

Leeds's hands any number of ways. The killer obviously put it there."

"Yes," Detective Berk says, looking up. "But why?"

Why indeed? I ponder this, thinking through possibilities as best as the white pills allow. The white pills make thinking *so* hard. "Are we in danger?" I ask. "Is the killer going to come after me?"

Detective Berk pauses. The dark mark pulses on her arm. It's grown larger since the last time I saw her. Half her forearm is black and charred looking. "That is a possibility we are aware of."

Aunt Bel mutters something like a curse under her breath. "So we're suspects and potential victims. Which is it, Anne Marie?"

The detective's brows pull into a warning frown. "If I knew, we'd be having a different conversation."

I feel like my head is floating three feet above my body. But I can hear the pounding of my heart and feel the sweat on my hands and understand that the police are thinking that maybe *I killed this woman.*

Because of the Wickerton curse.

Because who else do they have? I'm the one they picked up last year, yelling at Craig Murphy's dog to give back the First Avenue trees, which had been cut down that morning. *I'm* the one they had to restrain, because poor Mr. Murphy was afraid I was going to attack his seven-year-old Saint Bernard, Willie. I would *never* have done that, but that dog laughs at me *to this day* about the incident. I don't like him. So, I shouldn't be surprised if the investigators think maybe I'm disturbed enough to murder someone. Doesn't make it less terrifying, because I'm certain I did not murder anyone.

"We'll be assigning extra patrol officers to your street. I recommend keeping the doors locked and not going out alone. Stay vigilant. Be aware of anyone following you or showing unusual attention. Don't hesitate to call me with any new information, no matter how minor it seems." She gets up, signaling the end of this meeting. "And like I said, stick around town, please."

"I'm ashamed of you, Anne Marie. You have no other leads, so you're targeting my poor girl. Hasn't she suffered enough?" Aunt Bel's words come out sounding tremulous, like she's holding back tears. But I've never seen Aunt Bel cry, not even when she should.

"Actually, a past of neglect and abuse can manifest in violent behavior later on, so says the psychiatrist we consult with."

Gee, I wonder which psychiatrist that is? Dr. Roberts is the only one with a practice in Concordia. Choices are limited.

"That's bull crap and you know it." Aunt Bel surges to her feet. "Come, Essie. We're leaving. Unless you plan to make an arrest?"

Detective Berk sighs. "No. Of course you can go."

I get up. My legs are wobbly, and my mouth is packed full of sand. When I open it to say goodbye to Detective Berk, a whole load of it falls out and plops on the floor. I cough and wipe my mouth and apologize for making a mess on the floor.

Aunt Bel puts her arm around my shoulders and leads me from the police station. She leaves a smoldering trail of cooked hair behind her. I don't know how I'm going to stand being closed up with it smoking like that. "Aunt Bel," I say. "I can't breathe in the car with your hair doing that."

A moment of incomprehension passes over her face before she opens the car door with a tired smile. "We'll crack the windows, okay?"

"Okay." I lean back on the headrest and gaze out on Main Street. The strange man with the strange eyes and that big floppy hat stands smack in the middle of the intersection, seemingly unconcerned with the cars whizzing inches from him, whipping up his coat with their wind. He is still and staring at me. Cars drive past him, but not around him. I don't think he's real.

I dig out a peppercorn from my pocket and pop it in my mouth before Aunt Bel comes around to her side of the car. I crunch, wince at the explosion of pepper in my mouth.

Aunt Bel's hair instantly stops letting off smoke, but the man is still there. Maybe I need something stronger than peppercorns. Aunt Bel puts the car in drive, and we move toward the intersection.

The man gets closer and closer as we approach. Close up, he's not as much scary as he is sad looking. Or maybe he's not trying to be scary this time, like he was when I saw him through the window of the sandwich shop. He looks tired and sad and...lonely.

I know all about lonely.

I put down my window to get a better view of his face. There's definitely something off about it. The wind makes the sound of the ocean. Rain spatters on the windshield, sprinkles on my nose and cheeks. As we pass the man, I get a good look at him. Finally, I can see what's wrong with his eyes—they're sewn shut. His mouth, too—small, even stitches close up eyelids and lips. For a moment, we're face to face, a few scant feet apart. He raises a hand, although greeting or warning—it's not clear. I lean out the window, but we've passed him. I lean out farther and look back at the forlorn man standing in the middle of the intersection.

Aunt Bel grabs a fistful of my shirt and yanks me back inside. "Get your head in this car," she barks. "I won't have a decapitation on my watch."

I pick peppercorns from my teeth and give her a sideways glance. "Are you mad at me, Aunt Bel?"

She looks surprised. "Why would I be mad at you?"

"Because…" I slouch low in my seat. "Because I'm hard to live with. Because everyone's going to think I'm a murderer now."

"Everyone is *not* going to think you're a murderer."

"They will," I say. "If the police start asking a lot of questions about me, people will know I'm a–a…suspect." The word tastes bitter.

"They can think what they like, as they always do," my aunt replies mildly. "They'll be proven wrong when the real killer is found."

"*If* the real killer is found." I twirl my finger in my hair, making a nest of the dry, blond strands. "Maybe he'll kill me, too."

Aunt Bel sucks in a hard breath. "Don't you talk that way, Estelle Wickerton Roane." The bones of her hands stand out as she grips the steering wheel. "I won't hear it."

I drop my gaze and say nothing more. I honestly don't know why that upsets her. Being my guardian can't be fun. Unless you enjoy witnessing mental breakdowns and saying *stop digging at your arm* for the fiftieth time, because *there are no ants in your veins.* There's nothing to be gained from caring for someone like me. Or two, in Aunt Bel's case, as Grandma Edie doesn't realize how difficult she is sometimes. I'm also aware of all the things I want and will never have. Career. Love. Home. Children, someday. Independence.

We pass house after house. Cars in driveways, play sets on the front lawn. Sprinklers watering brown lawns. They don't know what they have. Even the worst off of them have what I would give anything for.

15

Essie

the laughing
moon

I curl into a ball under my blanket. It's past eleven o'clock at night, but I'm awake, but after basically sleepwalking for the past week, it's a relief to be awake. After telling Aunt Bel what I did to Dr. Roberts's carpet a few days ago because of how the new medication made me feel, she talked to some of the doctors she works with at the hospital. They told her they think my dose is too high and to say so to Dr. Roberts—who is annoyingly well respected at the county hospital. Instead, my aunt started cutting up the white pills. I only take a quarter each time and I feel a lot better now. We aren't telling Dr. Roberts. The last time I saw him, his hands had turned into claws.

There's a hum outside my open window, a pulsing hum that sounds a lot like—

I turn on my bedside lamp and leap from my bed. I throw open the curtains and there, in the dim light, I see the bees. It's an undulating swarm on the other side of the screen. There must be thousands of the tiny dark specks clustered into a buzzing cloud. It must be *him*.

Two weeks ago, this sight would have frightened a shriek out of me and a cry for Aunt Bel to get the spray can of Raid. But tonight, the swarm of bees makes me weak with relief, with happiness and, if I'm going to be honest, something a little bit more than both of those things that I won't even begin to ponder. Admitting to myself that I've been waiting for him for over a week is more than a little pathetic.

With practiced moves, I pop out the screen latches and remove the aluminum frame from the window. I place it against the wall and wait for him to come inside. For years now, I've enjoyed sitting in the window frame. It makes me feel free, in what little way I can. I know Aunt Bel would disapprove, but balancing there is a bit of control over myself that no one knows about but me. And now, Dresden.

The swarm remains outside. I bite my lip and circle my hand forward. "Please, come in," I say with a giggle, well aware that only a crazy person would invite a swarm of bees into her bedroom. But these aren't really bees, of course. They're a boy named Dresden, and inviting a boy into her room is something girls have done forever, so maybe I'm not so different, after all.

I hold my breath as the bees pour in like a small tornado. It's shocking to see—they could surround and sting me to death in moments—but they cluster into a column of yellow and black, flying so fast I can't make out individual bees, just the collective swarm. I've seen him do this before, and it's hard, keeping my smile in check. I back up to give him some room, bumping the backs of my legs against the bed. The bees gel together like they're stuck on flypaper. Wings and bodies and legs coalesce into human skin and hair and clothing. The buzzing quiets to the dullest of hums, and Dresden stands in front of me, head lowered. Black hair falls in his face. For a moment, I think he's going to turn back into bees and fly right out the way he came, but then he lets out a great sigh and lifts his head.

He's here, in my room, looking at me like the sight of me is relief and wonder and sadness. A confusing mix of emotions settles in the furrow between his brows. I know the brows belonged to someone else, once, but it's Dresden who moves them, now. Dresden who looks at me with a longing that I suspect is mirrored in my own face. I wish I could see inside his head. I wish I could slip in there and *know* what he thinks of me, of himself. My smile goes big—too big. I tone it down. "Hello. I'm glad you came."

He shifts so his face is more in shadow. "How are you?"

"I'm okay. How are you?" What's wrong with me? I sound annoyingly cheerful, like I'm trying to sell him Girl Scout Cookies.

"Concerned." His gaze sprinkles over me in quick assessment. "The times I saw you over this week, you seemed not to be yourself. You looked unwell. And I heard the body of the woman was found."

"Yes. She was. I knew her, you know. She tutored me in science." It makes my gut clench and my heart race, remembering the scene, and now knowing it was Miss Leeds…

I have dreams about it some nights—wild nightmares about knives cutting off my toes and a sewn-shut mouth laughing at me. No worse than my usual dreams, but these are rooted in real things. "I can't imagine why anyone would hurt her. Miss Leeds was *nice*. Detective Berk doesn't tell us much about the investigation…" I bite my lip and look away. Oh, I *can't* tell him the police suspect me. It's embarrassing. Like I'm the automatic default suspect. I don't want him to see me that way and honestly, I'd like to forget for a little while. When I'm with him, I just want to enjoy my quiet mind. "The police think it's connected to my family, somehow."

"You must be extra aware, Essie," he says in a growly voice. "This person is very dangerous. I am keeping an eye out for you, but you must be careful and on your guard."

"I am." I refuse to roll my eyes, even though I've been getting the "be aware and on your guard" lecture every day, several times a day, from Aunt Bel. "My aunt met with a security system company yesterday. She's having cameras put up outside the house." I wince, shake my head. "Not that we can afford it."

"She values your lives more than money. Wise woman." He pauses. "I saw you at your doctor's. You were ill there. Are you better?"

I hitch one shoulder and give him a flirty grin. "Are you spying on me, Dresden?" I wave a hand when he flushes. "I'm fine, now. Dr. Roberts loaded me up on a medication that upset my stomach and turned me into a zombie. I'm taking a much lower dose now, but don't tell him that."

"You need a new doctor."

"I know." I sigh. "I turn eighteen in a few months. I plan to petition for a little more freedom, then."

He wants to say something else but bites his lip on it. I don't press, neither does he. People don't like to be pressed.

The worst type of silence constricts the air between us. It's heavy, unsure. The room feels tiny and boxlike.

"I was hoping you'd come," I say quietly. "All week, I was waiting."

"It was…difficult to stay away from you." He turns back to the window, hands shoved deep in a pair of jean pockets. "I had to see you." His voice is tinted with wonder. "I couldn't fight it."

I reach out and pull one of his hands from a pocket and bring it between us. His hand is capable and strong, made interesting by a few ancient scars along the back and knuckles. He has the hands of a fisherman from a life he barely remembers. I lay my hand on his, feeling the bones, muscles beneath. I curl my fingers around his hand and gently squeeze. He releases a small gasp. Warmth spreads through me, both expected and a surprise. "I missed you."

Dresden stills. His gaze lowers to where my hand holds his. This point of contact between us takes a life of its own. It's an exploration, but neither of us knows where it will lead. Slowly, he turns his hand over until our palms touch. He's slow about it, giving me ample time to pull away. My fingers slide between his. His slip between mine.

A current zings into existence. My mouth goes completely dry. I don't know what to do with my other hand. It wants to touch, find out more about him, about myself, about *this*, but I'm balancing on an edge with Dresden.

The clarity of thought I gain when I'm with him comes with the knowledge that there will be no happily ever after for us. I hadn't before considered what might be at stake for him in regards to our friendship—if it could still be called that—but maybe I should.

"You want me…to stay?" he asks in halting breaths.

"You need to ask?"

He closes his eyes. Long lashes sweep over flushed cheeks. "It doesn't make sense that you'd want to be around me."

"Why?" I'm genuinely curious. "Because of the bees? Or your face? Or because at one time, you almost stung me?"

"All of those things," he replies in a growl. "And more."

"I didn't let you." I take a tiny step closer to him. "In the park that day."

His brow puckers. "You knew that was my bee?"

I tilt my head, working to understand why he seems so stricken over this. "Yes. But I heard someone say my name. Wasn't it you? When I looked up, I saw the bee and whacked it." I squeeze his hand, drawing a sharp breath from him. "You would have felt terrible about it later, if you'd done it. I couldn't have that."

He looks like he's having difficulty swallowing. "It took everything I had to send that bee. I thought I had no choice." His other hand comes up slowly. Fingertips brush along my jaw, leaving tingling trails in their wake, before falling away. "I swear to you, Essie. I will never sting you. For as long as I am here, I will do everything in my power to keep you safe. Whatever spoke your name and made you stop that bee, I'm grateful to it."

"It wasn't you." I frown at the floor. "Perhaps it was a lucky delusion."

"Perhaps."

My knees are getting a little shaky. I tug his hand and sit on the edge of the bed. He eases down next to me. I look at our linked hands. "You should have come sooner. Why didn't you?"

"Because I shouldn't."

"If you're worried about my aunt—"

"Your aunt is the last thing I'm worried about."

"What, then?" I ask. "I'm not going to hurt you."

He cocks his head. A rueful smile pulls at his lips. "Are you so sure? I'm powerless to say no to you, and yet the day will come when I'll have to leave, and this town is…" He trails off, shifting so hair falls over his face.

"Stop hiding your face." I tilt up his chin. "I know what you look like."

"I wish you didn't."

"Why? Do you think I'd think differently of you if you had only one face?"

His brows raise. "I would hope so."

"You make no sense at all." He doesn't. If he thinks all I see are those other features, and not the true person beneath, then he doesn't *know* me at all. "What were you saying about this town? Is something about it not to your liking?"

He sighs. "The only thing I like about this town is you," he says, and my face warms. "But really, the problem with this town is that the crows are here. They show up to places where—I shouldn't be talking about this with you."

"No, you should. Everyone treats me like I'm made of glass. Believe me, my head shows me things every day much scarier than anything that could come out of your mouth."

He grins, and it's not restrained, or practiced, or sad. It's just a grin. "You've seen what comes out of my mouth, Essie."

And I laugh. I plaster a hand over my mouth so I'm

not too loud, but I really laugh. "You made a joke."

"I did." He looks surprised. "The very reason I am here is a problem. Something…unfortunate is going to happen in this area. Something that will cause the deaths of many. I intend to do everything in my power to make sure you survive it."

I try not to react to his words. He's watching me closely as it is, and if he thinks I may get upset, he'll start to edit himself. Just like everyone does. "What kind of unfortunate something?"

"There's no way to know. I am here with a group of… people. Harbingers of death who are cursed in a way that's similar to myself. They can sense when terrible events are going to occur. They are drawn to these events, as am I."

"That boy with you at the parade?"

"Yes. His name is Michael."

"So like, a bomb is going to drop on us?"

"I would be very surprised if that happened."

He sees me frowning at the wall, considering all the different ways a bunch of people could be killed in Concordia, Missouri, and turns my face toward him with gentle fingers. "Please, don't worry. I told you, I won't allow harm to come to you. We'll get you out of town and away from here when the event is close."

"Oh, I can't leave."

He blinks. "Why is that?"

Oh crap. Crap, crap, *crap*. So much for leaving out the part about me being a suspect in the murder. I have to tell him the truth, now. "Because Detective Berk says so."

His gaze darkens. "They can't seriously think you—"

"They don't have any better leads and they found my

hat stuffed in Miss Leeds's hands," I blurt out. "She thinks it's a long shot, but…"

He shakes his head. "You won't stay a suspect for long."

"How do you know that?"

"Because I've known quite a few dark minds, like the person who killed your Miss Leeds. The fact that he brought her body to a public place—the park—tells me that on some level, he *wants* to be discovered. He will make a mistake." He brushes his fingertips over my cheek, so light I almost don't feel it. "So yes, I'll be spying on you until this person is caught. If he tries to hurt you, he'll have to get through me, and I'm quite indestructible."

"Indestructible?" I smile through a blush, so very unsettled—in a good way—by his words. "And here I was beginning to think you were such a nice, ordinary boy."

"Your turn to joke," he says with a fading smile. "I'm *not* ordinary, Essie."

"That's true. If you were, you wouldn't like me."

He goes still. "If I were, I wouldn't have to enter through the window to visit with you. I'd use the front door and greet your aunt in a civilized manner."

I look straight at him, studying his changeable face. He's not lying—he is simply unaware that he's wrong. Or perhaps he'd *like* to think that he'd be interested in me if he was an "ordinary" boy, but I've been around enough of them to know how they see me.

Dresden. If you were ordinary, you would not be sitting with me in my room. You wouldn't even see *me.*

But he is here, looking at me in a way that makes my hands sweat and my throat dry. I can't hold his words against him because it goes both ways. If I were an ordinary girl, I'd probably miss him entirely, like all those people who only see the shape of a young man, but not the young man himself.

Maybe we're here to give each other what the rest of the world can't.

Just then, a woman's lips appear as his mouth. They're full and young and contrast with the old-man nose just above them. They could have easily been my lips, if he'd let his bees sting me. But he didn't, and that choice is the reason I'm here with him now, heart pounding, feeling cloud light and painfully clearheaded. Wondering if this is what falling in love is like and experiencing every possible conflict about that.

All those days ago in the park, Dresden saw me, and I saw him. Like, really *saw*. And everything changed.

On pure impulse, I reach out. He only flinches slightly as I touch the soft skin around his eyes. I pull my hand from his to rest my fingertips next to his temples. Thumbs, on the bridge of his nose.

"What are you doing?" His voice is wary.

"I don't know." I'm breathless, a little giddy. I don't know what I'm doing, but the blood thrumming through my veins brings a surge of euphoric power. Perhaps the possibility of falling in love makes all other possibilities seem more possible. "I want to see your eyes," I breathe. "*Yours.*"

His face folds into an expression of hurt, sadness, infinite pain. "They're gone, Essie."

His hands close around my wrists, and he tries to pull back, but I press my fingers harder and he stills. "No. They're there." Sweat slides down my neck as I watch the shifting features of his face. A shudder rattles through me, but I don't release Dresden.

"You wouldn't know the difference anyway," he says, letting his hands drop away. "You can't know my eyes from the others."

I don't know how, but I'm certain he's wrong. It's as if the image of them swims behind my own eyes, just beyond my consciousness.

A pair of dark brown eyes shifts to blue, then to a rheumy gray, barely visible below a heavy, wrinkled brow.

Then, slowly, they turn a clear, gold-green with a thick fringe of dark lashes. Black brows arch over them. They fit his face with such perfection, I gasp and cup my hands to his cheeks.

"It's you." My breath hitches. "*Your* eyes. You can feel it, can't you?"

Those glorious eyes widen in surprise. He stares at me in wonder and something that looks a little like fear. Good grief, he's beautiful beyond words. Far too beautiful for a defective piece like me, I think with a spear of worry, but his beautiful eyes don't stay. They are swallowed up by a pair of heavy-lidded ones and are gone like an impression in the sand.

"When it's my features, it doesn't hurt. It's been so long…" he says roughly. His hand comes up. Shaky fingers rub his eyes, which look at me with an intensity I've never seen from him. "I don't understand. You shouldn't have been able to do that."

"But I did. I can." I bite my bottom lip as the room fills up with bright pink bubbles. "You're beautiful, Dresden."

"It was a long time ago," he says distantly.

I laugh and try to be careful about the pitch. My laughter can go high and piercing when I'm happy. I also sometimes forget to stop laughing, which I've been told makes people uncomfortable. I tilt my head and lean back on the bed, bracing on my elbows. "I can't always tell the difference between what's real and what's not. I hear and smell and feel things that no one else can. You know what people do when they see me reacting to the stuff my mind makes up? They cross the street, move their seat, leave the store. They're afraid of me. Grown men look at me with fear. Like I'm a monster."

"They're fools," Dresden says with a frown.

"So are you, for thinking that of yourself," I say. "You're beautiful to me. You see me. I have scary faces, too. You're the only one, aside from the people living in this house, who sees *past* them. You have no idea how much that means to me." I lay a hand on his chest, very gently. Barely touching. It's buzzy and warm with all those bees in there. He jerks at my touch and winces, but his hand brushes my thigh, just above the knee, then tentatively settles there. His gaze drops to my mouth.

"Essie." He breathes my name. He's close. The air between us zings, honey-scented and charged. "You are the furthest thing from a monster. You are light and grace and all the things I thought I had forgotten. It's agony for me to be near you, yet I can't stay away."

Oh my God, there is no resistance for that kind of talk. I smile at him, brimming with everything. Just, all of it, including a load of emotions I've never felt before in my life. My bones are jelly. In two seconds, my heart is going to burst straight out of my chest. "Just think," I whisper. "If my great-great-grandmother Opal Wickerton hadn't spontaneously lost her sanity before having six children and beginning the Wickerton curse, we wouldn't be here today. Maybe it's fate that brought us together."

"Your great-great-grandmother's mental illness came on suddenly?"

"Mm-hmm. Right before some religious massacre in the mid-1800s. Why?"

Dresden goes completely still. My vision goes gray tinged. "What's the matter?"

He eases away from me, climbs off the bed with shaking hands. "I have to go."

"Why?" I scramble to my feet. "I don't understand." He looks at me from the corners of his eyes. I can see the whites—crescent moons of fear. It's a look I've seen too many times. "Don't do that." Tears burn my eyes. "Don't you dare look at me like I scare you."

He lets out a sound of anguish and rushes toward me. His hands close over my upper arms, just below the sleeves of my nightshirt.

"I'm not *scared* of you," he grinds out. "I think I just figured out...I think—" He cuts off, tips his forehead to mine. "I adore you. You make me forget that I'm cursed. You make me believe huge, impossible things. You make me want..." He shakes his head and sets me back firmly. "I will watch out for you, keep you safe, for as long as I am able, but I don't know if I can come to you again."

My heart pulls at my ribs with an icy ache. My skin crawls with the sensation of skittering mice. I hug my arms around my torso to keep from touching him, but I step close. Too close, for sure, but they say the devil's in the details. I want to see *all* of Dresden's devils. "This makes no sense," I say. "Why might you not come back?"

His face is in shadow again, hiding his emotions from me. "Because I think I did something a long time ago that makes this thing between us even more unnatural than it already is. I have no business even thinking about you, and you…" He looks to the window with anguish. "You are defying the laws of nature by having a single kind thought about me."

"If it's unnatural to enjoy being with you, so be it." My chin jerks up. I'm all breath, no voice. "Dresden, I care for you—"

"No!" He surges away from me as bees roar from his mouth. They encircle him like a buzzing tornado, forming a wall. His face is pure misery. His hands are tense claws dragging through his hair. "Stop, I beg you." He backs toward the window.

"I want to know why—"

"I can't!" he gasps. "I've done enough damage. But I'll keep you safe. And I…I'll find a way to free you. So help me, I will." He turns to the window.

Free me? I stand up and am swamped by a wave of vertigo. This night has been a barrage of wild, swinging emotions—too many extremes to reasonably process. It's taking a toll. My ceiling, the whole roof is suddenly gone. Only the walls remain. I sit down on the edge of the bed. Above me, stars glitter in a black sky, and a low-slung crescent moon chuckles softly.

"Dresden, I don't want you to go." It's all I can say. It's all I have left.

"And I would give anything to stay," he rasps. "But I want you to live, more."

His eyes close, and he disintegrates into a heavy swarm of bees. It streams through the window and is swallowed by the night.

I watch the last bee disappear and sink onto my

bed, curling into the fetal position. Blisters boil up and break on my hands, arms, that spot above my knee—all the places on my skin where we touched. The pain is tremendous, but the ache under my ribs is worse because I know that one is real. It's like invisible forks are twirling the veins and muscle sinews like spaghetti. I curl my hands into my sheets and let the tears come. They come and come and come until my room is flooded by them. I fall asleep, sinking into a salty sea of my own tears, under sharp white stars and a moon that just won't stop laughing.

16

Dresden

a spoonful
of honey

I t's raining.

I pound a fist against the harbingers' motel room door. It's the sort of place that accepts cash and hasn't been updated in decades. The door is metal, but I'm very strong and my blows are causing it to rattle on its hinges. I rarely do this—visit the harbingers at their residence. They don't like it. Aside from Michael, they don't like *me*. The other three who travel with Michael tolerate our association, but prefer we keep it away from them. I've obliged, until now, as I stand here pounding on their door in the middle of the night.

The door is jerked open by Lish, a tall woman with dark brown skin and a mouth not given to smiling. I've been following these individuals for a long time, and I admire this harbinger, despite her clear antipathy for me. Her body has lost a few things in her forty-some years—an eye; a finger to a knife fight; a gunshot wound gave her a bad limp—but her mind is powerful. Her group follows her without question.

Lish scans me with her eye. "What?"

"Michael." By all the gods in the universe, I sound menacing. Bees fly all over the place in a disorganized mass. No wonder she's looking at me with more disgust than usual.

"He's busy." She moves to slam the door shut.

My hand shoots out, braces the door open. I'm faster than a harbinger. "I need to see him."

"No." She says it through her teeth.

Another thread of control snaps, and my mouth floods with bees. I open my mouth with a growl, and they burst out, swarm around her in a chaotic, anxious cloud. I've never done this before—allowed my bees to purposefully frighten someone. It's a new low.

It doesn't work, anyway. Lish's dark eyes narrow, turn assessing. "Dresden—that's your name, right?" She damn well knows my name. "He can't come out right now."

"I'm not leaving." Somewhere under my mania is a prick of alarm. There's a bad edge to her voice.

"Please," I say, making a supreme effort to sound civilized. "It's important."

She pauses, watching me carefully. Weighing something in her mind. Her full lips thin to a line. "Contain the insects and you may see him."

I must look desperate. I've never been invited in before. My bees corral back into my chest. She nods to the others inside.

The two other harbingers who are not Michael make noises of protest, of alarm. One raised hand from Lish and they cease. She presses a finger from her intact hand to my chest. Her teeth gleam white against her skin. "Don't make me regret extending you this courtesy, beekeeper."

"I won't."

Lish steps aside. I find Michael on the bed looking quite poorly. Lish and a male harbinger, who is new enough I don't know his name, move to the rear of the cramped motel room to give us room. Or, perhaps, to stay as far from me as possible. Clothes are folded into piles on the other double bed. Food is stacked neatly on the desk. Garbage packed inside the waste bin. All evidence of a comfortable, tidy transient family.

A third harbinger, a girl no more than twelve, is poised over a gaping hole in Michael's abdomen with a needle and thread in one hand and a turkey baster full of clear liquid in the other. Her name is Adele, and she blinks at me before turning back to Michael's wound.

It's important to not be fooled by harbingers. They're far older than they look. Every time they die, they're reborn and come back as children, but keep their memories and their skills. They don't find true death with any frequency. Even then, their curse is transferred to some other unsuspecting human on the brink of death. Bad luck finding worse luck. Michael claims he was in the death throes of some awful seventeenth-century disease when the curse found him. I know nothing about Lish, but Michael once told me that the first thing Lish did as a harbinger was hunt down a particular man and kill him. Slowly.

I don't know how Adele became a harbinger. She is delicate and fragile, and bears some telltale features of a long-extinct royal family I vaguely remember. I do know she has been a harbinger longer than anyone in this room. She has sewn up many bellies during that time.

I don't ask what happened to Michael, this time. Something is *always* happening to harbingers. The ashen color of Michael's skin isn't good. If he dies here, he'll turn back into a crow. After a few months to a few years in bird form, he'll start all over again as a child. He usually comes back around ten years, but once, he returned at age six.

"Are you going to survive this?" I ask him.

"Dunno," he rasps. "Got the bullet out, but…"

I sit on the side of the bed, carefully. My frenzy has died to a heavy sadness. "I need to ask you something."

Michael winces as Adele shoots a stream of the liquid—saline, I'm assuming—into his wound, and I'm reminded once again how lucky I am not to feel most pain. There is one advantage to being less human than the harbingers.

"You may need to be quick about it." His voice is thin, breathy.

"I just came from Essie's house," I say. "Do you think it's possible that I am the cause of her insanity?"

"Why would you think that?"

"A woman I stung back in the mid-nineteenth century. I followed you to a town here, in this territory. It was a religious massacre. My memories are hazy on the incident." I close my eyes, rub a hand over my face. "I stung her, but she didn't die. You harbingers have more contact with one another. You share more information than beekeepers do, so I want to know if you have heard anything that might affirm that Essie's condition was carried down from an ancestor who I stung but didn't die."

"Possible, but unlikely," Michael pants softly. "There

have been a few counts of people surviving stings."

"Any idea what happened to them? If they—" I can't finish. I'm so horrified with myself. "I think I may have made a mistake. A temporary imbalance can be mistaken for a target. The bees can sting if someone steps on them or swipes at them."

Not that that excuses it.

"I don't remember stinging this woman, but it's too much of a coincidence. That woman is Essie's great-great-grandmother, and she began the so-called Wickerton curse shortly after we were here. She survived to old age, passed the condition to her children, and through the generations. To my Essie. What if—" My breath catches in a gasp. "Michael, *I* made the monster. That's what the Strawman told me." Agony cracks my voice. "A thousand slow deaths is too good for me."

"Take it easy, Dres." Michael sighs. His eyes close briefly, reopen slowly. "Could be your connection to her. Told you…it wasn't a coincidence."

"Yes, yes. You were right." I give his wound a critical look. "You really must pull through this time. I need your help. Besides, you're a thoroughly irritating child."

He chuckles, but the movement pulls at his wound, and he cuts off with a grimace. "It's not good, buddy."

Buddy? Thankfully, he's never called me that before. Adele stares at me with big, moist eyes. I imagine how strange I must appear to her: the emotionless, stoic beekeeper unraveling over a human girl. I look away from her and back to Michael's wound. She had only just begun stitching. It *is* a bad injury. The bullet clearly damaged him internally in places that can't be stitched.

I've seen Michael die numerous times. The pale, sickly

gleam of his skin, the tight, gasping breaths are all signs of his imminent passing. The death of a harbinger is disappointingly anticlimactic: the black fog pours from their mouth and envelops them, and there's a crow sitting where the dead body was.

I never gave their death much thought, and Michael never made a big fuss when he has gone through it. No screaming, or moaning, or writhing about like humans tend to do. Harbingers are accustomed to physical pain. Michael grips fistfuls of sheets, his only real indicator of discomfort. How awful it must be, to be essentially immortal but stuck with the limitations and miseries of the human condition. I give Michael credit—he bears his impending death well. My fingers brush a thick, raised scar along the side of my thumb—an ancient injury from my time working one of my family's fishing boats. I had been afraid I'd lose the finger, but my mother had slathered it in honey, fresh from the hive, wrapped it in wax and linen, and it had healed.

Honey. On impulse, I unhinge my jaw and stick a finger far down my throat. I can reach quite far down. I scoop out a hearty glob of honey. My bees make it. It coats my throat and everything inside me. In the rare event that a beekeeper does get injured, our honey heals us very quickly. Perhaps it has the same effect on harbingers.

I smear the honey into his wound, as deep in as my index finger can reach. Michael groans. Adele stares at me in open-mouthed horror.

"I would be grateful if he lived," I say in explanation, but her shock doesn't abate. "He's my only friend."

The room is thick with silence. My bees rumble,

sensing my unease.

Adele shakes her head and points at Michael's stomach. "You just saved his life."

"Maybe," I say warily. "I don't know how the honey works with harbingers of death."

"You've had so many chances to help over the years." Lish puts her fists on her hips. "Why now? Because there's something you want?"

"Yes," I say, with a quick baring of teeth. "I want him to live. And *yes*, I want his help, and he can't do that as a crow or a three-year-old trying to remember how to use a toilet."

Her eyes narrow. "You watched him suffer so many times."

"I did." I return her gaze, feeling the faces twist over my face with increased speed. "He—all of you—are *cursed*. You exist in a cycle of pain and death that I cannot interfere with. Michael is my friend, and if I patched him up every time he got a scratch, I would grow to hate him. Worse, he would come to hate me."

Lish holds my gaze for a moment longer, then nods to Adele, who picks up the needle and finishes stitching Michael's wound.

Lish looks at the others, raising her chin. "We're going to help you," she says. "Michael is no longer your only friend." She angles her eye to give me a piercing stare. "As long as you keep the insects contained."

The other harbinger in the room is a young man, standing against the back wall. He's the newest of all of them, having caught the curse only a few decades ago. I've never heard this one say a word, which is fine, as he has made an art form out of becoming invisible. He studies me with dark, shadowed eyes and nods.

Something akin to panic shudders through my bones. As it had been with Michael, it appears I don't have a say in this new, group friendship. Did they consider that maybe I don't *want* them all as friends? I wasn't trying to win their favor. I just wanted Michael to live.

Harbingers are tortured creatures, too, but not one of them remains from the beginning of the curse. All of those found a way to die. *They have a way out,* while I do not. We beekeepers have endured since a time erased from history. These harbingers staring at me cannot understand the weight of knowledge I bear. They cannot know that *feeling* and *attachment* are the things that can break even my sanity, and that is probably the most isolating part of my existence.

Michael smiles weakly. "You may regret that," he says to them. "He's a cranky pisser."

"So are you." Lish pinches his nose. "There are degrees to all things. He's proven something. And if he's going to try to break the curse, we'll help."

"See? This is what you get for doing a good deed," Michael says to me while glancing at his sticky wound. Already, the tissue is knitting together. "A few more people willing to talk to you."

My head is spinning a little. Sharing a little honey did not warrant this reaction, but harbingers are sentimental creatures—emotional, and so very human in temperament. I won't say no to help. I will likely need a considerable lot of it in the coming weeks. "I'm... grateful," I say. "I don't know if I can break the curse, but I would like to learn more about that rumor you told me the day we arrived here. You said there was talk about the curses weakening."

Michael looks to Lish, who shakes her head. "There's no secret harbinger of death online group," she says. "When we say there is 'talk,' we mean brief communications, usually shared while traveling on the wing. We don't know specifics."

It wouldn't have surprised me if there *was* a secret online harbinger of death group. "Is there a way to find out?" I hate to ask a favor. Favors always result in another one owed, and I have little to offer. But for the first time, a tiny spark of hope flickers deep and quiet.

So many long-held beliefs have been burned down since I arrived in Concordia. That I am alone. That no one could ever care for me as I am. That I am content being alone. None of them are true anymore.

I have someone to live for.

Someone to fight for.

Impossibly, someone who cares about me. It makes me wonder what else is possible. The slight chance of freedom for Essie is worth finding out about. And possibly, maybe, there exists a crack in the curse that has controlled me for hundreds of years. Maybe the cryptic words of the Strawman mean something helpful, after all.

"We'll see what we can do." Lish runs a hand over her short, natural curls. "Do you promise you won't do harm with any information we may find?"

Can I blame them for still seeing me as a danger? It was only Essie who only ever saw my humanity. It was she who reminded me of the person sleeping beneath all my hideous masks.

My course of action shifts from something I want to do, to something that I *will* do. It's hard to speak through the bees clotting in my throat. "Of course. I won't harm anyone."

"Good." Lish's gaze sweeps the rest of them. "We'll find you something, Dresden."

"What about the event? It must be approaching soon," I ask Lish. Of all of them, Michael refers to her most often when trying to predict the type of event. She is often correct.

Lish purses her lips. "There's a violent taste to the air," she says. "I think the event will involve the weather. And there are a few weeks left, yet."

That's actually incredibly helpful.

Tornado, hurricane, flooding. It could also be fire. The nuclear power plant two towns over could turn the air toxic.

Actually, there are a number of things that could happen to Concordia. "Thank you," I say again. I can't recall the last time I uttered those words, but today I've said them twice.

"Dres, I don't want to disappoint you, but you may not be able to recreate another scenario, if there is one," Michael says. "Your situation is unique. Just…be prepared to hear that there is nothing you can do to help or save her."

"Aren't those the same thing?" I ask.

"No." He doesn't blink. "I know you want to free her from her condition, and protect her from this killer, and save her from the event. None of those things may be possible."

"I must try." I get up and move toward the door.

"You're right, you know." Michael struggles to sit up a little.

I pause. "About what?"

"I would have hated you," he says. "If you used your honey to heal me every time. My suffering makes us equals."

I bark out a laugh. "No, it does not."

"Shut up, Dresden." Michael sends me a weary smile. "I bet you have no idea you called me your friend for the first time just now." He chuckles as I stand there in appalled silence. "Thank you for the help this time, but don't ever do it again. I'd rather you be my friend than whatever you'd become as my honey dispensary." He waves a hand. "Go. Find a way to save your girl. Then tell us how you did it."

They're all quiet. I can't take the way these harbingers are looking at me—all shining eyes, as if they are so proud and pleased I want to do something noble and good for our kind. But it's only Essie I care about, and that makes everything I'm doing right now as selfish as it gets.

"I know something." This from the silent man standing in the back—the new harbinger I've never heard speak. Everyone turns to him. He watches me with eyes that are more crow than man.

"I heard something in passing," he says. "A few months back a beekeeper found his death and a harbinger gained freedom from the curse. The humans stung by the beekeeper were cured of their psychosis, but it wasn't clear how."

Michael gives him a slow blink. "Seriously, Jonas?"

So that's his name. Jonas nods. "What do you intend to do with that, beekeeper?"

Ah, so, sticking to titles with this one, I see. I take a moment to digest, but can't control a shudder. The stab of elation that jolts through me steals my breath. It had been done. Curses have been broken—recently. It didn't matter who lived and died, just that the humans infected by the venom had been freed. "If this is true, then there's a way to free Essie from the effects of my bees' venom. And I will find it."

Essie

the beginning of dark

We are in the car, returning home from grocery shopping. The last of the flavor ebbs from my watermelon bubble gum, and Aunt Bel sings along to an old Simon and Garfunkel song about the sound of silence. She has perfect pitch, and stays on key, but sings everything in a high octave and in this tremolo voice that turns head splitting very quickly. I can tell by the flush in her cheeks that she thinks her singing is magnificent.

We turn down our street, and my aunt slows the car. Her singing cuts off in a snarling curse word—one that earns me a slapped hand when I say it. One she only reserves for encounters with a particular person.

My father's car is parked on the road in front of our house. Today, anxiety takes the form of a red, late-model Acura.

Aunt Bel pulls in the driveway. "Stay in the car." She gets out and disappears inside. Immediately, I can hear the yelling. Something crashes inside the house, and I get out of the car in a series of jerky moves. I walk puppet-like toward the house, controlled by the desire to help my aunt, not by self-preservation.

Dread. Panic. My knees lose some of their rigidity when my hand closes around the front doorknob. I should hide in the car and wait for him to clear out, but I hear Grandma Edie's quiet sobbing and Aunt Bel's strained voice. She's trying not to yell. He is not returning the effort. His voice twists my belly into achy knots. There is no sound I hate more.

I smooth back my hair and go inside, trying to look as together as I can. I ignore the urge to pull at my hair, pick at my arm. A twittery voice in my head begins counting by twos.

He's in the kitchen, leaning against the counter. My father lives well outside of town and works at the college. He's a professor of psychology, of all things, which is why he and Dr. Roberts are such pals. I can't explain what he looks like beyond the basics—blond hair, brown eyes—but if you ask me what fear and pain looks like, my mind draws up an image of Bradley Roane.

I don't remember specifics of my time living with him. I was younger when I was taken from him, although a very expensive lawyer ensured that he still has say in my care. What I do remember are basic feelings, sensations. Hunger, for example. The need to hide, and the comfort of small places. I hid to avoid my father's drunken rages, but that resulted in more hunger, because he wouldn't feed me if he couldn't find me. I remember pain and fear and a pungent sense of betrayal, desolation. All things children shouldn't feel. All things I still feel, acutely, whenever I'm near him.

My father leans against the counter. His suit appears fresh from the dry cleaners. "Goddamnit, Essie, it took you long enough to get in here."

"I'm sorry," I say quietly. "Hello Father."

"Lazy brat." He tilts a small, label-less bottle to his lips.

"Bradley, don't speak to her that way," Aunt Bel says.

"I'll speak to her any way I like." He kicks a chunk of a shattered coffee mug. There's a brown splatter mark on the wall next to the refrigerator. He must have helped himself to a cup before we arrived. "She's *my* daughter."

"She's as good as mine, according to the law." My aunt holds her own against him, but her usually rosy cheeks are colorless. She's terrified of him.

"Don't I know it," he snarls at her. "I give you enough of my hard-earned money for her, don't I?"

I don't know how he hides this side of himself at work. I see him in the newspaper sometimes, all smiles while accepting an award of recognition or dispensing student diplomas. He talked himself into rehab and out of a jail sentence for his treatment of me. Intelligence is one quality my father doesn't lack.

Grandma Edie sits at the table, rocking and tearing her napkin into tiny pieces.

I need to take my medication. *Now.* I move to the refrigerator with the slow, deliberate movements of an animal handler inside the tiger enclosure. This is what it's like when he's here—walking on eggshells, knowing that one will break, and it will be because of something totally unavoidable and benign, like breathing too deeply.

I take out the orange juice and reach for my pill dispenser. I pop open the day marked "Friday" and shake the contents into my hand.

Oh God. My arms are covered in long cuts, deep slices that are crudely sewn up with oily black thread. Blood oozes from the cuts, smears on the counter. *My back is to them. They can't see.* I reach for a towel to wipe up my blood, then force myself to put it down. He'll see me do this. He'll know I'm cleaning up something that's not real. *Not real.*

I close my eyes and try to focus. I need my pills, but my hands are too unsteady to pour orange juice. I drop the pills into the pocket of my T-shirt and turn around, slowly, knowing I'm going to see something horrible.

I almost groan at the sight of him. His face is shiny scarlet, and a pair of pointed horns curves out of his hairline. He looks like the devil, but the Halloween-costume version. His devil is so clichéd, I'm actually comforted. A little.

"I hear you can't tell the difference between real people and the ones walking around in your crazy head. And now you're being investigated in the murder of your tutor."

"I–I didn't hurt anyone." I swallow thickly. "I just… found her."

"I know you didn't murder Meredith. I knew her, too, you know. The college is a tight community. You're too weak. But how do you think I feel having to answer questions about it? My own daughter implicated in the killing of a lovely undergrad student. I don't enjoy it, Essie. It's embarrassing. I have a good job. If I lose it because of you…" His upper lip curls in disgust. "Forget it. I'm telling Dr. Roberts to double your dosage. Maybe you won't be able to do any more damage that way."

With each word he speaks, slim metal razor blades

fly from his mouth and imbed into my sore, torn skin. It takes everything I have to stand erect. To not scream and curl onto the floor in a whimpering puddle. My fingernails scrape my palm in a telltale repetitive movement, but I can't help it. It's too hard to keep still. "Please don't do that. I'm fine now."

Grandma Edie lets out a sob and pushes from the table. I can't see her very well, though, because that set of blades came at my face and blinded me in one eye. Blood flows over the other and down my shirt.

"Bradley." Aunt Bel's voice could cut steel. "Leave now or I will call the police."

"Go ahead and call the police," he scoffs. "I have the legal right to see my daughter. And I'm not saying anything that isn't true. She is not, nor has she ever been, *fine*." More blades fly from his mouth. They spray all over, me, the floor, slicing into Aunt Bel, who doesn't react.

I force my frozen mouth into a smile. "I'm much better."

He pushes a knot of blond hair from his watery, bloodshot eyes — the only indication of his intoxication — and aims a finger at me. "Let me put things this way, so there's no confusion. If anything else happens that causes Dr. Roberts to call me in the middle of the night, you're going straight to Stanton House. I'll get a judge to grant me the right to commit you, and you'll go." He swigs down the last of whatever's in the bottle and throws it in the sink. "I'm through with this. Your mother would never have left if you'd been halfway normal."

He couldn't have found crueler, more punishing words. I turn back to the counter as a sob shudders out of me. I touch my face and all I feel is a mess of gashes and

protruding razor blades. I pick them out and drop them
on the counter, one by one. He can't see. I don't care
anymore if he can. The part of me that works so hard
to stay positive about myself crumbles to dust. A dark
fantasy skitters through me of how better our lives would
be if he weren't in it. If one of these days he took a bad
turn and wrapped his car around a tree. It could happen.
As far as I know, he's never driven sober. It's a terrible
thought, though. It makes me no better than him.

"Enough!" shouts Aunt Bel. "You are a cruel bastard."

"I'm realistic." His voice pitches into a strange key,
making me think once again that maybe he contracted a
touch of the Wickerton curse, after all. "Listen, Belvedere,
this little institution you're running here—*with my
money*—isn't helping Essie."

"Like you'd know what's helping her." That's it for
Aunt Bel. Her voice raises to a bellow. "You just want her
locked away! Out of sight, out of mind. This 'institution'
is the home of your child." Aunt Bel puffs up like an
enraged cat. "Now get out of *my* house!"

He slams a hand on the counter—making every dish
rattle—and storms out without a backward glance.

We hear him shout, and my aunt leans over the sink
to see out the window. "Looks like your father found a
swarm of bees. He's flapping around like a one-legged
chicken." Her lips curve up into a tight bow. "I hope they
sting him up good."

Dresden. I can't organize my body in any way that
would allow me to walk to my aunt and look out the
window, although I'd like to. "They won't sting," I say,
dimly aware that I'm speaking at all. "That would make
father more dangerous than he is, and Dresden wouldn't

do that to me. The bees are just to scare him."

Aunt Bel pauses, gives me a sidelong look. "Who is Dresden, dear?"

Oh, right. I just said that out loud. Ah, well. I don't care. It's astonishing she even asked. And I'm not up for concocting a lie. "The beekeeper." I wave a hand. "He's my friend. Well, he *was* my friend. I don't know what he is now." My silent protector. A memory.

She narrows her eyes. "I've heard you say that name before."

I can't tune into her anymore. My arms hug my torso, fingers curling into my shirt. If Dresden were here, it would be his arms around me, siphoning off my fear, my dark edges. He would make me feel that calm clarity that only comes from being around him. His deep, rumbly voice would murmur reassurance, and I wouldn't be slowly lowering to the floor right now with my eyes squeezed shut to avoid looking at the bloody kitchen. I wouldn't be curling my knees up to my chest, rocking, humming.

Aunt Bel sags at the sight of me. On top of her head sits a perfect little birds' nest with three dead, freshly hatched chicks draped over the edges. Their little beaks sit wide open, as if they died waiting for a worm. The kitchen stinks of rotten eggs. "Oh, Essie," my aunt coos. "You should have stayed in the car."

"I couldn't leave you to him," I sing to her in a high, terrible trill. "It's me he wants to hurt, any-way-ay."

"It's not you, my lamb." She squints out the window, where my father is peeling out of the driveway in his nice red car. "It's all him."

I swallow hard and peek at my arms. The cuts are gone, but my skin is tender everywhere, like I've been beaten.

"Maybe I should just go to Stanton House."

My aunt smooths her hair without touching the sad little nest. "How about maybe we find you a new psychiatrist? I'm through trying to pacify Bradley Roane." Her mouth twists. "We'll need a second opinion, anyway, if that slippery bastard follows up on his threat to have you committed."

My shoulders slump. I am so exhausted, I could fall asleep right here on the kitchen floor. "You should go see to Grandma Edie."

"I will." She lumbers down to the floor next to me. "In a minute. She's okay. It's you I'm worried about."

"Why?" I ask her. "Why do all this for me?"

"Because I love you, my girl." She brushes a hand down my cheek. "I'll protect you, Essie."

For as long as I can.

She doesn't speak that last part aloud, but I can hear it. I wrap my arms around Aunt Bel and rest my head on her powder-scented shoulder. A portion of anxiety drains from me like a leaking balloon.

The rest remains, wrapped around an aching knot of longing and loss that pulses with the name: *Dresden.* I know that was him out there, frightening my father with all those bees. I love him all the more for it. And I wish. *God*, how I wish…

"Interesting, how easily he used that girl's first name," my aunt says.

I lift my head. "What?"

"He called her Meredith." She shrugs, but her teeth are showing. "So what if he knew who she was from the college. It's a strange thing, calling her by her first name like that. So familiar. So personal."

A chill rolls over my skin. "Do you think he—"

"Of course not," she cuts me off. Bites her lower lip. "Probably not. I don't know. He has…multiple sides." I don't understand her face now. Her eyes are soft and hard at the same time. She hugs me tighter. "I just don't want you in his care again. Ever."

The chill turns into a shudder. Maybe there's a reason I don't remember much from the brief time I lived with my father. Maybe I've blocked things out. If that's the case, I'm happy to live with the amnesia.

But there are some facts here, sprinkled among the theories, and one fact is that my condition is not getting better. I drop one hand to the floor, and it falls on a shard of ceramic from the mug my father threw. Turning it over, I recognize it as a piece of my aunt's favorite Garfield mug. It used to read: *I hate Mondays.*

I hand her the piece. "I'm sorry about this."

"About what? You didn't throw it." She wags a finger. "Don't apologize for other people, Essie. They won't thank you for it." She takes the shard from me and tosses it up into the sink. "I'll clean it up."

If I follow the pattern of my other relatives with the Wickerton disorder, my condition won't improve. Already, it feels that way. I struggle more these days, and not just because of Dresden. Reality, and the reality my mind creates for me, are becoming indistinguishable. Maybe I won't even notice when they finally lock me up for good.

18

Dresden

all the
impossible things

I wanted to kill him. I did seriously consider the option. It took every bit of willpower to remain hidden when Essie exited her aunt's car. I knew who he was the instant I saw him. The similarities in bone structure. The fair hair. He was her father, and my bees wanted to sting him. He stunk of a particular variety of darkness that sang to my bees like a siren.

All I did was scare him, as stinging him would have turned him into a homicidal monster. Good for the harbingers, but not for the women inside that house. He hates them. Deeply. It would take so little for him to turn his rage on them. Essie is surrounded by dangerous men.

I didn't want Essie going inside that house, but hindering her free will is a line I will not cross. I interfered in the course of her life by allowing a bee to sting her great-great-grandmother. I will not take one of the few things she has left.

However, if I had known he would be that horrible

to her, I would have crossed that line and intervened, anyway. There is no excuse for abuse.

Instead, I watched her go inside and face her horror of a father through the eyes of a half dozen bees buzzing around the hydrangea bush.

My brave, brave Essie. I can't imagine the things she saw. The terrible things her mind created for her while her father yelled and smashed and spewed his poison all over. If I could have gotten inside, I would have. Thankfully, I couldn't. I probably would have scared Essie's grandmother to death. It's a good thing bees can't hear. I didn't want to know the wretched things that beast was saying to Essie.

Seeing the result was bad enough.

If I was charged with energy, I could kill Essie's father with one blow. However, satisfying as that may be, killing the man in cold blood would not do good things for Essie's mental state. And as I told her—I'm not a murderer. I can think about it, though.

I cluster myself as bees in Essie's neighbor's peach tree and watch her father's little red car tear an erratic line down the street.

This man will have his day. I am certain of it. I will *make* certain of it.

I'm too weak right now to challenge Essie's father in my human form. If I followed him and tried a physical assault, I'd possibly lose. We beekeepers are compelled to release bees to sting the dark-minded, but fear is what sustains us—fear and all the chaotic, destructive emotions that come with it. Granted, the fear in that house was high, and I did absorb some of it, but I have stayed close to Essie these past weeks and that has left me physically weakened. Avoiding the center of town, where fear has begun to pump through the community like blood in a thick vein, has taken a toll.

I'll need to amend that. I'm no good to Essie if I'm depleted. There's much energy to consume in the heart of Concordia. People are frightened. There are killings, with a murderer at large. An uptick in suicides. A scent on the air that makes those touched with even a bit of natural intuition turn a wary eye to the sky. Many know something is coming. They are afraid. But I am reaping none of it, staying away from the areas of public concentration.

I'll have to divide my time between looking out for Essie and getting myself charged up. I have little else to do until the harbingers learn more about the curse being lifted. Jonas's words still burn in my mind. There is a way. It's been done. And I will find out how to free Essie and perhaps even myself.

I separate from the tree and swarm in the air, looking for a good place to settle, when a figure steps into the road. If I had a head to turn, it would be twisting straight off my neck right now. As it is, several thousand bees turn in unison.

It's her. Standing barefoot in the road. Her skin is so pale it's almost transparent. Her eyes so wide they seem to swallow her face.

"Dresden."

I can't hear her, but I can see the shape of her mouth around my name.

And I ache.

There is no going to her. Partly because the old woman living directly across the street has her face pressed to the window. Changing to human form is out of the question for that reason alone.

Give me a mouth to speak with right now and I'd be declaring my feelings to her.

Maybe I should do that.

She reaches up toward me, and I disperse my swarm, scattering bees in all directions. I can't stand her looking at me like that, with all that need and hurt on her face, and not be able to go to her. Bees land on trees, roofs, lawns. They fold their tiny wings and go silent. Essie lowers her arm and her head and turns back toward the house.

The neighbor with the too-big plastic glasses and too-thin front curtains shakes her head and shuffles back to her kitchen.

I position a few bees on Essie's gutter and peer over the edge to get a good view of her. There's a cut on her hand. Tears on her face. She's looking for me, of all the impossible things. I send one of my bees—one I am in control of—off the gutter and down in front of her. Instinctively, she holds out her hand. The bee falls into it, crawling over the pads of her palms, along the lines that denote love, life, heart.

She cups her mouth over the bee and her mouth forms the words: *Thank you.*

"What are you doing?"

Essie whips around to see her grandmother in the doorway. Her hand closes around the bee, which buzzes nervously.

Suddenly, I'm regretting the decision. If she squeezes, I won't be able to stop it from stinging her. I watch Essie and her grandmother through the eyes of many bees, watching their mouths, reading their words.

"Nothing," she says to her grandmother.

"I saw you with the bees." A bony hand locks around Essie's wrist. The other one, without the bee. "You know him, don't you? The bee-man?"

Essie nods on a sigh.

"He and death walk hand in hand."

"No." Essie's eyes harden and soften at the same time in an expression I haven't seen yet. "He's protecting me. He-he… I think he cares for me."

The grandmother releases Essie's arm on a sigh. "Ah, sweet child. He's not here to protect you. He's here because something terrible is coming."

"Like what?" She looks exasperated, or very tired. I can't tell.

"Plagues. Fires. Earthquakes."

Interesting. I wonder how she knows anything about beekeepers. Maybe knowledge was carried down with the venom in their veins.

"Earthquakes in Missouri?" Essie says. "I don't think so."

The bee trapped in the cage of Essie's fingers begins to squirm. She raises her hand, as if just remembering it's there, and opens her fingers. Granddaughter and grandmother watch the bee crawl to the tip of Essie's index finger, then lazily take off, disappearing above the house.

"You're dooming yourself," her grandmother says. There is a quiet in the old woman's eyes. "Some creatures are not meant to be loved."

"Neither are some people." Essie lowers her head and enters the house. She says something else, but her face is turned away from all the bees in the area and I can't make it out. Her grandmother stands outside a few moments more, face turned to the sun, eyes scanning the small, parched yard. "Don't harm my Essie," she whispers.

If I could, I would tell her that my intention is just the opposite. I wish I could say how sorry I am that she and her granddaughter suffer from agony I inflicted, but talking to this woman would be a mistake. All I would do is terrify her. And that would upset Essie.

Quietly, I draw my bees away from the house and settle in a tall oak tree two houses down. To wait.

The way time moves is usually of no interest to me. Slow or fast, the passage of it has been irrelevant for a very long time. But now, suddenly, I'm acutely aware of the slow tick of the sun tracking over the horizon. The interminable length of a day. The endless slide of stars across the night sky. The layers of me are peeling back like an onion, unrolling me back to a far earlier version of myself. I can't stop the memories any more than I can speed up time. And I can't speed up time any more than I can travel backward in it.

I've never been so eager for anything in my entire, ceaseless life.

I've never wanted to live more.

19

Essie

another
dead person

I am tired of people dying in my town.

I'm tired of hearing Detective Berk's voice and seeing her face and answering her questions. I don't like the looks I'm getting from the neighbors. It's as if a toxic bubble has popped up around our house. Cars don't even drive by as much, but I might be imagining that part. Probably, I am. I can't imagine anyone would go all the way around the next block over to get to their house, just to avoid driving past our residence. That's just ridiculous.

But anyway. It's been two days since my father's visit. The cut on my hand isn't healed yet. The cuts inside aren't, either, but I've bandaged them, too, with pills of all colors and a daily injection, which isn't fun. Detective Berk is in our kitchen again, eyeing the new brown coffee stain splattered into the plaster wall, courtesy of my father. We'll paint over it, but we haven't gotten to it yet. There's a man with her who is not from around here.

He says his name is Agent Gray and that he's from St.

Louis, but I don't believe either of those things. He smells like Windex. His suit is the same bland brown shade as his hair. He's middle-aged, or thereabouts, but his skin bears the creamy, smooth-skinned look of someone who spends little time outdoors. He's a listener, by evidence of the lack of lines around his mouth. Listeners are the ones you have to be careful about.

Detective Berk and Agent Gray are in our kitchen because a young man was murdered last night, and some remains of another woman floated to the surface of Pember's Lake the day before that.

The young man was a soon-to-be freshman from Florida, visiting family in Concordia while taking summer classes. He'd been planning to study horticulture, although why Detective Berk felt *that* detail was important is unclear. His name had been mentioned, but blood had been roaring in my ears so loudly, all I got about him was Florida and horticulture. The guy had been strangled, then moved to a bathtub. This hadn't taken place in his dorm, but a vacant house for sale on the other side of town. A real estate agent and their prospective buyers noticed a smell when they'd entered the house, apparently, and made the discovery in the upstairs bathroom. He had been there for several days.

The woman's story was even worse. After her head and torso floated to the surface, divers found her feet tied to cast-iron cookware, like my great-grandmother had been found. Although the medical examiner hadn't finished his full exam, she suspected the woman was strangled, too.

Killers seem to favor strangulation, according to the murder shows my aunt likes to watch.

"What does this have to do with Essie?" Aunt Bel must be weary of asking this question. And never getting a solid answer in reply. "I mean, you can't think Essie overpowered this man, then hauled him upstairs into a bathtub. Or-or tied frying pans to that woman and—" She cuts off, the back of a hand pressed to her lips.

"She clearly couldn't have," Detective Berk said, drumming her blunt fingers on the table. "Also, there was a perfectly fine bathtub on the first floor. The problem is, some details in Ray Archer's murder"—*that* was his name—"exactly match those of the late James Roane's suicide, as I'm sure you are aware. His wrists had been cut, although that was not the cause of death. And then there's the, ah…carving of a Bible passage onto his torso."

I groan. "Was it Revelation 21.5: *Behold, I make all things new*?"

"Why, yes." Agent Gray perks up. "How do you know this?"

I never met my Uncle James. He died before I was born, at the age of seventeen. *My* age. Detective Berk doesn't show us the picture of the new victim, thankfully, but I know how the carved words would look. It's a short sentence, but actually a lot to cut into oneself.

Uncle James was committed to his task, no question. He even did it upside down, starting with "Behold…" below his belly button and working up his chest, so he'd get it right. "Grandma Edie describes it in detail during every Christmas dinner," I explain. "He was her son."

Aunt Bel clears her throat and glances back to the hall to make sure her mother isn't within earshot. "James was her youngest and my brother," she said in hushed, clipped tones. "This is very unpleasant to relive. I can't believe someone would recreate these horrific events."

"And you know, the female victim, who has yet to be identified, died in identical fashion to one…" Detective Berk glances at her notes, "Jessica Webster-Wickerton, a great-grandmother of yours. *Ours.*"

"We now have three murders staged to imitate suicides of past members of your family." Agent Gray folds his hands on the table. He leans forward as Detective Berk leans back. "With a little investigating, it has been determined that all three victims have genetic links to the Wickerton family."

"What?" Aunt Bel asks sharply.

"*Miss Leeds* was a Wickerton?" I look between Detective Berk, who I know, and Agent Gray, who I don't, and wonder where they're going with this conversation.

Agent Gray nods. "Mr. Archer is your second cousin, once removed. Miss Leeds is your third cousin. We thought it odd that the connection hadn't surfaced sooner"—he glances pointedly at Detective Berk, who shrugs—"until we discovered that those in your family who don't suffer from the Wickerton disorder are quite determined to disassociate themselves from the rest of the family."

There's a cigarette clenched between Aunt Bel's index and middle fingers. She taps ash into a glass sugar bowl whose life as an ashtray began about fifteen minutes ago.

"Oh yes. It's quite a stigma, being a Wickerton," she growls. "So whoever killed these people has an obsession with the condition that afflicts some of us and is targeting living relatives." Aunt Bel has seen a *lot* of true-crime TV programs.

"It's a strong possibility." Detective Berk's gaze is heavy as it moves between me to Aunt Bel. "Which is why I've been taken off the case. I *am* a Wickerton, as you know."

Aunt Bel gives Agent Gray a distasteful look. She is not trusting of outsiders. "And now the FBI is taking over?"

"Yes," Detective Berk replies. "Agent Gray is taking over the investigation, but I agreed to stay close to the case, to help. And to make you feel more comfortable, Essie."

I don't feel comfortable. Not at all. My gaze falls to the black, burned handprint on Detective Berk. It's now encompassing her entire forearm, spreading like a rash. "Why isn't that healing?" I ask her, momentarily forgetting to stay on task.

Her brows twitch into a frown, but she dips her arms beneath the tabletop. "There's nothing on my arms, Essie."

"Okay, so what do we do?" Aunt Bel cuts in, ignoring my question to Detective Berk. "Do we go into hiding? Move into the witness protection program?"

"Nothing like that, Ms. Roane." Agent Gray's smile is mild and condescending. "The FBI is in on this because the male victim was a juvenile. As well as the likelihood of these murders being linked. We'll be investigating, the police will be closely watching all known Wickerton family members, but at this time, there's no reason to believe the killer is targeting you. Remember, all the victims have been those unaffected by the disorder."

"What about me?" Aunt Bel asks. "I'm not affected. Am I a target?"

Agent Gray gives her a level look. "You do not fit the current profile. The victims have been young adults. Teens, early twenties."

"Is Detective Berk considered a target?"

He nods. "Possibly. It's why her help is so welcome."

"A goddamn serial killer is running loose in Concordia," Aunt Bel mutters, but if we weren't in the middle of it, she would be eating this up.

My aunt is a head nurse at the trauma unit, caretaker to Grandma Edie and me, yet she watches murder investigation shows in her free time. Sometimes I think she submerges herself in death and pain and sickness so she doesn't glimpse all she's missing in life. If that's the case, it's the saddest thing ever.

"We don't care for the words 'serial killer,'" says Agent Gray. "It incites panic."

"As it should," is my aunt's tart reply. The air is thick with smoke. She forgot to open the window, and the agent from St. Louis is starting to look a little green from breathing it. "So I assume you FBI agents are going to question us all over again?"

"Yes, and explore more of your family history, anyone who has access to these details or has shown more than average interest in it."

Aunt Bel throws up wild hands. "Everyone has access to it. It's all well-documented in the town library. There was a book written about it that you can find easily enough. Plus, there was that horrible news segment that ran a few years back."

"I know," he says. "We have the footage. And a copy of the book."

"Did you actually read it?" I ask with a totally inappropriate snicker that everyone ignores. But really, *The Wickerton Curse* is a terrible book. Like, truly, *truly* awful. Much of it is wild speculation written to sound like facts. The thought of this Agent Gray spending nights in his motel room reading it makes me pull up the neck of my T-shirt over my mouth and giggle behind it.

"Look, we're going to keep many details quiet." He ignores me. Everyone is doing that these days. "But there's going to be renewed interest in your family. In Essie."

Aunt Bel casts a worried glance my way. "We're not equipped for this sort of thing. You *know* how things are."

"I'll be okay," I put in, but again, no one's listening. My voice comes out wispy, faraway sounding.

A pang of despair twists behind my ribs. I'm starting to slip. I can feel it. My father's visit, and oh, these poor people being killed. No matter how hard I fight, no matter how many pills I take, I can't turn back an avalanche. Eventually, I'll get buried. It's just, no matter where I turn, there's pain, anxiety. Worrying that Bradley Roane will get me committed to Stanton House. Worrying about the disastrous "event" that's going to happen in Concordia, the one that drew Dresden here, and *oh*, Dresden. I miss talking to him. I wonder what he's doing right now.

Also, there's the worry that the murderer will come for me or my aunt next, although that's actually not at the top of my worries. It should be, I guess. I'll add that to the list of things wrong with me.

"Essie, has anyone recently approached you? Shown undue interest in your family or you?" Agent Gray asks, but he isn't looking at me when he asks. He isn't talking to me at all, but rather the space around me. He doesn't see me as a person. To him, I'm an object, like an inkjet printer, which sometimes works and sometimes doesn't.

"No," I answer. "Just you and Dr. Roberts. But he's always asking weird questions."

He jots something in a notepad. Checks his phone. "How did you lose the hat which came to be in Miss Leeds's hands?"

"These questions have been addressed already," Aunt Bel cuts in, her tone sharp with warning.

"Yes," Agent Gray says. "And will likely be addressed again."

"It fell off in the woods," I reply. "I wasn't aware of it. I didn't—"

"Thank you, Essie." Agent Gray looks up with another smile that doesn't reach his eyes. "I'm looking forward to talking with you further," Agent Gray says. "I have a background in psychology, you know."

Ugh, another one. Aunt Bel's eyes narrow to slits. "Well. Isn't that fancy."

Their voices begin to fade. Aunt Bel's cigarette smoke becomes a fog that envelops the room and sets me adrift in a sea of fragmented thoughts. The space between me and the people around me stretches, lengthens, until they're reduced to a vague idea I don't find interesting. I'm sliding away from the noise, the questions, the fear. I could fight it. I could push back like I usually do and force myself to stay present, but it's easier to retreat into the soft edges and discordant noise of oblivion. For once, the manifestations of my damaged mind are not as disturbing as reality.

20

Dresden

the truth
in rumors

The harbingers of death are living well off the misery of Concordia.

People die here, like everywhere, but the murder rate is currently higher than it's been in years. Henrik and I are to blame for that, although mostly *me*, with my bees' excessive stinging, and now the town is really starting to hum with fear. It's crept past the town center and into the sleepy residential streets. It emanates off residents like static, and helps charge up my depleted, corrupted cells. It soaks into my blighted self like water to a dried-up sponge.

It feels *good*. I'm less tired, and my bees are content rumbling around in my chest, rather than pinging against my teeth at the whiff of an unbalanced person.

It's a small bit of peace in a sea of turmoil. And I will need the energy when I leave Concordia and find this person who used to be a harbinger. They could be anywhere, and compared to harbingers, beekeepers have a short battery life, to use a modern metaphor. As in, we don't thrive straying from our strict pattern of following harbingers to new places of imminent disaster, squatting there, then following them when they leave. We lack the homing skills they possess.

I suppose we could go anywhere, sting away, and create our own chaos, but since no one does this that I know of, it's safe to assume we've all become dependent on the fear energy generated by a big chaotic event. Perhaps it's laziness on our part, but the charge is so powerful, we can't stay away. It's a foul thing to live on, people's fear. It's utterly disgusting to feel good from it.

I don't react as Michael sits on the chair next to me. We're on someone's front porch, diagonally across the street from Essie's house. The occupants are not home, and judging by the condition of their yard, haven't been for quite some time. They were thoughtful enough to leave some folding chairs on their covered porch, which come in handy for observing Essie's house under the cover of darkness.

Michael sits gingerly, as the hole in his gut isn't done healing. This is our first meeting since I smeared honey in his wound. I have conflicted feelings about that, now that I have some distance from it. I'm relieved that I won't be expected to cough up some honey every time one of those harbingers get a scratch, but I'm also surprised that I did it at all.

A few short months ago, saving him wouldn't have occurred to me. I meant what I said to Adele—I have as much business interfering with the cycles of his curse as he has meddling in mine. I also feel a weird, uncomfortable pride. For once, my bees and I did something constructive, rather than destructive. My curse brought relief, rather than pain and death. It throws the definitions I have of myself into question.

"Hey, what's up?" he asks.

It's a nice night, as nights go. No wind. Quiet. Aside from a few glowing TVs in the windows, most of the neighborhood is asleep at midnight.

I can just make out the peak of her roof, the back end of her aunt's car. Her aunt, who apparently had to take a leave of absence from her job to stay close to Essie and her grandmother because the home aides who used to come have quit.

"Nothing." We speak in hushed tones, so as not to be overheard.

"Ah, in a mood, are we?"

"No," I say. But yes, I am in a mood.

"I wanted to say th—"

"Don't even think of thanking me again. Once was enough."

"Okay," he says conversationally. "Actually, I wasn't going to thank you for saving my life. While I'm grateful to not be dead and stuck in a crow's body, it's your act of mercy—as self-motivated as it was—that I'm thanking you for. It's raised the spirits of my group. They don't hassle me about hanging around you anymore. That, alone, is a wonder."

I shake my head. "Who knew Concordia would be filled with such a thing?"

"Yeah. Wonders are rare in our world." He sends me a quick grin. "You go and do two things no beekeeper has ever done before—fall in love and save a harbinger's life. Seriously, don't do that last one again."

I grin back briefly. "I won't. And it was self-motivated.

Don't forget that."

"You can't deny it anymore. We're friends, Dresden. That means something to you." He keeps his gaze on the yard in front of us. "It means something to me."

Bees rumble in my chest as I tense up. I am hating this conversation, hating that he's right. I *do* care. I suppose I can thank Essie for uncovering this mess of emotion, although it's not something I'm grateful for. It's the purest agony I've ever known. "I was sparing myself years of you as a child," I say to him. "You are an utter wretch until you turn twelve or so."

"I am, aren't I?" He leans back, pleased with himself. "Intolerable."

Michael laughs, then sees the house my eyes are glued to and falls silent. He nods toward Essie's home. "How is she holding up?"

"Decent, I think," I reply. "I hope."

"You mean you don't know?"

"I know what I can see from a distance, or what my bees can see."

Michael raises his dark brows and scratches his impressive jawline. "You should talk to her."

I let out a sigh. "I want to. I'm not sure I should."

"Why?"

We go still as a police car glides down the street. They patrol every ten minutes or so, and I'm glad to see it. The more sets of eyes on her, the better. "Because I don't think clearly when I'm with her. I fear telling her my true feelings and frightening her."

"Really?" he asks. "Even though it seems she feels the same way?"

"Does she?" I murmur. "Or is it some variant of the

curse that's causing her to have these feelings? She says her mind clears when she's around me. Considering that I am the one responsible for this condition she endures, that's hardly a coincidence."

"So you think she likes you because of the bee venom she inherited." He scratches his chin. "I can see why you'd think that. But I'll tell you this: I've seen a lot of reactions to your venom. The infected do many sorts of things, but falling in love has never been one of them."

I nod slowly. He's right. But there's no telling if what Essie is feeling is love. "You know the curse works in bizarre ways. I can't continue on with her while she's still infected. If she lacks choice because of the bee sting to her ancestor, then nothing between us is real. I won't take advantage of something she has no control over." Only my lips move. The bees are quiet. "No matter how real it is to me."

After a pause, Michael says, "What if there is no way to cure her?"

I let my eyes fall closed. "Then there is no cure."

"Then, that's it?"

"What other option is there, Michael?" I look at him, genuinely open to suggestions. "I can't stay here if I can't cure her, and currently, between the Strawman and this psychopath on the loose, the best way for me to keep her safe is to watch from a distance."

Michael snorts. "Spoken like a true martyr."

"Martyrs are noble."

"Martyrs are idiots," he replies. "You are staying away because you think it will hurt less when you have to leave. *If* you have to leave."

I turn slowly, look him right in the eye. "I would kill

everyone on Earth to keep her safe."

He rolls his eyes. "Please. Speculate all you want about how the curse may be interfering with her feelings. The truth is, you're over here watching her house like some vigilante because you're afraid of going over there and telling her that you're falling in love with her."

His words hit me in a very uncomfortable spot. There's some truth to them. But if I tell her the truth about *that*, I'll also have to admit that I am the ultimate cause of her condition. It may be cowardly of me, but I never claimed to be particularly valiant. "Will you please *go?*" I grip the armrests of my folding chair so tight the plastic warps. "Surely there's someone nearby who needs the death energy siphoned from their failing body."

"No, I'm good," he says with a wave of his hand. "I get why you're worried about the murderer—four deaths, at last count. And we didn't sense any of them, which is weird. No question the Strawman had *some* hand in it. So you can do one of three things." He holds up three fingers. "You can go try to find the killer, go talk to Essie, or continue sitting here and stare at her house."

"I am going to continue doing the third, and hope the police do the first. I would like to do the second one day, but not until she is cleared of the venom's influence." I don't allow my thoughts to linger there. The possibility of that is an unlikely sliver of hope.

"Fine." He laces his fingers behind his head. "Nothing to do but watch the clouds come in, then."

Coming in they are, like great, deep purple carpets unrolling across the sky. Stars blink out, one by one. "Is it going to be a storm?" I nod toward the sky. "The disaster that's coming—does Lish still think it'll come from up there?"

He shrugs. "Wouldn't be the first time a bad storm hit these parts, would it?"

I swallow, my throat thick with coagulated honey. There were always bad storms. Sometimes they had nothing to do with the weather, but the people themselves. It was another town in another time, or maybe Concordia was built on the rubble of a previous town, but I suddenly *remember*. I groan against the memory shuttering to life behind my eyes, of an earlier time, more than a century ago, when I came across a young woman. I didn't know her name, then, but I know it now: Opal Wickerton.

The scene is incomplete, more like a scattering of snapshots than the reel of a movie. Beekeepers do not have flawless memories. I've lost many things over the years. I don't want most the memories I *do* have. But this one comes to focus, vivid and crisp, as if it had been just waiting to surface. The woman hangs out laundry in the whipping wind. Her green skirts conform to the shape of her legs. Long, blond strands pull free of her hat. I remember thinking, in a detached sort of way, that the men here would find her appealing. They would fight for her attention. One of them won her affection, apparently, as she wears a simple silver band around her finger.

The woman in my memory is Essie's great-great-grandmother, but where Essie is fine-boned and delicate, Opal is Artemis. Detective Berk, it would seem, inherited Opal's sturdy build. She is strong and powerful and looks as though she would be equally at ease bearing a crown or a broadsword. Her only real resemblance to Essie is her hair, and something in the shape of her mouth. All her other features were sifted out with generations, resulting in the girl I love—slender and delicate, but no less magnificent. Essie would wield magic rather than a sword.

I remember when I looked at the woman—Essie's ancestor—I felt ravaged and weak. Shaken by something raw, achy, desperate. The woman sets off my bees. I don't know why. I could have been depleted and tired, like I was when I met Essie. I honestly don't remember.

I push the memory, try to recall if I felt any dark, violent energy from her, but I can't recall if I did. All I know is they wanted to sting her. I suppose you could say I took the bees at their word and frankly, I lacked the strength of will to deny them. One bee left my mouth.

One bee. Little did I know then that it would change the course of this entire family for generations to come. It stung her, and that was it. I didn't think about it—or her—again. They wouldn't have stung her unless she was a valid target, right? They don't make those types of mistakes. Neither, I thought, did I. But they were wrong with Essie. I suspect they were wrong about her.

Yet here I sit, more than a century later, freshly sliced by the recent memory of Opal's great-great-granddaughter's arms around me. I'm forever altered because of her affection for me.

"Do you remember when we were here last?" I ask Michael quietly.

"Not very well," he replies. "What do you remember?"

"I remember stinging Essie's ancestor. It's my fault that Essie's family has been plagued with madness."

He makes a noise of frustration and smacks the back of my head, hard.

"Hey," I say. "What's wrong with you?"

"What's wrong with *you?*" he replies. "Don't you get it? You're trying to find a way to break your curse. Don't you see that what is going on with you and Essie is an omen?"

"No."

"Dres, I'm a harbinger of death. I can sniff out an omen."

"You can sniff out *death*." I say it gently, because I feel some pity for him. Michael is so hopeful for his curse to be broken, he's finding cracks where there aren't any. "It's very much the opposite of what you're looking for."

"Dresden, you fell in love, after...how many centuries?"

It's as if my jaw has been wired shut. I can't open my mouth to deny it or affirm it or tell him to go piss off. "Too many."

Love. It's a word meant to be uttered on a sigh, proclaimed from a rooftop, whispered through weeping. I would do anything to ensure Essie's well-being. I'm attracted to her, although I'm well aware of how fruitless that line of thinking is. Knowing her has changed me. My feelings for Essie feel so much larger than one simple word.

"And here you are, watching her house, rather than being inside it with her."

"Unfortunately, I am *this*," I say, waving a hand over myself. "I'm not capable of a relationship with her in this state, Michael."

"You were a man once, with all the usual emotions." He tosses his head back, flipping his floppy mess of hair out of his eyes. "Maybe you call him up and have him tell her how you feel."

"Maybe I should have let you die in that motel room."

"Yeah, yeah. Hey—" His laughter fades as he points to a spot across the street from Essie's house. "Look at that."

A figure leans against one of the oak trees lining the road.

Bees drop from my nose, buzz around my head at the sudden shift of my mood. The person is in shadow. I can't see what they look like. "Is it the Strawman?" I ask. He has sharper eyesight than me.

"No," Michael says. "Guy's tall but dressed in black pants and top. No hat. Shall I do a stroll-by?"

"No. People don't 'stroll' at one in the morning." I sink into observation, fixing my gaze on the still figure against the tree. It could be her father, sick bastard, or that twisted psychiatrist she's forced to have appointments with. It could be anyone.

Michael fidgets in his chair next to me. He's not good at waiting, watching. He's much more action oriented. It makes him a good scavenger, but a terrible observer.

For a long time, the mystery person remains right where he is, unmoving.

"He's on the move," Michael growls. "I can go."

"No." I rise to my feet. "I'm going."

"I'll come with you."

I don't argue. Two supernatural creatures are better than one in a possible confrontation, and I admit, I haven't confronted anyone in longer than I can remember. We start forward, easing down the porch steps and cutting across the neighbor's lawn. I'm a quiet walker, but my companion is not, and it only takes a poorly placed step on a crispy patch of grass for the guy to swing around.

Michael grunts out a curse. No more than ten feet separate us from Essie's possible stalker, who is still in shadow. He wears black from head to toe, like a ninja. Even his face is covered in black. My hands form tense fists. Bees buzz my head like flies. "Who are you?" I demand.

In a quick move, he grabs for his belt and takes out a gun, points it at me.

Oh, bloody everlasting *hell*. I wasn't expecting guns to be involved, and this person clearly knows what they're doing. A bullet wouldn't hurt me, but Michael is still recovering from a grave wound.

I slowly raise my hands, trying to keep my face in the shadows. It's very likely I'm dealing with the person who slew Essie's relatives. I mustn't sting him. "Relax. Just taking a walk."

"The hell you are," says a low, warning voice. "On the ground."

"We haven't done anything wrong—" Michael begins.

The guy jerks the gun toward the ground. "Now."

I hear him sigh and get to his knees. I do the same, but slower. Something about the way this person moves or their body shape is familiar, but I can't place it. It's definitely not a voice I've heard before, but if I was near this person in bee form, I'd have no idea what their voice sounds like.

There is a ripple to this person's energy that sets my bees on edge. Something unsettling and dark. Interestingly, he's radiating fear. Waves of it. It gives me a bit of energy, but it's mixed with that rancid, sharp-edged hatred that sets my neck hairs on end.

"Why are you watching this house?" I ask, hoping to throw him off balance. His body tenses in the dark. Who *is* this person? It's infuriating that I can't tell more about them. I commit as many details to memory as I can, but there's little to see. The streetlamps are not on us.

Headlights turn the corner, illuminating the three of us. The gunman closes the distance between us and in two quick, efficient moves, slams the gun into my cheek and rams a booted foot into my gut. I double over from surprise and the sudden expulsion of bees. They burst out of me, furiously buzzing.

"What the—?" My attacker's voice goes high-pitched as he wheels away from the bees. Inexplicably, they make no move to sting. One shaking, gloved finger points at me. "You stay away from Essie," he snarls, but the police patrol has spotted us. White and blue lights flash.

"Stop where you are," a loudspeaker calls out.

I roll to the tree and flatten against it. Michael moves with effort. He's in no condition for this. "Get out of here," I tell him. "*Go!*"

He gives me a stricken look but lets the black fog flow from his mouth and turn him into a crow. One loud *caw* rips from his beak before he takes to the sky.

There's a moment when the big oak tree sits between me and the police as they clamber from their car. I take it, change into bees, and follow the person who had been watching Essie's house. He ducks into a driveway to hide from the policemen's view, but there's not many places to hide here, with each house surrounded by fences.

But then I see a figure I *do* know, standing in the front yard of the next house over. The Strawman is still, blending into the shadows, in his long, dark coat and wide-brimmed hat. The man who hit me bolts directly for the Strawman.

I can only watch as the Strawman draws Essie's stalker into his embrace. The second before the police spotlight lands on them, the two of them vanish in the air. The sight is momentarily dumbfounding. I stifle a shiver.

This is a complication I hadn't anticipated. Never in all my years have I seen a Strawman take a human like that. But it makes sense. Whoever that was has been touched by the Strawman and now belongs to him. Which makes finding and stopping this killer much more difficult.

I watch from high in the peaked eave of a house as the patrol officers get out of their car and aim flashlights down the driveway and into the bushes. They know they saw *something*. Their mouths talk furiously as they poke at Michael's discarded clothes with their toes and peer into dark windows. Eventually, they get back in their car and drive off.

21

Dresden

the
calling

"**Y**ou have a bruise."

"Impossible." I don't know why I came here, to Essie's room. To check on her, I told myself. Once the idea took root, it was as if ropes were fastened around my limbs and pulled me straight here. When she heard my bees pinging against her window screen, she opened it and I went inside willingly, eagerly, with no interest in whether it was right, or responsible, or even ethical to do so. To be near her was to breathe again.

"You do." She touches just below her eye and points to me. "Just there. On your cheek."

I bring my fingers to my face and jerk back in surprise. My right cheekbone is hot and swollen. Surprise sparks a current from my gut to my head. Either I'm turning a little bit human, or the Strawman's minion has powers that make him stronger than a normal human. I don't know which is more unsettling. "It's nothing."

Essie frowns. "It's *something*."

I take her hand and hold it in both of mine. "Don't worry about me," I say with a quick grin. "I'm pretty tough."

"Whatever." She squeezes my hands. "I wasn't sure I'd see you again."

"I wasn't sure I'd come here again," I say honestly. "I just…I couldn't stay away. I wanted to see you." The words choke out of me. I hate how vulnerable they make me sound.

A smile spreads across her face. "Good. I wanted to see you, too. You made it sound like you weren't coming back."

I allow my fingertips to slide down a blond lock of hair. "I tried."

She doesn't look the same. Her skin is pale, and dark circles hang under her eyes. There's a fatigue to her that concerns me, and a rumpled look to her that I hadn't seen before. The energy she gives off is dull and almost nonexistent.

"You're different. What's happened?" I ask her. "Aside from your father's unpleasant visit?"

"New medication. Slows everything down." She smiles faintly. "Thank you for scaring him, by the way. He's so horrible. I don't like being related to him. Makes me worry how much of him is in me."

"You are nothing like him." I would know. I can feel the energy of a person. Essie and her father have completely different vibrations.

She shakes her head sadly. "You say nice things, but I can't tell if they're really real."

I tilt her chin up. "Try a peppercorn."

"If only that worked." She breaks away, walks to her

desk. "Will you promise not to leave again?"

I push my hands into my pockets. My heart feels like it's twisting and sinking at the same time. "I can't."

"Why not?" Her eyes flash, hot and sharp. It's a relief to see the emotion on her. The pills haven't snuffed out all her essence.

"I'm a beekeeper." As if to emphasize that point, my bees surge in my chest, buzzing loudly. "As I am, I cannot promise anything." I sweep a hand over myself. "I'm ruled by the curse that made me thus." *As are you.*

Essie lowers her head. Delicate shoulders sag. "I can't take this, Dresden." She scrapes her fingers through her hair. "I care about you, and that's not a delusion. It's real and true and has nothing to do with my mental condition. But coming and going; making me say goodbye, then showing up again—it's bad for me. I don't deserve this half-in, half-out thing." She straightens her spine. "It hurts. And I'm hurting enough."

She *doesn't* deserve it. Not long ago, I would have said that I didn't deserve her, but when I play that through my mind, a surge of fury ignites, rather than sad resignation. Before I arrived in Concordia, the idea of caring for someone was foreign—a distant scrap from my long-gone human years. But now, I burn with purpose. Yes, I am responsible for her condition, but I will do everything I can to free her of the venom. Whatever it takes.

Then, possibly, I can make promises. I can stay.

I'm searching for a way to help you. I want to be with you more than anything I have ever wanted. I want to be worthy of your love. But I don't say those things. Instead, I edge toward the window, belly in a knot. "I'm sorry, Essie."

Three words that I wish to rip from my throat. Did I

think myself immune to pain? I was wrong.

"Me too," she says very softly, to the floor.

Just then, a crow swoops up and lands in her open window frame, startling both of us. Essie slaps a hand to her chest, mirroring the gesture I've seen by her Aunt Bel. The crow angles its dark red eyes to Essie, then to me. It tips its head up and releases a gravelly *caw*.

In the past, I would have assumed this was Michael, but now I'm not sure. It could be any of the four harbingers of death. It could be the Strawman, borrowing one of the harbingers. How irritating. My once-predictable life has become as uncertain as a human's. One thing that is certain is that the crow wants me to follow it. If it's the Strawman, I want to get it away from Essie as quickly as possible.

That won't be difficult. She's not even looking at me. Turned partly away, she watched the crow from the corners of her eyes. "Just go, Dresden," she says. "And—if you can't be someone who sticks around, don't come back, okay?" Her voice hitches. "Don't do that."

Oh gods, it was a mistake to come here. My heart is a chaotic mess, full of feelings I can't begin to process. My heart twists at the hurt in Essie's voice, even as it soars for the possible reason the crow is here. The harbingers wouldn't interrupt me at Essie's unless they had important news for me. The words are there—*I will stick around.* But I can't say that, yet. I have to be human first. She has to be free of the Wickerton curse first.

Without another word, because I don't trust anything my mouth would utter, I move to the window and change into bees. The crow flies in the direction of the harbingers' motel. *Good.* It's probably one of them, then, and not the Strawman.

It lands in front of the room they're renting. I cluster my bees in between two cars and do my best to transform to human shape as discreetly as possible. The crow pecks once on the door, and Lish opens it.

She narrows her eye at me before motioning for me to enter. "Beekeeper."

"Hello." I go inside. Only she and Adele are here. No evidence of a bloody near-death remains in the room. The bed Michael lay in is tidy and clean. Black fog engulfs the crow. It transforms back to Michael. I watch as the transformation is completed with the inky smoke forcing itself down his throat.

"What happened to your face?" Adele asks me, stepping forward to peer at my bruise.

"I was hit by a human claimed by a Strawman." I hold still while she pokes a finger at my cheek. "Could that be why his strike injured me?"

"It's possible," says Adele, the little royal harbinger, as I've come to think of her. She pauses, a frown gathering between her brows. "Were you able to find out who it is?"

"No." I sink into the chair in the corner of their little motel room. "He wore a mask."

Her lips compress. "This doesn't make things easier."

"I'm aware."

Michael pulls on a pair of shorts. "He touched someone who is now obsessed with killing her family members. Only the ones not affected by the curse. *Not* Essie."

"Yet," I add.

"He warned us off." Michael shrugs. "It seems like the Strawman is trying to send you a message with all this.

Also, with the things he's told you in your little meetings."

"I have zero interest in his message," I say harshly. "I am only interested in keeping her safe until the event passes and this newly created psychopath is captured or killed. And I can't even get her out of town because the police have restricted them from leaving."

"Why?" Lish asks.

"She's a suspect."

The leader of these harbingers laughs. "You've got to be kidding."

I let out an exasperated growl. "I wish I was. They have no one else, so naturally they're looking at the girl whose missing hat was found with one of the victim's bodies. Her condition doesn't help her ease their suspicions."

"Dresden." Lish stands between the two beds, arms crossed. Her face is unreadable. "We called you here because we have his name and location."

"Whose name?" I ask wearily.

"The boy who used to be a harbinger, but isn't anymore," Lish explains. "You wanted the origin of the rumors we heard. We found it for you."

My chest contracts, unsettling the already-unsettled occupants of my rib cage. I clamp my teeth closed to keep bees from coming out, as per Lish's request. I mustn't give her any reason to withhold information now. "Who is he?" Speaking with my mouth closed gives me the appearance of sounding angry when I'm not.

"Reece Fernandez," she says. "He found a way to return to full mortality. The beekeeper he had an altercation with died."

"Who was he?" My throat is tight.

"He went by name of Rafette."

Rafette. I recall him. He always had a cruel edge and was terribly in love with his own visage. It must have broken him utterly to lose his features to those of his victims.

"There was also a girl involved—Angie something. Apparently, she had a role in what happened."

I immediately begin scheming how to locate this person. No easy task. There's surely more than one Reece Fernandez out there. I'll have to find a computer, "borrow" a cell phone—

"We have an address." Adele folds her hands. "Promise you won't hurt him."

"The young man? Why would I do that?"

Adele's gaze goes intense. "It's a long journey. You may not have full control over your bees."

"You have my word. I won't harm him."

"You'll share with us what you learn." Lish doesn't ask it.

My head snaps up. Something raw haunts her eye—a desperation I have seen enough times to know it's a plea for an answer. For an end to this existence we've all been relegated to. "Of course. Where can I find him?"

She gives me an address in Philadelphia, and my gut clenches. I don't know the miles, but Pennsylvania is a long way from Missouri. That will pose problems for me, energy-wise.

"Can you make it?" Adele asks. "Maybe you should you wait until after the event."

"No…" My head is spinning, and not just because I got punched in it. "I need to find him now."

"You should tell Essie what you're doing," Michael says.

"She asked me not to visit her again."

He makes a face. "That's not *quite* what she said."

"Nevertheless, I will respect her wishes." I turn my gaze to the floor. "I won't hurt her again." *Or myself.* If I can't be honest with her, I can be honest with myself.

Michael shakes his head. "We'll watch out for her."

"Thank you."

I make for the door, but he grabs my arm. "Be careful. Come back with answers."

"That is my intention."

His face is a complicated twist of emotions. "I've known you a very long time. You've been the constant. Everything changes, dies, is reborn. Except for you."

I've never been the back-slap, hugging type, and I won't start now. But Michael is looking at me like a dog just dumped at a shelter. He must be more worried about me than I thought. I clasp his arm. He's been my constant, too. Even when he is a pain-in-the-ass kid. As many times as we've swiped at each other, we've been unlikely brothers through the changing world. Each other's steady rock to turn to after seeing things that can't be unseen. When there has been absolutely no hope.

I can feel the heavy gaze of the other harbingers. They watch silently. How strange they must think this is, this friendship between beekeeper and harbinger. Perhaps now, they understand.

Or perhaps they're just counting the seconds for me to leave.

I squeeze his arm, release it. "Nothing truly remains unchanged through the ages, not even I."

I burst into a cloud of bees and fly east.

22

Essie

the avalanche

I know I'm in trouble when I can't tell the difference between dreams and reality. When things get so blurred and twisted up, my reality looks like a Picasso. Not one of the pretty ones, either, but one of those twisted cubists. I'm not sure how I got to this state. It wasn't gradual. I went to bed the night after Dresden came to visit and woke up with glass skin. Too many fears pressing around me, I guess.

Killers. Disasters. My father. Dresden.

Too much sadness, worry, anger. The pressure would bend the strongest mind. It snapped mine, transforming me into something sharp and brittle. It dropped a veil around me, and I can't summon the effort or desire to claw out of it. I can hear Aunt Bel talking to me, but she's speaking a foreign language, Chinese, maybe—when did she learn that? I'm glad she has time for some personal enrichment, but I wish she'd remember that I only speak English and some Spanish.

I don't understand why her eyebrows are worried. And why she's always there. Good grief, she won't leave me alone. She's always next to me, spooning food in my mouth, leading me to the bathroom, pulling a nightshirt over my head—ah, that pink one with the cat on it. The cat is nice until I fall asleep, then its claws come out and it scratches the hell out of me.

But whatever.

Now, all I want is to sit still and quiet, but Aunt Bel is bent on torturing me. Every time she moves me, my glass skin breaks and I have to wait and wait for all the cracks to smooth out again. The woman is relentless. But she doesn't know, of course. I can't tell her because my voice is gone. Worms have eaten away at my voice box. It's a miracle the food Aunt Bel feeds me doesn't just fall through the hole in my throat.

I'm glad Dresden is gone. I wouldn't want him to find out that I'm nothing but a porcelain doll, an inanimate thing to dress up and sit on chairs. Useless. A curiosity.

I'm sitting outside on the back porch with Grandma Edie. I'm on the wicker love seat and she's in the matching rocker, watching the small TV Aunt Bel puts out there for her on nice days. For the past two hours, my grandmother has rotated between *The People's Court*, a marathon of *Gilligan's Island*, and a repeat of last night's baseball game. She rocks the chair at an agitated pace with one foot, muttering that no one on the goddamn television is doing what they're supposed to be doing.

I know what's wrong. She's out of sync is all. It happens to me sometimes. The soundtrack doesn't match the video, so you have to try to match the actions with dialogue that happened ten seconds earlier. Except it's worse when your brain is out of sync with the show you're watching. That's what's happening now. If I could move, I'd turn the TV off, then back on again, and she'd be fine.

But the only things I can move are my eyes.

"Son of a bitch," Grandma Edie snarls, taking a swig of Coke from the bottle. "Bastard couldn't throw a pitch if his life depended on it."

That might make sense if she wasn't currently watching *Gilligan's Island*. But who knows? I might be the one out of sync. I can't tell anymore. I don't care anymore. I just want to sit still and not break myself.

A crow lands on the porch railing behind Grandma Edie's rocker. It cocks its head, studies me with dark garnet eyes, then starts preening its feathers.

I've seen this crow before. Outside my window. On my windowsill the last time I saw Dresden. I watch it, turning my eyes so far into the corners they start to water.

It fluffs its feathers and settles in. It looks like it's waiting for something.

Grandma Edie switches to the courtroom show and says something about there being no damn way they could make a coconut do that. She clucks her tongue and goes quiet about it. Aunt Bel had to run out to the store and I can't move, so she's just going to have to stay out of sync until Aunt Bel gets back.

I'm switching between eyeing that crow and the TV, but then I notice that Grandma Edie's foot stops rocking her chair. Her head is slumped forward. The remote is clutched in one hand and the bottle of Coke in the other. It's tipped over and dripping on the blue, painted planks of the porch floor. She fell asleep. She'll be pissed when she wakes up and finds her Coke empty.

The crow hops down to the floor in front of us. It blinks up at my grandmother, then opens its beak. Thick black smoke-fog-stuff pours out of its mouth. I suck in a breath, wishing more than anything I could move right now. The smoke smells like a blacksmith shop and envelops the crow like a dark cloud, growing larger, larger until it's the size of a person. I can see long, lean limbs through the smoke. Bunched fists. A shoulder and back puckered, disfigured with burn scars. The black stuff flows over his body to his mouth and funnels inside. What's left is a guy crouching on the floor, head bowed. He's naked. Totally nude. I've never seen a naked guy before. Well, a couple times on cable. What an exceptionally pretty delusion he is. Maybe he'll stand up and I'll see his—

He lifts his head and looks at me. I blink my eyes, and the delicate glass of my eyelids crunches. That, I can't help. Blinking, I mean. But I know him. Well, I don't *know* him, but I've seen him before. He's that guy Dresden was talking to a few weeks back at the parade before they both left in a hurry, all freaked out. He's not a man, either. He's a teenage boy. And if he's Dresden's friend, there's a chance he's real. I wish I could eat a peppercorn and find out for sure.

The first pang of panic twists my gut.

"Hi Essie," he says to me. "I'm Michael, Dresden's friend. I need you to stay calm, please." His eyes are soft, the ends of his words turn downward, like he feels bad about something. He kneels, angles himself so his privates are hidden behind his leg. It's probably a good thing. I'm staring like a weirdo. But then, he was a crow just a few moments ago.

I can't say anything in reply. It's hard to speak since

turning to glass. My jaw is locked and only hinges opens when Aunt Bel pulls it open with her fingers and spoons soup in there. A tiny noise escapes my throat. A whimper.

"What's wrong?" He scrutinizes me, then an understanding eases his gaze. "Ah, okay. You're stuck. Can't talk." He winces, then turns his gaze to my grandmother, who is still sleeping. He closes his eyes and opens his mouth and inhales long and deep, like he's inhaling something that smells wonderful.

I wonder what he's doing. Grandma Edie's going to wake up and freak out. It's been a while since she's seen a naked guy in real life, too, I bet. And from her angle, she'd see everything.

"I'm so sorry, Essie," Michael says, then does something strange—he reaches toward Grandma Edie's face and gently closes her eyelids. Until that moment, I thought they were already closed. I thought they were closed...

Ice pours through my veins. A cold, painful sadness uncurls through my belly. It feels worse than my father's cruel words. Worse than the most sickening delusion. Because even now, I know this *isn't* a delusion. For once, I wish it was. I can't turn my gaze from my motionless grandmother. Just a few minutes ago she was cursing at the television.

"No." The word slips through my frozen lips.

Michael leans in close to my grandmother and closes his eyes again. What *is* he doing? He looks like he's smelling her again—but his face flushes and his jaw slackens on a sigh. He stays that way for a long moment, and even though he's gentle, reverent with her, I want to rip him away. Whatever it is he's doing, it's too intimate. Too personal.

I'm her granddaughter. I should be the one closing her eyes, holding her cooling hand, and acknowledging her passing—me and Aunt Bel. But I'm trapped on this chair in this glass body.

When Michael leans back and looks at me again, there's a slight radiance to him that's not natural. His eyes shine bright and they're a little watery. He all but glows with an odd, euphoric vibe. I want to slap his face until it's gone, but then I remember something Dresden told me— harbingers of death. They survive off the particular energy given off by the dying. They're drawn to places where bad things happen. Where people die. Well, Concordia is certainly a place where bad things are happening. The town, and I, it seems, are steeped in death. Drowning in it.

That must be what Michael was doing—taking in her death energy. My heart contracts. Michael—the crow— came because he knew my grandmother was about to die.

He knew and didn't warn anyone!

A scream builds below my heart, but it's stuck somewhere in my throat. It can't leave my mouth.

"I'm sorry you've lost her," Michael says gently, peering at me. His eyes are concerned. "There's nothing I could have done. I can't interfere with death."

Liar! He could have done *something*. He could have called an ambulance; he could have told me!

"You need to call someone," Michael tells me. "You can't sit here with her like this. Your aunt won't be home for a while."

I'd *like* to move. I'm not *choosing* to sit here in stillness. Doesn't he understand that? Fury, hot and pressure cooked, puts a red tint to my vision. My grandmother just died, and I can't move. I can't *move*, because of this broken, defective brain I was born with. I'm drowning in death and all I can do is sit here like a fragile, useless doll.

"Seriously, someone needs to be notified right away." Michael looks out over our small, fenced-in yard. The neighboring houses are quiet, empty. It's a work day. Only the old and the crazy are home right now.

The scream has moved up my throat. I can hear the creaking rasp of a thousand hairline cracks fracturing my glass skin. It hurts. Oh, the pain is terrible. Pain over my skin and under it. Suddenly, it's all too much. The glass shatters. My head tips back, and my gaze goes skyward. The scream rips from my throat. Unbearable. Unending.

Michael says something I can't make out. I catch a glimpse of that black fog, and then a crow streaks off the porch in a blur of black feathers.

Everything breaks down. The broken pieces of me: fractured and jagged and precariously stacked up in this seat. Every single bit of me is shattering. Defined in this one moment of undoing and the piercing shriek coming out of me.

And I know, in my last moment of lucidity, there is no coming back from this.

Thoughts, deconstructing.

To feelings. Basics.

The beginning of it.

And the end.

An avalanche.

23

Dresden

the boy
who changed

The bees are at war with me.

They went along with it for a while, this departure from Concordia, but now, after two days and two nights, they are in revolt. We shouldn't be leaving the place of nourishment, where fear is running higher than it has since we arrived. In the past—distant past—when I attempted to defy the curse that defines my existence, the bees have kept me in line. They've taken over, forced me to sting. They are insects, merged with the intellect of a man. The original design of the beekeepers was to secretly infiltrate an enemy community, destroy it from the inside. We did that very well, for the brief time we were used for that purpose. Before the magic users began the purge.

None of them considered what would become of us *after*. None of them considered that they wouldn't eradicate all the magically altered blights they'd created. Just as they previously believed they'd controlled their power, they believed they'd effectively wiped it out.

Mistakes, both.

And now, here I am, stumbling around Philadelphia at night, leaving a trail of dead bees dropping from my mouth. The rest are tearing up my insides in pure misery. I can't reason with them. I can't explain things to them. Changing to bee form is a trial. The swarm that I become is more powerful than the swarm inside me, but the struggle takes tremendous energy.

I touch the fading bruise on my cheek.

And I continue on.

I don't think this neighborhood is a great one. I'm counting on that. A group of four men congregate in the alley between two buildings. I head for them, walking quickly, hating myself for what I'm about to do.

The men turn at my approach. One lets out a warning. They're standing in the small pool of light given off by an exit door lamp. I see a flash of silver, glass, before it's tucked inside folds of clothing. I spread my arms when I'm sure they can see me clearly and release a torrent of bees from my mouth.

The men scream in terror as the bees whirl around us. Three bees break from the swarm and make for the men. The three targets howl in pain as they're stung. The fourth isn't a target and bolts from the alley. He's going to tell what happened here and someone might believe him. But I don't care.

Fear pours off the men, potent and piercing. It hits me like a drug, so good I tremble in the sensation. It's like a sugar rush to humans, this kind of fear. It's a powerful shot, but doesn't last long. Not like the slow-simmering dread that's currently back in Concordia. Plus, scaring people like a Halloween prank is the most shameful way to get the energy I need. I've sunk to a new low.

The men run to the back of the alley, waving their arms wildly, screaming as though they've been gutted. Some lights blink on in windows. I pull the bees back into my chest and swiftly walk away, toward the address singing in my head.

Stinging and the absorption of fresh fear energy leaves the bees slightly more manageable. I'm as prepared as I'm going to be to speak with the young man who used to be a harbinger. I promised Adele I would not harm him. I mean to keep that promise.

Part of me still doesn't believe such a person exists. According to the address Lish gave me, he does, and harbingers are not prone to deception. It's the reason I'm here, against every instinct. The ex-harbinger lives in a pleasant neighborhood, in a nice brick building.

Charming little window boxes overflow with flowers. The iron railing beside the steps still smells of fresh black paint. I slip into the building by following a man delivering food. Reece Fernandez lives on the third floor. I take the stairs. Apartment 3B is the second on the left. My hand isn't steady as I knock. No answer. I rest my ear to the door and hear nothing. All this way to come to an empty place.

It's a simple decision, as beekeepers *are* prone to deception. I change into bees and enter through the space under the door. It's a most impolite thing to do, but I simply must speak with this guy.

I take human form in the kitchen, which is right off the entry. I have nothing better to do while I wait, so I look around. The apartment is lightly, but tastefully, furnished. Pretty tidy, too. After glancing at the clothes inside the wide-open closet, it's clear that Reece lives here alone. However, evidence of the girl who supposedly helped free him from his curse is all over the place.

A stray hairband on the coffee table. Small white flip-flops next to the couch. Green sunglasses with pink lenses. A framed photograph shows the two of them, smiling. I peer at the boy in the photo and—*there!* I see it: a weary hardness to the eyes. He *was* a harbinger. Shedding his curse did not lift the burden of sorrow, pain, death. He will carry that for the rest of his days.

But there is joy in his eyes, too. Love. Belonging. Hope.

Envy, the likes of which I've never known, starts a riot in my chest. I've never known anyone to rid themselves of a curse, and it strikes me as monstrously unfair that the rest of us haven't known this joy. Why did Rafette die? What caused *him* to be deprived of a life without bees? The first frissons of worry rattle through me.

After I've sufficiently annoyed myself with the photo, I sit my restless self in the recliner across from the dark TV and wait.

And wait. I'm about to get up and start pacing when I hear voices at the door and a key turning the lock. The girl is with him. A shock of nerves makes sweat break out on my palms. The bees, which had been crawling around my insides, roll toward my sinuses, trying to get out. I suck them back forcefully. I'm going to give these two a scare. Best not make it worse by allowing bees to fly around the room.

The harbinger enters first, followed by the petite young woman in the photo and the pungent scent of Thai food. He turns on the kitchen light, drops a takeout bag on the counter, and says something into the girl's ear. She laughs and turns to face him, raising on tiptoes to kiss him. It starts out playful, but quickly deepens. His arms go around her, and he backs her up to the counter, lifts her up on it. The rest of the apartment is darkened. They don't know I'm here.

My chest constricts. I would give anything to kiss Essie that way. To kiss her at *all*, for that matter. I look away from the couple, swallowing another wave of envy. I'm going to have to interrupt them, as I obviously can't sit here while they make out or do whatever they're going to do. The trick is making my presence known in such a way as not to terrify them in the process. If that can be avoided.

"I beg your pardon," I say.

The girl lets out a little shriek, and the harbinger, or ex-harbinger—*Reece*—steps in front of her in one swift move. "Who's there?" He reaches for the phone in his pocket.

He can't see what I am yet. He thinks I'm an ordinary intruder. For some reason, I hadn't considered that. I get to my feet and come forward quickly. "I know my presence here is terribly rude," I say, moving into the kitchen light. "I'm not here to harm you. I need your help."

A hint of the bird Reece used to be still shifts at the corners of his eyes. "I don't know you."

The girl's expression goes belligerent. She hops down from the counter and shoves around Reece, peering up at me with all the fury of an angry kitten. "You need to *leave*."

Against my better judgement, a smile moves over my mouth. "You're not afraid of me."

"Of *course* I'm afraid of you. One of your kind stung

me over a hundred times. I almost died." She bares her teeth. *"Asshole."*

Reece is more calculating. His hands are curved and ready. The guy is tall and physically impressive. If evidence of the hockey equipment in the corner is an indicator, he's a powerful athlete. "We can't help you." His voice is low, sharp with warning.

He says it so matter-of-factly, I collapse against the wall, suddenly spent. "Please. I've come a long way," I say through my teeth to keep the bees contained. They don't want to sting these two—it's my nervousness making them clamor for release. Although Reece gives off some damaged vibes, he's not dark and violent. His energy carries the stories and the scars of all he endured during his time as a harbinger. It always will.

I hold up my hands and back off, feeling absolutely wretched. "I need to know how you and the beekeeper broke your curses."

"I wish I could tell you it was magic words, a potion, but it was nothing like that." Reece's expression is wary, guarded. He didn't have the relationship with his beekeeper that I have with Michael. "I guess you could say it was love that broke it," he says with a small shrug.

I raise my head, meet his watchful gaze, which is now tinged with pity.

Reece's expression eases a fraction. "I'm sorry. I know the curse is horrible for you. You beekeepers have it much worse than harbingers."

Love.

Hope, need, certainty—so many emotions unfold within me. My faces are changing so fast, my whole head aches. I must look absolutely gruesome like this, but I walk up to them. They tense up, but don't back away.

I don't know how to prove myself. I don't know how to show these strangers that I am here for a noble reason. I close my eyes and conjure an image of Essie behind my eyes. The first time we met—her sitting on a swing and eating peppercorns. She told me I was pretty and wished I was real. I didn't know it then, but I was lost to her that day.

"Love," I quietly say, "is the one thing I have." When I open my eyes, my vision is blurry with tears. "Will you help me?"

A curious smile quirks Reece's lips. "You're…in love?"

A few dead bees fall from my nose and for some reason, I find it humiliating. I move to gather them up, but the girl waves me off. "Go, sit down." Her voice is brusque. "You look like you're going to drop. I'm Angie, by the way."

Reece nods to the living room, which is a few steps from the kitchen. He sits on the couch. I take my previous spot on the recliner.

Angie joins Reece on the couch. "Why are your bees dying?" she asks.

"They're starving," I explain. "I left the town we were feeding off of."

"How are you keeping control of them?" Reece asks, narrow eyed.

I offer a closed-mouth grimace. "With considerable difficulty."

"Wow." Angie leans forward. "You must really love her. Him?"

"Her name is Essie," I reply with a smile. "And yes, I do." Just saying her name brings a shudder. "I'm afraid, many years ago, I stung her ancestor—*accidentally*," I add, not that it matters. "Her family line was infected with my venom, and my Essie suffers, too. They say that when the curses were broken, the humans who'd been infected by the beekeeper who followed your group were cured. I came halfway across this country to find a way to break the curse. To free Essie of the suffering I brought to her."

There. I said my piece. I admitted my sin to two total strangers. Neither of them says anything for a moment. The pause stretches. Perhaps they're going to throw me out.

"Are you willing to die for her?" Reece asks me.

That shiver of worry returns, stronger. "I would do anything for her."

"Look, surely you know that the beekeeper you're referring to didn't survive being freed from his curse. You probably think one of us killed Rafette, or there was an accident. None of that happened. He tried to turn me into a beekeeper."

"I would never sentence another to this existence," I say with a savage growl to my words.

"I'm liking you more," Angie says. "This girl, Essie, could do worse."

"Thank you." I give her a weak smile. It's all I've got in me. "Will you tell me what *did* happen to the beekeeper, Rafette?"

Angie and Reece exchange heavy glances. "We don't *exactly* know how the harbinger's curse was broken, but we do know that the beekeeper's curse was broken when his queen bee was killed. She's quite squishable," Angie added. "I'd know, because I'm the one who squished her." She splays her palm, where a light, bumpy scar mars her skin.

"What happened to us isn't something that can be recreated," Reece says. "I can't say there'll be a happy ending for you and your Essie. If you want to free her of your venom's effects, you need to kill the queen bee. Then, the rest of your bees will die, and so will you." He winces. "Maybe what happened to Rafette won't happen to you, but I wouldn't count on a different outcome."

"I see." The words choke out of my chest. *No happy ending*. None of the things I was so foolishly dreaming of. Hope is a double-edged blade, then. But it isn't extinguished. There is still the possibility to free Essie. And haven't I wanted to die since I was given this curse? It looks like there's a way to make that happen. There's a bonus, too. I can die to free a family from a curse they should never have had to endure.

My head feels lighter. A bizarre euphoria sweeps through me like balm to the soul. "So be it." I look at Reece and Angie. "How can I do this and free my Essie?"

"Well, killing a queen bee isn't easy. She doesn't leave your chest, does she? Rafette lured her out."

I always know the location of my queen. She and I share a unique connection. We can't communicate directly, of course, but we read each other, sense each other. The other bees come and go, but she never, *ever* leaves my body. She has never even ventured up my throat. But there must be a way to get her out.

"I wish I had better news for you," Reece says, and he sounds like he means it.

"Does Essie…" Angie pauses, bites her bottom lip. "Know what you are? Does she have feelings for you, too?"

"She knows everything. *Almost* everything," I reply. "And she does seem to have some affection for me, yes."

"Then maybe there's some hope." Angie takes Reece's hand and twines her fingers with his. "Rafette wanted only one thing—to die. He got what he wanted. That's not what you want, though, is it?"

I get to my feet. My body feels like it's weighed down with knowledge, with the dissolution of hope. With this impossible task before me. I'm ready to put distance between myself and these two happy people, who have exactly what I would give anything for. My bees roil with eagerness to return to Concordia. "I want very much to live, but not as I am now. As that appears not to be an option, I will try to make some good come of my death." I rub a hand over my face, through my hair. "I'm tired of only bringing suffering. I'd like to stop. Permanently."

Reece's face opens in a wide, handsome smile. "You are very unusual, beekeeper."

"My name is Dresden."

Angie gets up. She walks right up to me. "I hope you get what you want, Dresden."

I gaze down at her. "What I want doesn't matter as much anymore."

She smiles, slow and intrigued. "That's why you have a chance."

24

Essie

the remains
of myself

There are comfy chairs by the windows. I sit in one of them while the woman next to me quietly cries. Her fingers fly in intricate, repetitive movements. For the longest time, I couldn't tell what she was doing, but I stared at her hands long enough to figure it out—she is knitting.

Unfortunately, she's the only person who can see what she's making. She doesn't talk to anyone, so I don't know why she cries. Maybe it's because they don't let her have real knitting needles. Still, she's making great progress on her blanket. Every now and then, she straightens it out and checks her stitches. Maybe I can get her to make me one, since I'm not going anywhere anytime soon. I'm now a resident of Stanton House.

There are between twelve and fifteen women living here. I'm related to a couple of them, but I'm the youngest by far. Yesterday, I played checkers with my cousin Lori, who is sixty-five and hasn't spoken in almost a decade.

I'm in the Library room, which is full of comfortable chairs and shelves full of books. Most inmates, er, *residents*, prefer the Open room, which is bigger and has games and art and sometimes music. Everyone has to be quiet in the Library room, which doesn't always work out so well, but right now it's just The Crying Knitter and me.

I don't remember being brought here. One minute I was sitting on the porch with Grandma Edie and the next I was curled up on a strange bed in a strange room. Aunt Bel tells me Grandma Edie died in front of me and as a result, I had a complete breakdown. Some guy apparently heard me screaming and called the police. They don't know who it was, since none of the neighbors were home. At least no one thinks I killed *her*. She died of a massive, sudden stroke. Natural causes, they say.

My father is happy. Dr. Roberts is happy. Aunt Bel does not seem happy and says she's going to get me out of here, but I kind of wish she wouldn't. It just makes it all worse. I'm here now and I'll be here for a while. I lost several days to an episode I don't remember. From what I've been told, and if the bruises on my arms and legs, across my cheekbone, are any indication, I went demonic when they tried to move me. Worst of all, I hurt Aunt Bel. Don't remember it, of course, and they say it was an accident. I was resisting the EMTs. She thought she could subdue me and got my elbow in the eye for her efforts. She's forgiven me. I haven't.

I tuck my legs up and rest my chin on my knees. I feel better, tucked up like a turtle without a shell. My sweatpants are warm, and that's a good thing, since the nurses play fast and loose with the air conditioner. I've been treated well here. No one bothers with me. I haven't required any extra observation so far. There's two things that make it unbearable: the complete management of every minute of our conscious time, and the loneliness. I want to go outside without a nurse two steps behind me. I want to draw in my sketchbook, but I'm not allowed to have a sharp pencil yet. I want to look out my window and see my neighbors, cars, even that asshole dog who lives next door, but the only thing I see is the closed courtyard of Stanton House.

Then there's the medication. The drugs Dr. Roberts has me on shut everything down. It's like my emotions are smothered under a giant pot lid. I can't access them. Not even enough to properly grieve my grandmother's passing. I can think about her death, sort of, but it's like this faraway thing, not really real.

As scary as it is, I *want* to feel. Honestly, that's the thing I hate most about the stuff they keep giving me—the disconnect. Makes me worry that I'll lose what little of myself remains. That I'll never be anything more than a pincushion to be injected and corralled and managed. Like a cow. A zombie cow. Oh, that would be a terrifying sight.

But I *do* deserve this. I am where I belong. Not a burden or a danger to Aunt Bel, who is finally free of dependents. She can have a life of her own. Wean herself off those true crime shows. She *needs* to quit smoking.

The Crying Knitter—I should find out her name— gathers up her invisible blanket, sniffles, then scurries out without looking at me. Her chair rocks gently in her wake. Ah, I have the room to myself, finally. I gaze outside, where a lead-gray sky hangs dangerously low over the parched lawn. A blanket of humidity weighs everything down. Even the air conditioning can't fully dispel it, which is saying something, because the air conditioning is downright arctic.

There's a strange charge to the air. I recognize it— everyone in these parts does. The strange quiet that portends a bad storm. It's been hanging over us for a few days now. Heaven knows, we need some rain. Everything is turning brown and dry. I sink into the cushions and let my thoughts unspool. The Library room has a camera, but from where I'm sitting, it only sees me from the back.

Only when I'm in a place not facing the cameras can I think about Dresden. And I *do* think of him, more often than I'd like. He was one of the few amazing things that actually happened in my life. Happened: not imagined or fantasized or conjured up. I don't know why he left, but I believe he wouldn't have, if he could have stayed. He'll always be my friend. No matter what I said to him. No matter what he said to me.

The floor creaks. I open my eyes and rear back with a gasp. The tall, thin man with the farmer's hat settles into the chair next to me. Up close, he's an absolute horror. His skin is like cracked leather as he sighs through the stitches keeping his lips closed. He gazes out at the dusty lawn through sunken, sewn-shut eyelids. Careful, even stitches made by someone a long time ago. Black thread, sewing shut the ways a human is a person.

"You," I whisper.

I turn around to call for someone, but Stitches turns and leans toward me. I shrink as far into the corner of my recliner as I can get. A low, gravelly voice fills not the air between us, but the interior of my skull.

Don't scream.

"Why?" I ask out loud. I don't know if this telepathy thing works both ways. My heart is thumping so hard, I can feel it throbbing in my eye sockets. I can only look at him for quick moments, he's so terrifying to gaze upon.

I'm not here to hurt you.

He smells like rotten teeth and fresh-cut hay. An odd combination made more disturbing by how much I've always *liked* the smell of hay. "What are you?"

A mistake. The very corners of his mouth curve up. *Relax. Your fear is distracting.*

"Well, I'm sorry, but you're a scary dude. How did you get in here?"

Stitches ignores my question. *Yet you don't find* him *scary.*

"Who him? You mean Dresden? Of course not. He's my friend." I whack my palm against the side of my head, as if that will dislodge the man's unwelcome voice from resonating through my skull. "Wait, are you real? Are you really here?"

Yes. Hitting yourself won't help. I would prefer you not injure yourself.

I cast another quick glance at him. "*Why* are you here?"

I'm curious about you. You have tremendous power over him.

"What power?" My voice is different just after I've had my meds. I can't get crisp edges to my words. "He left. And I don't have power. Not even over myself."

You are full of power. You are *power.*

"I'm a mental patient who's been committed. They don't even let me use a fork."

That is irrelevant.

"Oh, sure." This is feeling like a chat with a cranky uncle, and it's making me tired. "The fact that I have psychotic episodes is irrelevant."

He's trying to help you.

After a pause to comprehend, my belly does a weird flutter. "He can't help me."

He can. Promise you won't try to stop him.

"Why would I try—"

Promise.

"Okay, fine. I won't try to stop him." I blow out a breath and wave a hand when a puff of woodsmoke comes out of my mouth. "You're crazier than me, you know."

A rough, creaky noise scratches down the insides of my skull. It takes me a moment to figure out he's chuckling.

I don't have the luxury of madness.

Oh sure. Being this way is a luxury. This guy is getting on my nerves.

Maybe he heard that, because he gets to his feet slowly, like an old man. His joints let out a series of noisy pops and crunches. The air fills with that strange stench of decay and hay. Bony fingers tip his fraying hat.

Good day, Estelle Roane. You've been most enlightening. He starts walking away.

I spin in the chair. "Wait."

He pauses without turning.

"Why do you think Dresden can…help my condition?"

There's no answer for a moment. It goes on long enough for me to think the telepathic link is broken and I can't hear his answer. Or that he's just going to walk away without answering.

Because he caused it.

His words punctuate like hammer falls. I freeze in a

state between *no-freaking-way* and *of-course-why-didn't-I-think-of-that?*

Dresden didn't sting *me*, though. I push my sluggish mind to think back to that weird conversation I had with Dresden. We'd been talking about…my great-great-grandmother, Opal Wickerton. *Oh, Dresden.*

Can you forgive him?

Stitches's back is to me, but he still watches me. He doesn't use his eyes, after all. I blame the medication for slowing me down too much to answer or ask another question quick enough, because in a flash of light, Stitches is gone and there's a circle of darker wood on the hardwood where he stood. I'm alone in the Library room again, facing that stupid camera, winking a red light at me.

I turn back around and huddle in my chair. My thoughts are a disorganized ball of thread, knotted into a single impossible mess. A nurse comes into the room. Her sneakers squeak. Keys jangle at her waist.

"Are you okay, Essie?" she asks. "You were talking to yourself and appeared upset."

"I'm fine." I work hard to keep the trill out of my voice. "Sorry about that."

She hesitates at the dark stain on the floor, then squeaks out of the Library room.

I slump against the chair. Oh god, no one saw Stitches but me. No one *smelled* him. I eye the chair next to me with mistrust. That guy was *here*, I think. I don't care if he didn't show up on camera. *How did he not show up on the camera?* Well, he's telepathic. He can probably do a bunch of things that no one else can.

Unless he wasn't real. Oh, I don't want to go there.

I reach out, touch the cushion of the chair next to me. It's warm. I snatch my hand back.

It's *warm*, and there's no way The Crying Knitter's body heat would have held that long. Of course, I could be imagining the warmth, too. I run my fingers through my hair and squeeze until my scalp hurts.

I'm so tired of this—of not knowing whether something is really real or if I'm existing in an imagined landscape of my mind. I'm tired of either being slow and foggy with medication, or aware and delusional and possibly dangerous.

I envy Grandma Edie right now. It's terrible, and Aunt Bel would be so mad at me if she knew my thoughts. But my grandmother is free of the Wickerton curse, and how nice must that be? I don't know how to live like this and not hate myself.

And if Stitches *was* real and Dresden did *cause* the Wickerton curse, what did that mean? If he stung Opal Wickerton, it had to have been an accident, right? He said he only stung bad people. Then there's that strange promise Stitches made me make. Why, if Dresden *could* cure my insanity, would I try to stop him?

There, teetering on top of the pile of all these questions and uncertainty, is the one question—the question that I think Stitches came to find out, but I'm not sure if he did—if Dresden cursed my family...

Can I forgive him?

There is no mistaking the meaning. It's as clear as an unmedicated day. Could I accept that Dresden stung my ancestor and love him anyway?

I backpedal from it neatly—I'd only played with the idea of love in the first place. I hardly knew Dresden long enough to know if I loved him the way people are supposed to love each other. I'm not sure I'm capable of it.

I chew my lip, staring blindly outside at the brown grass, the tall fence surrounding Stanton House.

Somehow, this question, and my answer, are important. My answer has power.

On the other side of the window, it starts to rain.

25

Dresden

the
storm

I left Philadelphia immediately. I wanted to speed back, but to say I was depleted would be an understatement. I passed by crime-ridden neighborhoods, hospitals, corporate bank headquarters, skimming off as much fear and pain energy as I could find. It was like eating crumbs, compared to the powerful waves produced during a cataclysmic event. Never in my life have I wished more that I could fly on an airplane, but not even I can avoid scrutiny in places like airports, and the bees are not happy in enclosed places like planes, or tunnels, or underground places. It makes them feel contained, I suppose. They don't mind trains, though, and I did attach my swarm to a freight train heading west, which saved me time and precious energy.

Perhaps I am getting soft or spoiled, because I don't remember feeling this much discomfort during times of low energy before. There was a time when beekeepers didn't trail behind harbingers. This is how we all lived—

hungry, exhausted, alone.

So here I am, tumbling into Essie's backyard well after nightfall, six days after leaving her. My body has developed a tremble. My route from Pennsylvania back to Missouri is littered with the tiny bodies of dead bees, but Essie's house looks peaceful. The car is parked in the drive, and the lights are out, except for the glow of a TV set in Aunt Bel's room. The sight reassures me that the Wickerton house did not receive a visit from the killer during my absence, not that I thought he would, with Michael watching out for her. Essie is safe, and I owe him for that.

I want to see Essie—just check, to reassure myself that she's fine—but I feel like I'm moving under the weight of a boulder. Sleep rarely beckons me, but tonight it calls me like a siren. Being mindful of the cameras Essie told me her aunt had installed, I tuck myself in the narrow, leaf-filled space between the shed and the stockade fence. Consciousness slips away. The ground is lumpy with sticks and abandoned plastic plant pots, but as long as I am near *her*, I can find rest on a pile of bricks.

My body soaks up the pulse of fear, which now permeates the community thanks to the murders, the episodes of people acting out violently—all thanks to my stings. Doors that have never been locked are getting new deadbolts. Children who have enjoyed free range of the neighborhood are being corralled in their own backyards. Fear travels through the ground like a current, pressurizes the air like an electrical charge.

I wake up in early morning, bemused by the fact that I actually slept all night. First feelings, then bruises, now *sleep*. My body is nowhere near full strength, but I'm functioning. The tremble has eased, thankfully. The first glow of light is pushing back the shadows, but not by much. The sky above rumbles and sends down a steady rain. Great masses of furious clouds roll across the sky. It's not good, the way the clouds are moving. My stomach tightens at the erratic, churning patterns.

A storm is coming. *The* storm. The one that will scar this community for generations. The one that will end many lives. The harbingers are never wrong.

I change to bee form. The bees are sluggish this morning. They're not trying to take me over today, at least. I fly up to Essie's window, starving for a look at her. For this girl, I will find a way to die.

26

Essie

the
storm

It started like a thunderstorm, like they all do. Rain and rumbles. A furious sky. We knew it would be bad.

The weather services was tracking a line of severe storms.

The staff gets twitchy when the tornado watch goes up.

I keep my distance when the "watch" turns to a "warning," as the nurses grow claws and great, leathery wings, as they swoop up and down the halls. I'm not sure what to make of their transformation—whether they're mad at us, or just worried in general. I stay out of their way, just in case.

The morning "goals group" is cut short for preparations. They think the residents don't notice their worry, and some definitely don't, but I do. The winged nurses haul cases of water, locked cases of medical equipment to the basement with cell phones clamped in the crooks of their shoulders. Logically, I know these people have children to account for and pets to bring inside and homes to secure, yet here they are, stuck with us. I gather up the courage to offer to help carry stuff, but it just stresses them out more. One of them bares gleaming fangs at me.

Go watch TV in the Open room, Essie, she says.

So I sit on a chair and watch the Disney movie *Frozen*, which someone has put on *again*. I feel like a useless lump, doing nothing while the rain beats harder and the wind rattles the windows. My least favorite nurse calls me to Dr. Roberts's office for our ten-fifteen therapy session. I swallow a groan and get to my feet.

"We're still doing this in a tornado?" I ask.

"Essie, the weather reports say the tornado is going to miss us."

"Then why are you doing all this?"

"Standard preparatory procedure." Her eyes snap at me as she hooks a thumb toward the nurses' station. "They say we're *not* going to be hit with a tornado. Remember to consider good possibilities, not just the worst ones."

My eyes water from the effort not to roll them. This is the nurse most likely to add extra meds for contentious behavior. An eye roll could land me a few extra milligrams and, well, no thank you to that. I nod and go to Dr. Roberts's office at the end of the hall.

It's the same office I've visited for three years, but now I enter it through the door leading directly to the Stanton residences. Sitting in this chair, I could almost imagine Aunt Bel in the waiting room outside, crocheting to pass the time for my appointment to be over.

"How are you feeling, Essie?" Dr. Roberts asks, like he always does.

"Fine."

"Can you elaborate, please? What do you feel fine about?"

I sigh and tell him I'm worried about the weather, about my aunt alone in this, and he tells me that it's good to think of other people. He asks me how my medication is making me feel, and I tell him it feels like my head is floating two feet above my body. He nods and writes something down on his pad.

It's the usual set of questions. I don't think about them very much, I just answer them in the most efficient manner possible to get me out of this room and away from this man who sits too close and touches me when there's no reason to. His eyes are black today. Solid black all the way around, like smooth onyx in his sockets. I can't tell exactly where he's looking when his eyes are like that. That dead raccoon is back on his head and oh boy, does it stink.

Then he asks me a question: "Who is Dresden?"

I turn my head so fast, I almost get whiplash. "Where did you hear that name?"

"From you." He smiles. It's ugly and gloating, as if he's won a game. "Nurse Jill noted that you said that name numerous times yesterday in the Library room. She said it didn't sound like you were referring to the German city."

I clamp my mouth shut. *What does he know?* "I don't know. I don't remember."

He pats my hand, reassuringly, then leaves his hand there. I can't pull it free, because if I do his hand will be on my knee. I sneak a glance at the door. The lock is in place. A line of sweat crawls down my back.

"Essie, who do you think you were talking to yesterday?" he asks.

"No one."

He leans forward. "You were clearly having a discussion with someone we couldn't see, but *you* could. Unless you share your inner world with me, I can't help you."

"You can't help me," I say, squirming my hand and leg away from his touch. "All you do is dope me up so I can't form coherent thoughts, which I *don't* like, thank you." I raise my chin, scraping together a bit of courage. "And I'd appreciate it if you'd keep your hands off me."

"That sounded perfectly coherent to me," he says, brows dropping into a frown. "And confrontational."

A particularly bright lightning strike is followed by a loud crash of thunder. I let out a surprised yelp, as my nerves are a bit frayed. The lights flicker but stay on. For now. I shift out of my seat and edge toward the door. "I'd like to leave now."

"We are not finished." Something about him has shifted. I'm facing the real prospect of being alone in this room with Dr. Roberts when the lights go out. I must assert myself. I know this, but I'm not sure *how*.

Acting on impulse, I step toward him. Surprise is clear in his widened eyes and open mouth. He's used to me bending into shapes to get away from him. "You can't keep me here forever."

"I can keep you here as long as I wish." His voice is a whisper. There's no mistake now that he's looking me in a way he shouldn't. Coal-black eyes move down my form with slow, sickening deliberation. I was trying to stand up, make a point, but I just provoked him. My heart starts to pound. I shrink back too late. He moves in, keeping the space compressed, fetid with his breath.

"It doesn't have to be like this, Essie," he says. "We don't have to be adversaries."

"Don't touch me."

He smiles. A long, forked tongue flicks out, brushing my cheek. "Don't provoke me."

I take a deep breath. A clear head is what's needed here. "Okay," I say slowly.

"We have plenty of time, you know." He reaches out, pinches a few strands of my hair between his fingers and rubs them. "Plenty of time for you to revise your thinking."

"About what?" I ask, gulping back a wave of revulsion.

"Who is Dresden?" he asks, ignoring me. "An imaginary boyfriend?"

"Not imaginary," I say, even as my voice cracks. I've never felt so trapped in my life. "Touch me, and he'll come for you." I believe these words and I don't. I told Dresden to leave me alone, but a part of him remains in my heart, always. My hands make tight fists on my lap. If Dresden can wander the world for centuries, I can stand up to one perverted, power-tripping doctor.

I jerk back and break free of Dr. Roberts's touch, but as if he expected this, his fingers remain tight on my hair. Pain nips my scalp where the strands are ripped out. Fear clutches my gut as Dr. Roberts rubs the blond strands between his fingers. There is a look of pity on his face. "Poor little Essie. I don't see anyone here to rescue you."

No. I will not be pitied. Not by him. He chose the wrong sentiment, at the wrong time, to belittle me with. All I've gone through in the past month concentrates in this moment. It stacks up like a teetering tower of experiences, feelings, words, looks.

There was the way Dresden looked at me—never with pity, only with respect and….something big and soaring and *more*. There was how hard Aunt Bel fought—*is still fighting*—to keep me with her. There was Grandma Edie, who'd confide in me all the things she couldn't tell Aunt Bel. Because I understood. Because I wouldn't dismiss her. And yet, I always thought of myself as a *burden*.

Ah, that word. It defined much of my life. My father… how often had he called me that? But when I think of him now, I see a man thin as paper, and just as fragile. I may have a condition that causes me to see things that no one else can, but I *am loved*.

Loved. Wanted. *Needed*. Something shifts in my heart and mind like a bone snapping back into its socket. And then, this singular thought: *it isn't selfish to want more than this*.

Anger, unfamiliar and unexpected, courses through me. "It's never going to happen. *Never*." I hold his gaze. "I'm going to report you to the police."

"No one will believe you."

"You're wrong. Someone will." I tilt my head. "You may be the doctor and I may be the patient, but between the two of us, you're the one who poses a danger to yourself and others." I flash my teeth at that last bit. He likes that phrase. It helped him get me committed to this place.

His face goes splotchy and red, and his lips peel back to retort, when the tornado siren rips through the air. It blares loud and clear, even over the roar of the storm.

Dr. Roberts rears back, looks around wildly, as if he's afraid someone *has* just shown up to rescue me. The siren is a signal that a tornado is approaching. We rarely hear it, and as far as I know, a major tornado has never directly hit the town. No one has died from one in the town of Concordia.

Based on what Dresden told me about the harbingers,

this time may be the first.

The door to Dr. Roberts's office bursts open. A wide-eyed nurse hangs through the opening, one hand on the knob, the other on the doorframe. "We're moving them to the basement."

"Excellent, Lorraine," says Dr. Roberts. "I'm sure it will miss us, but get everyone downstairs, just to be safe. I'll meet you there in a moment."

The nurse's gaze falls to the two of us and lingers for just a moment.

"That will be all." There's a bite to Dr. Roberts's voice now that has her snapping her mouth closed and scurrying off. *Coward.* People don't see what they don't want to see.

"Now, where were we?" he asks, all silky voiced, as if there is no blaring tornado siren, no storm threatening to tear the roof off the building.

My anger catapults to panic. "We need to go—"

"I say when we go," he says. "And I say this session isn't over yet."

"We're getting a *tornado*," I holler back.

"No, we're not." He grabs my arm, hauls me toward him. There's a gleam to his eye that's just not right. He's always been creepy, but this is so far over the line, it's like he's become a different person. "I've been waiting for this, Essie. I won't be denied now."

I don't think I can overpower him. He's a full-sized man with some madness burning in his eyes, and I'm a terrified teenage girl. Maybe it's the storm. Maybe it's the overall panic in the building. Whatever triggers Dr. Roberts isn't something I or anyone else is going to talk him down from. But I can try to escape. I twist my arm from his grasp and dart for the door.

His hand closes on the back of my shirt. I'm jerked back against him, hard enough to knock the breath from my lungs. Panic makes my ears ring and my vision blur around the edges. The desk is within reach. I sweep my hand over it, and metal touches my fingers. A stapler. I grab it. It's not great, but it's something

Another bright flash and immediate deafening crash of thunder. The lights blink out, plunging the room into uneven shadows. The brightest light comes from the transformer box on the telephone pole outside the window. It's burst into flame. The air snaps with the smell of fried electronics.

I open my mouth and scream, even though I know no one will hear me.

I fight, beating him with the stapler and kicking, even though I know I cannot win.

27

Dresden

all the rage

I cluster on a pane of her window, but Essie is not in her room. Her bed is made, untouched. I look in the other bedroom windows. The grandmother's room is empty as well, as is the aunt's, the latter of whom I find downstairs in the kitchen. Essie's aunt looks absolutely horrible—one eye is rimmed with a fading green bruise, and both are puffed up so badly I can't imagine how she sees through them. She looks like she lost a brawl a week ago and hasn't slept since.

Something is terribly wrong here.

I watch the aunt for a few more minutes as she sits at the kitchen table frowning at the TV and drinking coffee. I don't know what I'm expecting to see—she's not going to conjure Essie from midair. Her eyes are glued to the Weather Channel. A red bar at the bottom scrolls a tornado watch. Soon, it will be a warning. Not soon enough, for many of the people here.

I fly to the empty house across the street and take

human form in the privacy of their backyard oak tree so I can think. Changing in daylight, in a populated place like this, is a risk, but my capacity for complex thought greatly diminishes when I'm in bee form. I crouch on a branch deep in the tree and stare through the leaves at Essie's house.

Panic scratches up my spine. Where is she? What happened here? If only I could ask the aunt, but the poor woman looks upset enough without me showing up at her doorstep asking about her niece. If anything happened to her…

No. I can't think like that. I can't even consider it.

Michael will know. He said he'd look out for her.

I change back into bees and fly to the motel they're staying at. The town is oddly quiet. Only a few cars ease up and down the street. They move with great care, as if trying to tiptoe around the storm. I arrive at the motel to see the cleaning cart sticking out of the open door and the back end of a woman dragging out a bag full of trash. They've checked out. Gone. They could be anywhere in town right now. They know where the worst of the chaos will be, and that's where they likely are, but I lack that particular talent. I also lack the time to go scouring the streets for them, but that's what I'm going to have to do.

A black cloud moves in the trees behind the motel. It's a swarm of bees. Another beekeeper. He's trying to get my attention.

Fresh nerves unsettle me. What is this about? The beekeeper's swarm moves erratically. The wind is picking up, flipping leaves over to reveal their pale backs. Sleet hits like cold needles on my skin.

I fly into the trees and change back to human, and the

other beekeeper does the same. I feel a modicum of relief to see Henrik perched in the tree with me. But I don't like the way he's holding himself. Like he's preparing for a blow.

"What is it?" I ask over the wind.

"I have a message for you," he says. "From the harbingers. They regret they could not wait here for your return, but the event is imminent." He glances to the sky. "There is very little time."

"What is it?" And when did everyone suddenly become chummy?

"The girl was put into a home for the mentally ill."

Fury wells up. My jaw unhinges, and bees pour from my mouth, swarm my neck like a ferocious scarf. "They put her in an institution?" I snarl. "She was fine with her aunt. She's not a danger to anyone."

Henrik cocks his head at me. He's so terribly interested in my reaction. "She witnessed her grandmother's passing, had a mental breakdown. Apparently, she became violent."

The aunt's black eye. "Oh, Essie," I whisper. She must loathe herself right now, for putting a mark on her beloved aunt. "She didn't mean it."

"No one does, when they are not in control of their actions."

I look up suddenly, unsure of Henrik's meaning. If he means to reprimand me for caring for a human girl, he can go straight to hell. He can—

"Come. I'll take you to her."

I narrow my eyes. "Why?"

This could be a trick. Some punishment for what he and others surely see as my behaving far outside accepted behavior. For drawing the attention of the Strawman.

He looks at the sky again. "Because I made a mistake, too, Dresden."

"What did you do?" I snarl, fists bunching. So help me, if he stung her—

"One of my bees stung her doctor," he replies. "The one who treats her. I didn't realize until—"

I grab Henrik by the front of his shirt and jerk him forward. His eyes widen, and he nearly tumbles from the tree.

Sirens rip through the air. Our gazes snap to the horizon.

"Sweet gods, look at that monster," Henrik murmurs.

The tornado is indeed a monster—wide and black, lacking the capricious funnel that is often seen curving from the sky. It looks like a massive churning column. It's in the distance, to the southwest, moving slowly.

"Where is she?" I demand.

"One-fifteen Chestnut Street," he replies. "It's called Stanton House."

I know where it is. It's the in-patient residence connected to Essie's doctor's office. I burst into bees and fly toward town. We sail over the tops of cars to avoid the worst gusts of wind, but it's still difficult flying. It's a good thing I'm in bee form right now, because I can't form any complex thoughts anyway. Panic and dread and an unspeakable fury are unhinging my mind.

Essie in the custody of Dr. Roberts is *bad*, and there is a depth of that word I'm grateful I can't fully explore right now. I don't know when Henrik stung him, how long the venom has been percolating in the doctor's brain. The man should not be alone with her. Probably should never have been, but a beekeeper sting could turn an inappropriate attraction into an attack.

Henrik, in bee form, zooms his swarm up beside me, then pulls ahead. If I had teeth right now, I'd gnash them. I have a bad moment deciding whether to let him pass, or to run his swarm into the side of a building.

Lightning spears through the sky. A hard gust of wind momentarily scatters my swarm. Hail pelts cars, roofs with ominous thuds. I put Henrik from my mind. He can follow, if he likes. He can't do more damage than he already has. The only thing that matters is getting to Essie.

Finally, I arrive in front of a large, white house with multiple additions tacked on over the years. It's stark and old and made of wood. It bears a small sign beside the door: THE STANTON HOUSE FOR WOMEN. It was not built to withstand a tornado.

I reform right there on the front lawn of the place, in full view of anyone who might be looking. Henrik appears next to me. The siren still screams over the roaring wind. The telephone pole in front of Stanton House is burning steadily, and a long black scar runs up the length of a towering pine tree in the front lawn. Lights are off everywhere.

Henrik turns his face up to the ice-chunked rain. "I did not know he was her doctor," he says again. "My bees chose him."

It's an apology, beekeeper style, and also a warning that this man is dangerous. It's something I already knew, but I suspect that the warning is for me to be prepared at what I may find inside this place.

"This isn't your concern." After all, I only asked him to leave Essie alone, which he did. Perhaps what is happening to Essie and me is so unprecedented, it's giving hope to other beekeepers. "You should go."

I run up the steps. The queen crawls around the area above my heart. I'm extra aware of her location, now that I know I have to capture and kill her somehow. She is agitated, adding to my discomfort because she goes around stinging my insides when she's truly upset. I feel the first pinch as my feet hit the steps. The second as my hand closes around the handle.

The door is locked, of course. I turn back into bees to find a way inside this infernal building. Henrik is gone.

I spot a rip in a screen in an upper-story window and head for it. It's not ideal. I have a lot of bees to funnel through, then navigate a cluttered storage space and get to the main level. It takes time and tests my thin patience. Furthermore, all the patients and staff have been herded to the basement. I arrive down there to find patients and staff congregated under one of the main support beams of the house. I scan the faces. No Essie. And no Dr. Roberts.

I debate, briefly, whether to stay in bee form or change to human—which would cause the least amount of panic?—then decide I don't care. The quickest way to get to Essie is as a man, so I transform behind the washer/dryers and step out into the room. Most of them don't even notice me, but one nurse does. Her mouth falls open, and her hand claps to her chest. I walk up to her, ignoring the choking noise she's making. She can freak out later. Right now, she'd better answer me.

"Where is Essie Roane?" I ask.

"She-she's not here?" the nurse stutters out.

I lean in, and now one other nurse and a few of the patients have noticed me. It's dark down here. There are a few battery-powered lanterns, and a generator is cranking out some very low lights by the stairs, but I think most of them don't actually see me, thanks to a trick of the magic. "Where," I grit out, "is she?"

"She was in therapy session with Dr. Roberts," the nurse gasps out. "They should be down any minute. Who *are* you? Why are you—?"

I turn and race up the stairs, leaving the nurse blubbering at me to stop. A window is broken out. The floor glitters with glass shards. Great gusts blow inside. Stanton House groans like a falling tree.

"Essie!" I call out, running down the hall, poking my head into rooms. It's so loud, I wouldn't hear her if she was screaming. There is an increasing roar, a sound unlike wind or rain or thunder: the tornado. It's the sound of pure terror for humans. Waves of fear pulse through the ground, the air, injecting me with strength, speed, energy. The bees buzz gleefully around and inside me.

Any other time I'd be basking in this, soaking in the energy, letting myself feel the immense gratification that comes with being fully charged. It's so fleeting, after all. It wears off so quickly. But now, the intense pleasure of it is distracting.

The bedrooms are all identical—tiny boxes with a bed and a dresser. Very little in the way of personal items. Impossible to tell which is Essie's, not that it matters. She's not hiding in one of them—there's no place to hide in them. I race down the longest hall to a metal door at the end, calling her name, panic riding me hard. I'm more afraid than I can remember being. More desperate than I've ever been.

I burst through the door at the end, swinging the thing off its hinges. Then, finally, I hear her. It's a muffled cry, not even a scream. It's a pleading sort of cry. The cry of one who thinks they are going to die.

I smash open the office door, and my vision goes red tinged.

Essie. Grappling with that shameful excuse for a doctor. She's on the floor, fighting, kicking, as he pulls at her pant legs. Her face is red and terrified and utterly furious. Tears shine on her cheeks, but she grips something and pummels him in the head with it. She's contorted, trying to escape him, and despite his good hold on her, she's not losing. Her blows are adrenaline fueled, and therefore brutal. Blood flows down his face so thick, he probably can't see. His energy is the sickest, most violent form of need. It feels like needles all over the skin.

Bees flood from my chest, enclosing me in a buzzing cloud.

His nose is bleeding. *Good for you, Essie.* Soon, all of him will be bleeding.

I reach down and pluck him off of her in one movement. Essie scrambles to safety. This is an advantage of being fully charged right now—my strength is greater than a normal man's. Surprised, the doctor clamors for release. He's without his glasses and smearing blood out of his eyes, so whether or not he can see me is a mystery. "What the hell?" Terror drains the color that had been flushing his cheeks. "Oh my God—what *are* you?"

My voice is ice as I fling him backward. "Your death."

Fear rims his eyes, but he doesn't completely back down. "This is not what it seems," he insists, voice pitching to a moan. "I love her. I've loved her for so long."

"This is something, but it isn't love." I send a look to Essie, who is hiding behind a wing-back chair. I can only see a sliver of her in the dark room, but she is safe.

"She and I—this is consensual." His fingers knot on either side of his head. "She's of legal age. I wasn't doing anything wrong!"

My control snaps. My plan to dispatch the man—incapacitate him quickly and get Essie out of there—gets complicated when I charge him, grabbing him by the throat and smashing him back against the wall. His hands are out. His voice begs for something—mercy, maybe. But I want him to suffer.

I call back my bees, watch with unholy glee as the man's fear turns to stark terror at the sight of a swarm of bees funneling into my throat. He looks as frightened as Essie had been, trying to break his grasp. I don't care that he's been influenced by Henrik's sting. My hand squeezes, tightening the tender airways and arteries there. This is effortless for me at my strongest. I look in his eyes, giving him enough time to really see what I am, to get a good look at my horrible face, without the tricks magic plays to make me look normal to the passing eye. The stink of released urine permeates the air.

"Now you know how *she* felt," I say, and I don't know if the howling between my ears is from the tornado or from the rage pounding through my skull. All I know is, I'm going to kill this man. He touched her, and I'm going to kill him.

As if from a far distance, I can hear Essie's voice. She's calling something, but it's so faint, I can't hold on to it. My hand squeezes. The doctor's eyes roll in their sockets.

Then arms band around my chest, pulling me off the doctor. I'm yanked backward. A voice sounds at my ear, speaking in a language long, long dead.

"Be still, Dresden." *Michael.*

I'm not done punishing. I let a fist fly, clipping the gasping doctor in the jaw and knocking him out cold. I draw my arm back again, but Michael catches my fist neatly in one ready hand and lowers it with slow deliberation. He's in control. I'm not. I'm as wild as my bees. A creature.

"Look at her," he says through his teeth.

"Dresden—don't!" A bloody stapler flies across the room and hits the wall, cutting through my fog of rage. "You're not a murderer."

I turn in Michael's grip. She stands there, so close. Facing me. Eyes wide, overflowing with tears. No hatred. No disgust. No fear. I pull in a ragged breath, ludicrously close to tears.

Michael lets me go, and I move to her. She reaches out, and we fall into each other. Her face crushes against my shirt. Her body fits against mine so perfectly, the thought of letting her go brings physical pain. I've never been *this* close to her. Her hair smells like lavender, feels like the finest satin. My mind reels—her closeness is a gift I never imagined I'd experience outside of my own imagination.

I could die like this, with her hair in my hands and her scent in my head. A shudder runs through me, and I feel them—tears falling from tear ducts unused for centuries.

"Amazing," Michael murmurs. His voice is wistful, but rough edged.

"You came back," she says against my chest.

"Always," I reply hoarsely. "Are you okay? Did he—"
But I know he didn't. Aside from a tear at the shoulder of her T-shirt, her clothes are intact. Her faculties are fine, considering the circumstances.

"I'm okay." She leans back, wipes the wetness on my cheek—her, comforting *me*, after she was nearly violated by her doctor.

"Your doctor was stung by a beekeeper. *Not* me," I quickly add. "It turned his unhealthy attraction to you into a violent obsession. I'm sorry I didn't get here sooner. I tried to—"

"Ssh." Her fingers brush my mouth. "You're here now. Don't leave again, okay?"

I pull her close again, so she can't see the tortured expression on my face. I will not promise this. If I do what I set out to do, I *will* leave her, and this life. She will be free to live a life she deserves. Love someone worthy of her, if such a man exists. I doubt he does.

He certainly isn't me.

The man on the floor groans, staggers to his feet. He blinks at Michael, then at Essie and me. His expression turns livid. Foul energy sprays off him like acid. He's fully gone. Nothing is left in him but the darkness that had been nibbling the edges of him for many years before Henrik came along and stung him.

"You let this monster touch you, but not me?" he snarls.

Essie goes tense as a rod. "*You're* the monster." Her eyes flash with righteousness and her unique flavor of mania. "And a shitty doctor. I'm still reporting you!"

Michael is restraining laughter, but I am finished with Dr. Roberts. I won't kill him, but he has spoken his last words to Essie. I step forward, blocking her view of him— and me—and open my mouth. Bees pour out in a violent buzzing cloud and fan out between us. A profound dread rolls over his face, and a whimper escapes Roberts's lips.

Then he turns and hurls himself through the window behind his desk. Blood streams off him as he runs into the heart of the storm, shrieking.

"Oh no." Essie points after him, her face stricken. "Should we—"

"No," Michael cuts her off. His eyes have turned deep garnet, as they always do when he's about to harvest death energy. "His fate is irreversible. His choices have brought him here."

"But he won't survive out there." She swallows, clearly conflicted.

"Neither will you, if you don't get someplace safe." Michael turns toward the window. Wisps of black fog curl from his lips. He leaps through the broken window, disappearing into the torrent outside.

Essie gasps. "What is he *doing?*"

"He's a harbinger of death," I say, snatching her around the waist before she rushes after them. "He's following his nature."

It is then that I notice how quiet it is suddenly. Still. Perhaps the storm has passed by this area. I look to the window the same moment Essie does. The sky is black. On the street outside, a car rises from the ground, delicately, as if suspended by wires. It wavers for a moment, then disappears upward.

"Run!" Essie screams in the split second before that car slams into the side of the building.

28

riding out
the beast

The rest of the windows blow out. Glass sprays like rain. Dresden shields me from the worst of it, but this is really the *least* of it.

The roar is back, louder than ten jet engines, more deadly than a pack of demons. Wind howls through the punched-out windows, hurling everything that's not nailed down.

The carpet glitters with broken glass. Dresden scoops me into his arms like I weigh nothing. That may or may not be real. I close my eyes and hold on tightly when Dresden turns toward the door. Right now, I want to survive.

I've never been through a tornado like this. Little ones that can be seen in the distance, more of a curiosity than a threat, have been my experience.

I wrap both fists in the front of Dresden's shirt. "The basement," I scream above the screaming wind.

He pauses. His body tenses, but then he barrels

down the hallway, through a door torn off its hinges. The basement entrance is in the kitchen. He seems to know the way.

There's a crushing, splintering sound. Patches of dark light and wind pass through openings above us—the roof has been ripped off the top of Stanton House. Dresden lets out a stream of foreign words that must be curses in another language. "I'm sorry, Essie," he says to me. "We lingered too long in the doctor's office. It will be my fault if the tornado pulls you away from me."

I want to tell him to shut up. I'd be dead if I was still up there with Dr. Roberts. The whipping air steals my breath and is so clogged with dirt and dust I can hardly breathe. I tuck my face against Dresden's shirt and breathe through the fabric, letting the smell of honey flood my senses and calm me.

I peek up and I wish I hadn't. Through gaps in the torn-up upper story, I can see the mouth of the monster. It's wavering, as if trying to decide what to destroy, who to kill.

Planks in the wood floor overhead pop off like matchsticks, pulled into the vortex. The building shakes violently. Hiding in a doorway won't help. We have moments to get underground, seconds, if that. A desk slams into Dresden's back, but he only stumbles a bit. He bolts for the kitchen. He's fast, but not fast enough.

The tornado makes its decision. It shifts toward Stanton House.

Dresden flies down the stairs as the roar threatens to split my eardrums. He makes a cage around me with his body, and we tumble downward. Despite the buffer of Dresden's body, it hurts. White light fills my vision when my head hits the corner of a step.

I'm completely jumbled up and bruised when we hit the bottom, but Dresden rolls easily to his feet and plunges into the first room to our left—it's a small root cellar of sorts, located on the opposite side of the basement from where the patients and staff are taking refuge. A narrow plate glass window provides a small amount of light, but the thick, warped glass offers no view outside, which is just as well. This small space is packed full with file boxes and old office supplies—computer monitors, printers—but the ceiling and walls are brick.

Dresden wedges between some boxes and crouches next to the wall with me, holding my bruised body with care. He lifts my hand and rests it on my chest. I hurt in so many places.

The monster passes overhead. The sound is unreal. The house is being torn apart, but the individual sounds of tearing wood and flying debris are swallowed by the rolling roar of the tornado. Dust rains from the ceiling as dirt-thick air pours into the basement. It's so hard to breathe, impossible to hear. Dresden curves his body over mine. His mouth whispers reassurance, sweet words just out of reach. I count the seconds. Fifteen, sixteen, seventeen. It feels like it takes an hour to get to twenty, twenty-five, twenty-six seconds.

And then it eases. The noise. The wind. The destruction.

Suddenly, my breathing is the loudest thing, and I can't quite get a hold on it. It's hitching all over the place.

Dresden falls silent. He cradles me against his chest, gazing at me as if committing my features to memory. His fingers shake as they brush hair from my face. His thumb tracing over my cheekbone. "Essie," he says softly.

I gaze up at him, following the kaleidoscope of features molding, reforming over his face. He's different from the cold boy with the chilling words I met in the playground of Baxter Park a month ago. I can't imagine the Dresden I met then holding me in his arms, looking down at me with so much emotion my heart squeezes. I forget the sparks dancing in my peripheral vision.

Can you forgive him?

"Are you okay?" he asks.

I give him a lopsided smile. "I'll be fine. Are *you* okay?"

His lips twitch. "Of course. I bungled that rescue terribly."

"I'm here, aren't I?"

"You are too kind to me." He leans down, rests his forehead against mine. "My sweet, brave Essie. I was afraid I'd lost you."

Thick black hair brushes my cheek. It's the closest he's ever been to me. The few times he's touched me have been reluctant, wary, but the arms around me now are strong and sure. His hands move over my back, sliding up my spine, barely testing the curve of my hip. I close my eyes and breathe in honey and the unique scent of him that reminds me of grass and fresh air.

His chest quietly hums with bees. They vibrate against my arm. Somewhere along the line, the bees have become a sound, sensation of comfort, safety.

Dresden's gaze briefly falls to my mouth, then back to my eyes. The moment stretches, charges with a current I've only felt the edges of with him, but was never locked into like this. Even as inexperienced as I am, I can tell he wants to kiss me. And I am certain I would like him to.

It doesn't even seem weird, and it probably should,

considering I could wind up with a number of different lips under mine. But a funny thing happened somewhere along the way—he just stopped looking unusual. He just looks like *him*, changing faces and all. And I like *him*. I lean forward to close the distance, to let him know that I don't care which of his lips kisses me. That I don't care what features happens to be on his face—I want this kiss, but he pulls back.

"No, Essie," he says roughly. "I can't."

"Why?"

"I'm lucky to have seen you, briefly, through my own eyes, but I won't kiss you with another's mouth. Please, don't ask that of me."

My heart pounds hard. It aches like my ribs are too small for it.

Stirring can be heard from my fellow patients and the staff on the other side of the basement. There's a good deal of crying and talking. Someone starts wailing, but it doesn't sound like anyone's hurt. Just scared. Just a little more broken than they were before.

"Why did you leave like that?" I ask him.

He pulls back, retracts like a turtle into a shell. "If I tell you, you'll despise me."

There is distance here that wasn't a few moments ago, making me regret my question. "Really? It's that bad?"

"Yes," he says so quietly he's almost inaudible. "I've done something I will never forgive myself for. And neither will you."

There's nothing to forgive.

"How do you know what I would or wouldn't forgive, if you don't tell me the truth?" My heart pounds. Good grief, what did he *do?* "I deserve an explanation."

He closes his eyes. "One of my bees stung your ancestor. It was an accident, but it doesn't change the fact that I'm the reason for the Wickerton curse." His face contorts in self-loathing. "It's my fault you suffer."

Air rushes from my chest in a rush. It's only *that*, which I already know about and am so ready to move on from, but this is clearly a big deal to him. I get that, I suppose, and at the same time I don't want it to be this *thing* between us. "You know, you shouldn't shoulder the blame for every bad thing even remotely connected to you. What about the people who made *you* this way? Aren't they at fault?"

"I–I don't know." He raises his gaze on a shaky breath. "How are you not furious?"

"I don't blame you for my great-great-grandmother's condition." I tilt my head to the side. He truly thought I'd hate him if I knew. The thought is so absurd a laugh bubbles up. *Literally*. The air fills with big, pink bubbles. He sees me watching them, and his expressions fold into sadness. "Dresden," I say. "I knew already. Stitches told me."

He frowns. "Stitches?"

"Yeah. That man with the sewn-up eyes and mouth," I reply. "He visited me in Stanton House." I want to tell him about the rest of the conversation. About the part where Stitches told me about Dresden being able reverse my condition, and the strange promise I made, but my tongue seizes up around the words. It feels like another brick on his load, and he looks upset enough about Stitches as it is.

"He *visited* you?" he asks on a sharp breath. "Did he touch you?"

"No," I say. "He was nice. Polite enough, too. Why are

you looking at me like that?"

"Because 'Stitches' is a creature called a Strawman. He creates evil. He likely caused the person who is murdering your family members to become psychotic. Are you sure he didn't touch you at all?"

I nod. "Positive. Do you think it was Dr. Roberts?"

He looks at me like he has no idea what I'm talking about. "You think your doctor is the killer?"

"After what he tried today, it's possible," I say. "He didn't care that a tornado was going to kill us, he just wanted to—"

He closes his eyes and places a finger to my lips. "Please. Just thinking about that makes my bees want to sting someone. I'm not sure about him. I saw the killer once, although he was covered head to toe and…" He shrugs with a shake of his head. "I don't know. Something about the body types didn't match. I'd be very surprised if he was the guy."

"You *saw* him?" I gasp. "When?"

"Outside your house," he replies with a wince. "I was keeping an eye out, and so was he, I guess. The police arrived before I could get any answers from him, and the Strawman grabbed him, and they disappeared when the police showed up."

I smack his chest. "You should have told me."

"I was trying to keep my distance," he says gruffly. "I can't think straight around you."

That makes a nice little warmth unfold in my chest and a smile curl my lips. "Thank you," I say. "You have the total opposite effect on me. I'm remarkably clear thinking when we're together."

He shifts in his seat, and his skin darkens. "Yes, well.

Regardless, I'm relieved that the Strawman didn't harm you. They're not known to be 'nice,' as you put it."

"What makes him so dangerous?"

"His touch leaves a black scar on a person's skin that turns off the light in a person, leaving only the dark. The killer who is targeting your family was touched by him."

His description pricks a memory, but I can't hold onto it enough for it to fully form. Dresden leans back as someone shuffles near the doorway, then back to the group down the hall. "People are on the move. We should go."

"Is it safe to leave?"

"I will keep you safe." Dresden lifts me gently. Keeping his head down, he carries me from the tiny room. The stairs are blocked, filled with debris. We peek around the corner, around a bank of industrial washer/dryers. Part of the basement on the other side is caved in.

There's no immediate way out that way. With the stairs covered, the bulkhead would be the only other exit, but that's crushed under the weight of part of the roof and what looks like a refrigerator, but I can't be sure. Every single nurse is trying to make calls on their cells while comforting patients and handing out water bottles. I hear one nurse mutter something about giving everyone a good dose of sedative until crews come to get them out.

Dresden draws me back to the cellar room we'd been in. He places both hands on the thick plate-glass window and pushes. To my surprise, the window frame comes out, emitting a grinding noise and a fresh puff of dust. Through the opening, I can see outside. What little there is to see. Debris covers the opening, which sits only a foot above ground level.

In the other part of the basement, the nurse yells at everyone to get away from the stairs as a fresh cascade of wreckage slides down and piles up at the base.

Dresden shoves the debris out of the way. He takes my hand and boosts me through the opening he made, and soon we're both standing outside on a patch of sodden grass and blinking at the transformed landscape. The rain is lessening. Already, the sun is trying to break through.

I stifle a cry at what I see. A wide swath of Concordia is simply flattened. Where we're at, in a less densely populated area, it doesn't look that bad, but to the south, where the center of town used to be, is a trail of rubble. Cars, crumpled and overturned, lie in strange places, like the tops of trees—the trees still standing, that is. Homes turned inside out, their contents disgorged on torn-up front lawns. Leroy Stanton the Third's once-proud manor house, turned home for the mentally ill, is a pile of wood. The buildings that connected to it that housed Dr. Roberts's practice are completely gone.

Dresden picks up a golf ball–sized piece of hail and places it against my forehead, where a knot is forming. "The others won't be able to get up those steps," Dresden says. "But they have food, water, fresh air, and the rescue crews will find them easily enough."

Sirens are starting to wail. Not the tornado-warning kind, thankfully those have ceased, but the fire-and-ambulance kind. Somewhere overhead, helicopter blades whip. Rescue is on the way.

A sob pulls from my belly. "My home is downtown," I choke out. "My aunt...oh, Aunt Bel!"

Dresden catches me as my knees give out. "I'll find her. *Look*," he says, pointing at the street. An ATV with police markings bounces over debris. "You'll be safe now. Let me find your aunt."

I nod, recognizing the Concordia P.D. emblem on the side of the ATV. The driver is tall and strong, but unmistakably familiar. "It's okay, it's only Detective Berk."

He narrows his eyes on the driver. "Do you know her?"

"Yes, she's—was—on the murder case. She's my cousin, so a possible target, and they took her off."

"Your cousin?" He frowns at Anne Marie Berk for a moment longer than necessary. "Do you trust her?"

"Of course," I say. "She and I go back. Before she was a detective she had to…deal with me a few times when my meds were off. She was nice. And like I said—she's my *cousin*." I frown at him, this time. "Why are you acting weird?"

"Don't know. Just…" He appears to shake off a thought. "I can't let her see me, and you need to get to a hospital. She's your cousin and a police officer." His hands scrape through his hair. "I'm acting paranoid. I just want you safe."

"Thank you." I link my fingers with his and squeeze his hand. Tears prick my eyes. "You should know it doesn't change my feelings for you, what happened with my great-great-grandmother."

He sighs. "It should, but I'll make it right, Essie. You need to know that. I'll find a way to make it right."

"How?" We're running out of time here. Detective Berk is almost here.

He gives the ATV and driver a stricken look and brushes fingers down my cheeks. "I will find your aunt. Make sure she takes you to the hospital. No stops along the way. I'll meet you there. Okay?"

"Okay," I say.

He gently dissolves into bee form and flies away, toward town. Toward the destruction and my aunt's house. My heart is a heavy weight in my chest. I'm tired of watching him leave.

Tires scrabble on gravel behind me. I turn to see Detective Berk jumping off the four-wheeler. "Essie?" She runs up to me, grabs me by the shoulders. "Are you okay?"

"Yes," I say in a distant voice. "I'm…fine. I wish everyone would stop asking me that."

She looks at the hail chunk I'm holding against my head. "You're not fine, clearly."

"Better off than most. Have you found my aunt?"

"Teams are getting out now. The National Guard has been called. Resources are pouring in from all over the state, but it will take time, Essie."

I nod to the pile of wood that used to be the Stanton House. "I think everyone's okay in there, in the basement. Except for, um, Dr. Roberts. He ran off."

"Yet you got out."

"Yes."

Her eyes narrow. "Who did I see you talking to just now?"

"No one."

"Essie, I saw you with a man."

I smile up at her. A wide, unrestrained smile. "Maybe you were seeing things, detective. It's been known to happen in our family."

Her lips thin. "Let's get going. I'll call in this location to get crews out here for these folks, if they aren't already en route." She tugs a helmet on my head and motions toward the ATV. "I have an extra shirt you can put on. You're wet and cold."

I do as she asks, and after she gets on the vehicle, I swing a leg over the seat and sit behind her. "I need to go to the hospital."

She looks over her shoulder. Her eyes are two glowing balls of coal, smoking in her eye sockets. "You got it, Essie. Hold on."

29

Dresden

aunt
bel

The center of Concordia is a wreck. I don't see Michael, but I glimpse others, moving around in their quiet way, collecting the energy of the dying. Tapping into the dark current of death. There are some new harbingers who have just arrived, drawn by the whiff of fresh death. They *are* scavengers, after all.

I travel through the town to find Essie's aunt. I desperately hope the woman is still alive. Without her, Essie has no one.

Her neighborhood is in bad shape. Some of the big trees withstood the winds, but most of the structures were damaged to one extent or another. Essie's house is one of the ones badly damaged but not destroyed. The garage is gone. The house's roof and part of the upstairs exterior has been peeled off like the front of a dollhouse. A bed and dresser sit undisturbed and exposed in a bedroom. The massive maple tree in their front yard fell onto Essie's room. But this is encouraging. If the house still stands, there's a chance Essie's aunt survived.

I group my swarm under a piece of roofing that now lies in the backyard and change to human shape. I climb over the debris and into Essie's house through the front door, which is surprisingly intact. There is some unfortunate irony in that the only time I can enter Essie's home the proper way is after a tornado has ripped it apart.

This is probably unwise. If Aunt Bel is alive and conscious, she's going to panic when she sees me. I never would have interfered with a human's plight in the old days. The "old days" being before I met Essie, of course. Now I'm a veritable humanitarian, scrambling through a pile of debris to rescue an aunt of the girl I'm in love with. The area is quiet. My hopes of finding the woman alive falter.

I move efficiently, scrambling over the strewn contents. The living room looks as if someone shook it and rolled it like dice in a cup. Furniture is scattered all over. A rustling sounds from the basement. The basement staircase is blocked by the hutch from the dining room. I move it and head down the creaky steps. Aunt Bel is down there. She's sitting on the floor, holding a cloth to a head wound, which is bleeding enthusiastically, and brandishing a large kitchen knife.

"Hello," I say, trying to keep in the shadows. "Are you hurt badly?"

She squints, puts down the cloth to her head, and picks up a flashlight. The beam hits me square in the face. I shield it with my hand, not because the light is hard on my eyes, but because I don't want to frighten her with my face. This close up, and with her looking so closely at me, the curse may not be able to conceal my true appearance from her.

"It's *you*." Her voice is touched with awe. She puts down the knife and picks up the cloth again, presses it to her head. The flashlight remains trained on me.

I flinch. My gut sinks. My skin is itchy, hands twitchy, and it occurs to me that I'm nervous meeting this woman. Her opinion of me matters, which is the most absurd thing ever. I have no chance of winning Essie's aunt's approval. *Ever*. All I could earn is her fear and disgust. I remind myself, firmly, that I'm not here to curry her favor, but to make sure she lives. That's it.

"We haven't met," I say. "My name is Dresden. I'm a friend of Essie's." *Why did I tell her my name?* "I came to see if you were hurt."

"Oh, I'm plenty hurt, but this little scratch is not the cause."

"You really should get looked over by a medic," I say. "That looks like quite a cut."

"Superficial, but it's going to need stitches." she says. "Head wounds always bleed like a son of a bitch." She holds up a hand. "Be a dear and help me up, will you?"

I hesitate, truly unsure of what she sees when she looks at me. A person wouldn't reach for the hand of a monster. Maybe the curse *is* hiding my true face. I take her hand and help her to her feet. She wobbles a little, and I steady her with a hand to her shoulders. "Are you okay?"

She shines that beam in my face again, so close I can feel the warmth of the bulb, but I don't move away. No reason, at this point.

"Of course I'm not okay," she says, waving the flashlight around. "A tornado just tore up my house."

I breathe out a sigh. She's fine. She'll survive, and Essie won't have to endure the loss of another loved one. Time to get out, now, before she looks too closely for the curse to veil me and she sees what I really look like. I turn to leave. "I'm very glad to hear it. I'll let you be. Medical personnel are—"

"Hey there. You're not leaving me down here, bleeding out of my head."

I really want to get out of here. I firmly tamp down the few bees trying to crawl from my mouth. "I'll make sure the rescue cre—"

"I'd be grateful for help out of this basement," she says with a dust-crinkled smile. "In case the whole shebang decides to cave in on me. And why aren't you with Essie? My lamb isn't hurt, is she?"

That stops me. "No, Essie is safe. How do you know—"

"Oh, I *know* who you are, Dresden," she says with a dismissive wave. "I swear. All young people think everyone over the age of forty is oblivious. That we don't pay attention to anything. Sorry about the knife, by the way. I thought you might be someone else." She holds out her arms and I, lacking any reasonable alternative, pick her up. She's a large woman, but I'm pumped full of energy, power, and lift her easily.

"Oh! My, my," Aunt Bel twitters in surprise. "I see why my lamb likes you. You're certainly quite *strong*."

My nerves spark anew. In a few moments I'll have brought Essie's aunt to the trashed first floor of her house. The curse is most effective in making the human eye slide away from me. The veil which disguises me will grow thinner and thinner the longer we are in contact. She studies me *so* closely. Chances are, she'll see me just fine in the light of day. There's nothing I can do to minimize my appearance once the curse's disguise fails. It's a risk I'll have to take.

Aunt Bel gestures to a backpack, which I pick up and hand to her. She holds it to her bosom and I carry her up to the battered remains of the kitchen. I put her down and turn my face away, but Aunt Bel takes my chin in her hand and turns me toward her like a mother about to scold an errant child. She examines me with a practiced eye. "Look at you. Your face really does change like that— you know, she really drew the transition accurately in her sketchbook. Thought you were something she imagined, but clearly, you're not. Unless the Wickerton curse has got hold of me, too, all of a sudden," she says with a chuckle. "So tell me something, young man, what exactly *are* you?"

"Um." My mind blanks. Of all the reactions Aunt Bel could have upon seeing the truth of me, curiosity wasn't one of them. Maybe she *is* affected by the Wickerton curse.

"Well? I asked you a question."

Good grief. How to explain myself briefly. "I'm a… beekeeper." My voice comes out rumbly, mumbling, and I have *no* idea how to go about explaining myself to her. I want to leave in the worst way to check in on Essie at the hospital. At the same time, I'm amazed that this conversation is even happening. "Do I not…frighten you?"

"Frighten me?" She blows out a breath. "Son, I'm a trauma nurse. Seen a lot of things more scary than your face. I don't know what a 'beekeeper' is, as I'm sure you don't mean it in the traditional sense, but my Essie cares for you. *That's* what matters to me."

"I…" *love her. Would do anything for her. Am so thankful that you aren't screaming at me right now.* "Okay."

She keeps the wadded-up cloth pressed hard to her head and hands me the backpack.

"That's got to get to those FBI people — *not* the police," she says urgently. "My girl isn't safe."

I take the backpack. "Essie *is* safe," I say. Best not to mention yet that her doctor attacked her. That's Essie's story to tell, how she chooses to tell it. "I left her with that female detective cousin working with the two of you."

Aunt Bel seizes my forearm. "*What* did you say?"

"The detective arrived on a police vehicle," I say, puzzled by the color draining from the older woman's cheeks.

"No. My God, tell me that's not true." Her grip on my arm tightens like a vise. "You need to find her, Dresden. *Now.*"

"Why?" I ask. "I'm meeting her at the hospital."

She rests her head back against the wall and closes her eyes. She appears to be fighting for consciousness. Maybe she's losing more blood than I thought. "You won't find her at the hospital." She jabs a finger at the backpack. "Keep it safe...find her..."

Aunt Bel's head rolls to the side as she falls to unconsciousness. I rush to her side and pick up the bloodied cloth she'd been holding there. The wound was barely bleeding, and it really was just a scratch. She doesn't appear to have any other wounds.

"She fainted."

I spin around at the voice. It's Lish, standing over me in a wide-legged, crossed-arm stance. She's wearing a man's clothes, clearly taken from someone's home.

"How do you know?" I ask.

"I'd know if she was dying. She's not." Lish nods to the

door. "You should take her advice. Find Essie."

But if Essie isn't at the hospital—and Bel seems certain Essie is not there—then I have no idea where to find her. *The backpack!* Aunt Bel knew something, and that must be in here. I unzip it and find a laptop and a file of papers inside. I put the kitchen table upright and place the laptop on it. Lish helps me wake it up, because I have very little experience with computers, and find files and files of...

"Looks like surveillance footage," Lish murmurs, after opening one of them and finding black-and-white scenes of the Roanes' property.

"Essie said her aunt had security cameras installed after Essie's family became the target of a killer." I point to one file on the desktop that's separated from the others. It's from a few nights ago. Lish opens it and hits play.

The recording shows the front stoop of their house and part of the driveway. A car drives up, parks across the street. A figure gets out, dressed in black—the same figure I saw watching her house that night—and walks to the front door. The person unlocks the door, looks around, inadvertently giving the camera a full look in the face, then enters the house. This time, the scarf is not over the face, but hanging around the neck—*her* neck. There is no mistaking who it is.

"Detective Berk. Her own *cousin*," I say with a strangled cry. My head spins with this new information and with the dawning realization that I sent her off with this person. "I didn't know. I thought it was a man."

"Typical." Lish shakes her head. "No one ever expects the woman, but we can be every bit as savage as a man."

"No one expects someone to murder their own

relatives." A few bees escape my hissing mouth. "I sent Essie off with her."

Lish waves away my bees this time, as if they're just a nuisance. "Then get the hell out of here. We'll take this stuff to the authorities. Find her."

"I don't know *where*." My voice is even, somehow, but I'm a shaking mess inside. How could I have been so foolish? I scan the pages spread out on the counter. Copies of autopsy reports from the string of murders, medical examiner notes, test results, police documents she should not have. I don't want to know how she got them. I riffle through the papers with shaking fingers. *Somewhere* in here there must be addresses.

"Beekeeper," Lish says.

"What?" I ask absently.

"Be what you are," she says. "You can find her. You don't need a map."

My fingers go still.

"The curse will lead you," she says. "You're not the only one watching her."

"What do you mean?" I ask. "Wait. Why are you *here*, Lish?"

"I want you to succeed, beekeeper. I want to believe that what we are can be undone." She rubs her mangled hands on her pants. "I can't go on like this much longer. The others don't know how close I am to...requesting the *mortouri*."

I swallow hard, pushing back a clot of honey and bees. "Even if I can free myself from the curse and die, the rest of you won't be changed."

"Oh, yes we will." She turns her one eye to the door. I can tell she's ready to leave, to absorb more death energy.

"We'll know it's possible. It won't be *a* story, but *our* story. It will be the hope I need to continue on." She pokes me in the chest. "You need to trust. There will be other harbingers. The ones who are trapped as birds. Where they are, you'll find her. Finish this, beekeeper."

She wants me to go searching for *harbingers*? I trust Michael, and the rest of his group to a smaller extent, but hunting around Concordia for a murder of crows that *may* have followed Essie is a tremendous risk that could cost time—time she doesn't have. Still, I don't see an alternative to Lish's suggestion.

I rub my chest, where the queen is settled under my heart. I think a wish, then change into bees.

30

Essie

the end
of the line

"Why aren't we at the hospital?" I ask. It's a reasonable question. Perfectly appropriate. So I'm not sure why we're *here*, at a ramshackle farmhouse on the edge of the Parker farm. A leaning garage sits fifty or so feet from the house. Crows make a dotted line up on the sagging roofline. They preen their feathers and watch. I feel very much on guard, and I'm not at all sure why. The smell of gasoline is so intense I nearly gag.

"The roads aren't passable." Detective Berk gets off the ATV and helps me off. She's so careful to keep my arm protected. So considerate. I'm mostly curious why we're here. Only a niggling worry picks the back of my mind. She stood up for me. She's on my side. Hell, she's my *cousin*.

Sodden corn stalks bow to the hot, damp wind rolling over the fields. The road is about a quarter mile away. It's quiet out here. Sirens scream in the distance.

Why do I hesitate on the muddy driveway? Why are

my instincts telling me to run from this house? After all I've been through today, I should be grateful for a friendly face. Her face is very friendly, except for those smoldering eyeballs. But that's not real. Not *really* real. I feel for my pocket and the baggie of contraband peppercorns inside, but of course they're not there. What I wouldn't give to pause everything and bite down on one. What I wouldn't give for one moment of clarity right now.

"Come inside, Essie," Detective Berk says. She's standing on the dilapidated front porch, and suddenly, she looks like a stranger. It could be that I'm used to her standard baggy pantsuit and scuffed pumps. She's wearing a rain-sodden sweat suit, and it must be uncomfortable, soaked like it is.

My feet just won't move. I can't fight it when they do this. "No thanks," I say. "I'll stay out here, if that's okay."

Her face pinches in annoyance. "Essie, don't be stupid. Come inside so I can see to that arm."

I shake my head. This doesn't fit. Something is out of sync, like Grandma Edie watching her television shows. I don't like how Detective Berk is looking at me. My heart beats faster.

My feet have no problem moving backward, away from her. Away from that house.

A roll of thunder rumbles the heavy air.

I act on instinct and nothing more. I turn and run.

Detective Berk lets out a growl, much like an animal, but she doesn't give chase. "You can't hide, Essie. You're the final piece. You and me. We're the last Wickerton women. We're going to end the curse, finally. Forever."

Oh boy, that sounds bad. And crazy. I run around to the other side of the garage. There's nowhere else to go, really. Behind that lies acres and acres of corn. I don't think I can outrun her. She's bigger and stronger than I am, and I'm particularly out of shape after spending the past few weeks convalescing at that damn Stanton House. I flatten against the back of the garage and drop to a crouch. My hand closes around a wooden handle, long since separated from its tool. I pick it up. I need a weapon. This is better than nothing, even if the wood is rotten.

Berk comes from the right, gun pointed at me. She looks like a demon straight out of hell — red skinned and smoldering all over, not just from the eyes. I'm so surprised I freeze.

"You're coming to the house, Essie," she says in a silky voice. "We're finishing this the way our great-great-grandmother Opal did — in flames."

That explains the gasoline smell. Cold sweat trickles down my back. I don't want to die like this. "Actually," I say, probably unwisely. "She hanged herself."

"It was fire. Everyone knows that."

"I'm telling you, Opal hanged herself from her clothesline." I can't believe this conversation is happening, but it offends me that she's got such a well-known bit of our family history wrong. And if she's planning to *kill us* based on it, it should be accurate. I know it's weird to worry about something like that, at a time like this, but unlike her, *I* never claimed to be sane. "Grandma Edie said it was hanging and she would know. *She* was alive for it."

"We'll break from tradition, then. Flames, for us. No one will pass these genes on." She steps closer, closer. She's right in front of me, and I can't move a muscle I'm so scared. The barrel of the gun presses cold and hard against my forehead.

"That hurts," I say.

Her voice, face soften. "I've always liked you, Essie. It's a shame about this," she says. "I wasn't going to kill you. You weren't going to have babies, were you? There was no way you could attract a guy, or even know what to do with one. You were going to rot in Stanton House with our elderly relatives. But you had to get a boyfriend—*don't* deny it—I saw you two together in your bedroom. I knew then that there was a chance you'd pass it on."

"You *saw* me?" I ask, surprised. "You were spying through my window?"

"I was. It was hard, deciding what to do with you," she replies. "But I can still be merciful. Would you like me to kill you first, then burn you?"

A crow on the roof above starts up a noisy cawing. The other two join in.

Tears gather in my eyes, even though I feel very far removed from my emotions at the moment. There's little I can do against a gun pressed to my forehead. I survived a tornado, a crazed doctor, to be murdered by my own cousin. My throat closes so tight I can barely speak. "Yes, please."

She nods. "I can do that. There doesn't have to be unnecessary pain. I didn't make the others suffer long. I killed them quickly and I'll do the same to you." She motions me toward the house, to walk in front of her. She lowers the gun.

She thinks you've submitted.

It's a voice, rasping in my head. A familiar voice that I'm sure isn't mine.

She thinks you're too weak to fight.

I look around, searching for the owner of the voice —
ah, I remember! It's the man with the sewn-up eyes and
mouth who visited me in Stanton House. "Stitches!" I call
out. "Are you here?"

No one's answers. It's just me and Berk and all
those crows. I wonder if they're sometimes people, like
Dresden's friend Michael.

"Shut up, Essie. No one's here." Berk looks so smug, so
sure of herself. So certain that I'll go quietly and gratefully
to my death. My hand tightens around the broom handle,
which I'd nearly forgotten. With a sudden burst, I swing,
slamming it into her face.

Her hand flies up to her nose, as surprised as I am that
I just did that. Blood pours from both nostrils.

I break into a run. I may be able to get to the road.
Someone driving by might stop for me.

Bullets crack the air.

Pop!

Pause.

Pop! Pop! Pop!

Pain sears my right leg. I go down hard, skidding in
the mud, but more from surprise than anything else. Her
shot grazed me, missing meat and bone and skimming
my skin. I climb to my feet slowly.

"That was bad of you, Essie." Berk stands over me, a
river of blood flowing down her face. None of the woman
I recognize remains. She is a thing of my worst nightmares.
Her skin smolders. Her features are transformed into the
most horrid hallucination my mind has ever conjured.

"You'll suffer for that." She grabs my arm and propels
me toward the house.

Her gun is at my ribs, now, and it twists painfully

against me. I hiss in pain and walk as she pushes me. I'm still holding that broom handle and whack at her with it, but my efforts are feeble. She doesn't even bother taking it away from me. She pulls me up the front steps. Blood pours down my leg and soaks my sock, leaving red footprints in the mud. She drags me inside and throws me on the floor. The stench of gas is so strong, it's hard to breathe.

My mouth tastes of bile. My ears ring, and I can't stop shaking. This is hopeless. My fingernails scrape on the scarred hardwood floor.

Berk kicks my hand, sending the broom handle—my only weapon—clattering to a corner. She crouches down, looks into my eyes. "The Wickerton line finally ends here, cousin. With us. Ready to die?"

Dresden

the
queen

I see the house. Six crows circle it in agitation. *Harbingers.* Another favor owed to a harbinger. To Lish, no less. These birds are on the fringe—ones unable or unwilling to change to human form. They're here to see what happens with me and Essie and the Strawman, who everyone fears. They, like Lish, are desperate for hope that they can escape their cursed existence. I can see it in the red of their eyes and their low-held heads. Not long ago, I would have scorned them. Now, I'm more hopeful than all of them.

I smash through a windowpane in a tornado of bees— thousands and thousands of them. Essie is on the floor, bleeding, crying. She's in considerably worse shape than last I saw her. Blood seeps from a wound in her right thigh.

Detective Berk looms above her, gun in hand, flushed with the righteous purpose seen in faces of cult leaders and the psychotic. Dark, shattering energy pulses from her in hot, sharp waves. Although it's unmistakable now, I have no idea why I didn't sense this before. The Strawman may have been able to mask it. It may have been a dormant thing, only waking and raging when she was out of her police uniform.

Berk's head snaps up. Her mouth opens in surprise, fear, at the sight of a massive swarm of bees. Tears streak down Essie's face. Her lips are moving, saying things I'm too frenzied to interpret. I bring my swarm straight to Berk. I cover her, covering every inch of her with bees. They know better than to touch Essie. Berk flails, swiping, jumping around like a madwoman. My intention is to sting her death, but the bees won't do it, no matter how much of my will I try to impose on them. I have more influence in bee form, but to my immense frustration, I can get no more than a couple stings—not enough to kill or incapacitate her.

Of course. We were not designed to do this. We were never meant to *be* killers, only infect with madness. I'm asking the bees to do something they were not designed to do and have never done before. We've never killed on purpose. Not like this. I draw back and take human form.

My hands are fists. My faces are changing so fast, I doubt I look like anything resembling human. I'm a ball of emotions, trembling with this primal need to protect this girl I've come to love.

I should have told her.

Berk kneels behind Essie and hooks one arm around Essie's throat. Essie struggles, clawing at her cousin's elbow while gasping for breath. Her gaze locks on mine. Her eyes dart to the open door, back to me. *Go*, she's telling me with her eyes. I won't. If it's the last thing I do, I will get her out of here.

I want to tear Berk's head off her body and slow-roast it on a spit.

"Oh look, Essie's lover boy has arrived." Berk presses the gun hard against Essie's gut, and my own clenches. "Back up or I'll make it painful for her," she rasps.

"You're going to kill her anyway," I say, circling to the right, her weaker side, since it's opposite the gun. "Why don't you shoot me instead."

"And waste my bullets?" she snarls at me. "He tells me beekeepers are impossible to kill. That you and your insects are cursed." She watches me, pivots as I turn. "He says you are a creature to be pitied."

He? Ah, the Strawman must have told her many things. Things no mortal should ever know. How else would she know anything about me? And *pitied?* I'd find that humorous if I wasn't quite so angry. "Think what you like of me," I say in a growl, "but let Essie go."

"Get out of here or I waste her now." Her voice pitches to a wail. She presses the barrel harder against Essie's tender skin, twists. "This is a *family* matter."

I back up, chilled by the ice in her words. She will pull that trigger if I can't distract her soon. "You're not in your right mind," I say to buy time. "You need help."

"I *need* to do this. Essie and I are the end. Do you hear me? After we're gone, there will be no more children born to suffer. No more!"

"And those other people you killed? Your other relatives who showed no signs of illness? Did they deserve to die, too?"

"They carried the gene," she replies.

My chest tightens. "Genes have nothing to do with it."

"It's hereditary! My mother was sane, but I wasn't.

Do you know how hard it was to hide it all these years? To ignore the voices, the obsessive thoughts? You have no idea."

I don't think I could hate myself more. *God*, the suffering I've caused this family. I take another step forward.

She shifts her aim to the gasoline canisters sitting in a corner. "We'll both go painful, if you come closer."

"Please," I say softly. "Essie is innocent."

"She's a scourge. Just like me. Just like *you*, you abomination."

"You're right about me, but she is nothing like you," I say. "Nothing like either of us."

"I'm going to kill her." Berk's voice holds some real regret. She looks down at Essie, who has stopped struggling. Her eyes are closed, but I can still feel her energy. I can still save her. "I'm sorry," she says. "I can tell you care for her."

"I more than care for her." My face throbs, it's shifting so quickly. I imagine it is nothing more than a grotesque twist of skin. Something half made of clay and melting in the sun.

All the feelings I've shunned, all the everything built up over too many years of living too long, explodes within me.

Love. Vengeance. Hatred. Injustice. Betrayal. Pain. So *much* pain. And love again. In the end, it all comes down to love.

The queen bee moves inside me, pacing little circles next to my heart. If I could kill her, both of these women would be freed of my curse—*just* mine, though. Berk was infected by a far worse one—the touch of the Strawman.

However, it may buy Essie some precious moments to escape. That's all she needs. Just a chance to get out of this house and run.

Reach deep inside yourself. The answer is there.

That's what the Strawman told me.

And suddenly, the answer *is* there. So clear, I don't know how I missed it. So obvious, I throw my head back and laugh. It was there all along, waiting for me to be desperate enough to see it and do the deed.

The queen sits behind my ribs.

Right *there.*

I unhinge my lower jaw. Bees fly in confused disarray. I don't think about it—I bend over and plunge my hand down my own throat. My hand scrapes over honeycomb, sticky honey. I feel the flesh of my throat tearing, ripping with every inch my hand advances. The thought flits into my mind that this should hurt more than it does.

I'm glad Essie can't see this. Berk is staring at me in horror.

The queen is down there, right *there.* My mouth is bent at an unnatural angle. I'm not even sure how I'm managing this, physically.

It occurs to me then, in a shocked surprise, that if I succeed at this, these are the last thoughts I'll ever have. I'll be done. Dead. I should be happy about that. I shouldn't be mourning the time I won't have with Essie, but I'm allowed a selfish thought just now.

Lights dance at the corners of my eyes as I shove my arm in deeper. It's starting to hurt badly now. My fingers grope through bees and honey, which drips from my nose. It's taking so much concentration to keep doing this. Self-preservation is kicking in, and I'm fighting the instinct to pull my hand out. Only thinking about Essie keeps me continuing on, tearing myself apart. Only *her*.

Finally, I feel the queen. Of the few bees that remain, she's the largest, and as always, I know just where she is. My fingers close around the tiny body—the queen who has been my partner in this hell for so many centuries. She struggles in my grasp, stinging me over and over, but I keep my grasp on her. Only now do I pull my hand out. Stuff comes with it, parts of me, but I don't look. My vision swirls with colors. Flashes of light explode behind my eyes.

I have very little time. My strength, the power I'd soaked in since the tornado deserts me. Dizziness overwhelms. There's no breathing—everything inside me between my mouth and my heart is shredded. I drop to my knees, bee clamped between my fingers.

I squeeze.

She pops like a grape, her tiny exoskeleton crunching like an ordinary bug, not the immortal creature she is. *Was*.

I open my eyes. Dead bees—the sum total of my swarm—fall like rain, dropping by the thousands to the floor.

Essie is starting to recover. I can hear her coughing, pulling in breath. I hope she didn't witness this.

Berk's lips slide over her teeth. Her sleeve rides up above her elbow, and I see a dark mark on her forearm. It's the shape of a handprint burned into her skin. The touch of a darkness nothing can undo.

"Bad move," Berk whispers, lifting the gun to the gasoline cans again. Her hand is shaking as she shoots, thankfully missing the can, but hitting a pool of gas soaking into the floorboards. It ignites into flame.

No! She's going to burn down the house. I am barely

conscious—*dying*. How am I going to get Essie out of here?

Time slows to a crawl. Dust suspends in the air. Flames cease their undulation. All movement, including my own, stagnates to one-thousandth of its normal speed, and a tall, thin man appears out of nowhere to stand next to Essie and Berk. He wears a wide-brimmed hat and looks at me through leathery, sewn-shut eyes. It is the Strawman, come to, what—*delay my death? Draw it out? To punish me?* Life drains from me in a slow leak.

Then, to my surprise, Essie pushes herself upright. One hand presses to the wound on her leg. She's not frozen. The Strawman exempted her from his power, for reasons beyond me.

Stitches stretch as those ancient lips curve into a tight smile. *You have righted your wrong, beekeeper.* He still speaks directly into my mind. *You are free.*

Free, but helpless to do anything, I watch as he turns to the girl I'm desperate to save. She gazes up at him, wide-eyed. She says something to the Strawman, but I can't make it out. My dying mind is done with thinking— done with *everything*. One by one, my senses gray out. My eyes slide shut, but not before I see him bend toward her, reach out a hand…

32

take my hand

Everything is still. Everything is silent, except for me and *him*.

"It's you." I blink up at the figure bending over me. "Hello Stitches."

Hello Essie.

The way he says my name in my mind sounds almost kind, but Dresden has assured me this creature is *not*. "Did you do this to my cousin?" I ask him. "Is she a monster because of you?"

I breathed life into what was already there.

His gaze moves dispassionately to Berk. He runs his fingers lightly, almost lovingly, under her chin. Over her eyelids, closing them. The moment her eyes close, her body slumps, slides to the floor in a heap. Her face is peaceful. A quiet smile curves her mouth.

I gasp in horror. "You just killed her!"

There's a weary, defeated look to Stitches.

I took her life weeks ago. Her body was soulless. Finished.

My mind is a strange place. My thoughts are a jumble of string, slowly untangling. One by one, strands slide free. *Free.*

I look to him, my Dresden. He just did something impossible and stuck his *whole hand* down his own throat. Yes, I saw it, but I'm uncertain whether it was real. It doesn't seem possible to do something like that. He's on the floor now, way too still. His eyes are closed. His lips are parted, as if he was about to call out, tell me to run. But I can't. I won't.

Dresden is dying.

"He is not. Beekeepers can't die."

Stitches heaves a great sigh. He shifts his weight, making that crackling, snapping sound.

He found a way. For you.

Stitches mentioned something about this. He made me promise not to stop Dresden from helping me, but *this* was not what I thought he meant. And I'm not sure it worked, anyway. I don't *feel* any different. I crawl to Dresden, ignoring the burning wound on my leg. It's not far, only a handful of feet. My hand finds his cheek. It's ashen. Blood shines on his lower lip. I gently wipe it off. "Don't let him die." I send the plea over my shoulder. "Fix him!"

The tall man glides close to us, sending a waft of straw and rot into my nostrils.

I cannot.

"Why?"

My power grows weak with each turn of the sun. The centuries' toll, I suppose.

"He found a way to break his curse, but you're going to let him die anyway?"

For others, death would be the greatest reward, but not for him. A grimace stretches the threads in his lips. *I steal light and spend darkness. I don't bring life, as mine is lost.*

He sounds almost regretful about this, and I can actually believe he would do something if he could. But he's just *too tired* to do it. Too empty of hope and belief in himself as capable of bringing anything but pain.

He spreads his hands.

I was not always like this.

His words bump through me. They mirror the ones Dresden told me, weeks ago in my bedroom. There'd been a desperation to him, too—for me to see beyond the shifting face to the young man inside. I remember this one thing Dresden told me, once: *You are light and grace and all the things I thought I had forgotten.*

You are light. It was one of the nicest things anyone had ever said to me.

I turn to Stitches. Desolation hangs in every line in his face. He's *not* that different from Dresden, when I first met him. "I forgive him." I nod toward Dresden. "*And* you. Can you forgive yourself?"

He shifts to the side, clearly unsettled, or surprised. For a moment, the flames around us begin to move, as his control over them slips. But just as quick, they're stilled again.

My power wanes. Unsurprisingly, he ignores my question. *I have nothing left, Essie.*

"I just survived an attack by my doctor, a mega-tornado—*for God's sake*—being shot in the leg and nearly killed by my own cousin. And that's just *today*. So don't tell me you have nothing left. There's *always* something left." I reach my hand toward him, palm up. "Take my hand. Let's do something that's never been done before."

Are you a sorceress?

"I'm a Wickerton."

He hesitates, motionless, then slowly extends a bony, desiccated hand. It slides into mine. A chill skitters down my arm, making me gasp. The cold is unreal, like ice through my veins. I grit my teeth and push back against it. How many times have I done this—fought against delusions and illusions and hallucinations? Enough times to make this mental muscle I'm using powerful.

If magic is created by people with intentions, then people have the ability to mold it, change it. With one hand on Dresden's sallow cheek and the other in the Strawman's shuddering grasp, I push all of my intention into the power roiling through me.

Magic pounds through me, scratching through my bones and electrifying my skin. Breathing becomes difficult, like my lungs are filling with something heavy and churning. Bubbles explode from my mouth, but I'm not laughing. It's more like a purge. Something dark explodes from me, from every pore. Something unwinds. Something else lies down and slumbers.

I don't know what I was expecting. This isn't the kind of thing anyone can prepare for.

This will destroy you. The Strawman's voice threads through the chaos of my mind.

I've been destroyed many times, I think in return. My hand stays tight around Dresden's. Magic made him a beekeeper. Magic will unmake him. *I always rebuild.*

33

Dresden

one last death

Like a switch, I'm aware again. I'm alive, as much as I can be, for as long as I can be. Flames have resumed licking the walls. Detective Berk, or whatever the Strawman had turned her into, lies on the floor, motionless. She's dead, as she gives off no energy at all. My gaze scans the room for Essie, but I don't see her. Suddenly, an arm twines under my armpits, tugs me backward. Breath puffs at my ear.

"Get up!" a girl shouts into the back of my head.

Essie!

I dig deep, unearth a spoonful of energy, and pedal my feet backward, grabbing traction and gaining a semi-standing position. Essie's arm tightens over my chest. She pulls me toward the open door. The Strawman stands in the middle of the room, unmoving, as the flames lick closer to him. Closer, until they ignite the cuffs of his sleeves. Still, he doesn't move.

Essie and I tumble from the farmhouse. We manage

to get to the edge of the field and collapse between rows of corn. It's as far as we can go, both of us with our broken bodies. I brace myself above the dirt, then vomit, repeatedly, uncontrollably. Chunks of honeycomb and a stream of honey spill from my mouth. Never have I known pain like this. I feel like I'm being turned inside out, but then, I am dying. Death is not supposed to be easy.

I feel Essie's hand on my face. She speaks soothing words I can't make out over the roaring in my ears. I catch snippets: *Hold on, Dresden… Stay with me… I'm here.*

You're going to be fine.

I love you.

Blackness takes over slowly, with darkness stealing my peripheral vision, then closing in on my mind like a warm blanket. It's impossible to fight. I'm dying, as I should.

I'm dying, and my only regret is not telling Essie that I loved her back.

34

Essie

the dead bees

The boy bleeds honey from his mouth. He doesn't move.

Crows let out loud caws and alight from their perches. They surround us, staring with bright, red-black eyes. I wave a hand at them. "Go!" I yell, although it's more of a croak. "Get help!"

A few take flight, but most stay where they are, watching the boy with the face that *doesn't* change anymore leak gold from his mouth. They watch me cry over him. They throw back their sleek black heads and scream at the sky.

I touch Dresden's face. It's smooth and still. Young and beautiful. Utterly at peace. Only his eyes are familiar. I've seen them once before, in my bedroom. A few weeks or a lifetime ago. There's no difference.

Dresden.

He isn't breathing. I don't feel a heartbeat. Panic ices my spine. I was *sure* that whatever magic I did with

Stitches would save Dresden's life. The power channeling through me had overwhelmed all of my senses, but the Strawman worked *with* me. I could feel his will pouring into the darkness he wielded, trying to turn destruction into something life-giving. He'd given everything to not destroy me, and in turn, I'd transferred what he had to Dresden. I'd *felt* the life surge in him. I'm certainly not giving up on him now.

A few years ago, I took a CPR course at the hospital, at Aunt Bel's insistence. *It's important*, she'd said. *You never know when you may get to save someone's life.* Little did I know. I do it exactly as I remember: Clear his mouth. Tilt his head. Pinch nostrils and breathe. My palms go to his chest. I pump to a count. Repeat breath. Repeat pumps.

My lips come away from his tasting of tear-salted honey. The tears are mine. I pump and breathe, pump and breathe. Over and over. Until my knees are numb from kneeling, my arms are trembling, and my head is dizzy from filling his lungs as well as mine.

My back is warm. The air is thick with smoke, which doesn't help. The farmhouse burns behind me.

I vaguely hear the ambulance arrive. Hands pull me off him and place him on a stretcher. Voices call for paddles and tubes and milligrams.

A blanket over my shoulders. A clear oxygen mask over my face. And questions:

What is your name, miss? We're from the Marshall County fire and rescue—was this your home? Who can we call? Good heavens—is that a gunshot *wound?*

I don't know. *Help him. Save him. Don't let him die.*

My mind does not feel like mine. I am alone—vacant in my own head—and the world is a stark, stripped-down place that is familiar and alien at the same time.

People, buildings, trees. Things are as they are. The sky doesn't bleed, although my leg does. A gurgle of laughter escapes my mouth, but bubbles do not. The world is unchanged.

But everything is different.

Someone picks me up and puts me on a stretcher. What for? My leg doesn't even hurt anymore. Nothing hurts, aside from this crushing press in my chest, like my heart is being squeezed out of my ribs. And the residual cold—a chill under my ribs I wonder if I'll ever fully be rid of.

My gaze is locked on the boy being whisked into the ambulance. Doors shut, and the ambulance tears off. Tires spit gravel.

"Will he be okay?" I ask.

"We don't know yet."

Oh Dresden. You better live. After all we went through, you'd better damn well live.

Dresden

one last
life

"Son, are you awake?"

The voice is male and unfamiliar. The other sounds are foreign, too. Beeping, whooshing, shoes slapping on a hard floor. It's hard to move. My body weighs a thousand pounds, and it's oddly quiet. The bees are being so still…

"Young man, my name is Doctor Beecham." He enunciates each word, pausing between each one. "Can you hear me?"

"Oh, move over," a gruff female voice takes over. "Look you, my girl is worried out of her mind over you, so open your eyes or I'll put something nice in your IV to pep you up."

"Belvedere, you can't just—" Dr. Beecham is cut off with some muted muttering and a rustling of clothing.

"Go on now, Aaron," she huffs at him. "This one's mine."

I blink my eyes open. The round face of Essie's Aunt

Bel slowly comes into focus. She peers down at me, frowning, then perks into a bright smile. "There's my boy. About time you woke up."

"What—" I can't say another word. My throat throbs. I press a hand to my neck. It *feels* intact.

"You're in a hospital, kiddo. You can thank Essie for that, and *me*, for making her take those CPR classes." She pats my cheek. "But thank-yous can wait. It'll be a while before your insides are healed up, so don't try to talk." Aunt Bel's smile widens as she shakes her head. "You're a lucky young man."

It finally occurs to me what she said: *You're in a hospital*. My eyes fly wide open. I look around. How did I get here? I must be terrifying everyone. My face...

She leans close on the pretense of checking my IV, but whispers in my ear. "Calm down, Brando. Your looks have improved considerably since last we met. No one's going to run in terror from this face you've got."

Brando? I bring my trembling hands up, tracing features so long missing they're new to me. My fingers stay there, waiting for the inevitable shift, but the face remains. I try to remember this nose, this mouth. I haven't felt them for so long, I can't believe they're mine.

Aunt Bel watches me with a bemused smirk. I can't hide my astonishment, the strange mix of confusion and relief and fear, too. The curse is...broken? I wasn't supposed to break the curse *and* live. My memories are fuzzy. I recall the Strawman telling me I righted my wrong, and that I was free. I recall tens of thousands of dying bees, carpeting the floor. And Essie, like a superhero, pulling me out of that burning building. What happened in between those two events?

My head aches at all the implications, possibilities. I'll think about them later. Right now, one of Aunt Bel's carefully drawn-on eyebrows rises. "You must have a hell of a story, kid. I can't wait to hear it, when you're healed up."

I point to my wrist, like a watch, and give her a questioning look.

"You've been under for week and a day," she replies. "Doctors had fun sewing up your trachea, bronchioles— you name it. *Three* surgeries. They are curious to know what happened to you." She pauses, drops her voice again. "Essie filled me in some, but it may be wise to claim a memory lapse on how your insides got torn up and honey poured down your throat."

"Ess...sie..."

"She's fine. Better than fine. You two are the luckiest people alive to escape a psychopath. Anne Marie Berk's body was found in the ashes of that house, which was her mother's old place. Journals found in her apartment in town detailed everything she did. Plus, I already had that security footage." She pushes hair off my forehead, pats my cheek. "We'll take care of you, Essie and I, until you're healed up. Then, we can talk about whatever comes next."

My gaze goes to the sound of a breathless gasp at the door.

It's *her*. She's on one crutch to support her injured leg, but she's smiling. At *me*. I've never seen anything more beautiful in the whole of my life.

I automatically try to sit up, but Aunt Bel presses me back into the mattress with one capable hand. "Lie still, champ. Dr. Beecham won't forgive me if you bust your stitches."

Essie hobbles over to me. She sets her crutch against the wall and sits on the side of the mattress, carefully moving tubes and wires. She's done this before. She must have sat here while I slept. The thought makes my eyes burn with tears.

"Dresden." Her voice is soft. Her eyes bright.

Aunt Bel moves toward the door. "Essie, remember he needs rest."

Essie doesn't seem to hear. She touches my cheek, my nose. Her fingers dance along my jaw. It's the sweetest agony.

"You took so long to wake up, we were worried," she says, then wrinkles her nose. "It's weird to see you with just one face. I keep expecting it to change."

So do I. I can't drag my gaze from *her*. She's still Essie, but she's different than she was. Her gaze stays on me. It doesn't drift off to look at all the other things her mind would show her. The curse is gone from her, but there's still a hint of something about the edges of her that will always make her a little bit different. *Thank goodness.* The girl I fell in love with is still there—*here*. Looking down at me so tenderly. I've never wanted to speak so badly.

There's so much I want to say, to ask. *How did we get rescued? Is your mind fully free of the venom I infected it with all those years ago? Is this really* my *face you're looking at? And*—unreasonably, but overwhelmingly, important—*do you like it?*

Perhaps the last was readable on my face, because she raises one brow. "You are absurdly handsome. My aunt thinks you look like Marlon Brando."

A flush heats my neck. Well that explains *that*.

I raise a hand, bring it to her cheek. "You oh...kay?"

I breathe-whisper the words.

"I'm good." She leans into my touch. "As good as I can be. You can't live so long with a condition like I had, then suddenly be fine, you know? My new doctor says it's like living your whole life on a boat, then trying to adapt to solid ground. So, it's...not easy.

"But I haven't had any hallucinations or difficulties with reality since the tornado." She brushes back her bangs and shows me a fading greenish bruise on her forehead. "Nothing a nice concussion can't cure, right? They're saying head trauma re-scrambled my eggs, even though that has never happened before. They just don't have an explanation. Not that they ever did. No doctor ever figured out what the Wickerton curse was, either. I know it was you who lifted it." Her brows lower into a fierce frown. "Shame on you, Dresden. I'm not worth trying to kill yourself over."

"You...are..." I slide my fingers into her hair, letting thick strands slide between my fingers. "Worth a... thousand...deaths."

Essie's hand covers mine. "And you're worth a lifetime of delusions." She pulls a folded letter out of her pocket. "A certain guy who can turn into a crow wanted me to give you this."

I take it from her, but don't open it yet. There's a ripple of guilt in my belly. I'm not going with Michael and his group this time. The four harbingers will be without a beekeeper trailing them around for the first time.

"You were in surgery when your friend, Michael, came by. He said that they couldn't stay any longer, but that you can keep in touch through email. It's in the letter." Essie tilts her head. "He also said that he's happy for you, but annoyed that you're better looking than him, now."

I smirk. He *would* be annoyed about that.

It will take a while to get used to being around her without worrying about scaring her or containing bees. My chest feels filled up and empty at the same time. It's just me now. No hive, no queen. It's so *quiet* inside me.

There is only the sound of my beating heart, and it beats for *this girl*. The only worry left is that she'll send me away. It's hard to say what she'll want now. The future is open to her. She has so many choices. So many options that don't include me. But no matter what she ultimately chooses, she'll know one thing: "I…love you," I say it clearly, although it hurts. "Loved you…since met you… Promise…won't leave unless…"

"Shut *up*, Dresden." She dips her head. Her lips touch mine hesitantly.

My first instinct is to pull away, but this is *my* mouth. My lips.

I have one last lifetime to live. Just one.

I gently lean up and kiss her, giving her plenty of time and space to pull back. Instead, her hand fists in the front of my hospital gown and her mouth parts over mine. My fingers thread into her hair, and I breathe into this first kiss, for both of us. I close my eyes and melt into a euphoria I'd completely underestimated.

Her lips curve against mine. "You still taste like honey."

"And you…peppercorns."

She laughs, but it fades quickly. "I'll always be a little different, you know. If you're looking for a typical girl, I'm not it."

"Don't want…typical," I rasp out. "Want…*you*."

If I could fully speak, I would remind her that I spent

the previous untold years as an immortal monster with a hive of bees in his chest. I'm not exactly typical, myself.

"After you get out of the hospital and are well again, Aunt Bel is taking the insurance money we're getting from the house and we're starting over fresh. We're moving away from here."

My heart beats faster. "To where?"

"Don't know yet. Somewhere where no one has heard of the Wickertons." She picks the edge of her finger, where the skin is red and peeling. Some habits arc hard to break. "Maybe Rhode Island, near the art school I was accepted to. I think I'd like to go."

I smile with genuine delight. *That* doesn't hurt, at least. "Won...derful!"

"It is, right?" She grins back with a little shrug. It's clear she's scared about it, too. "I turn eighteen next month. After what my father did when he visited last, Aunt Bel's new lawyer got me fully emancipated from him. So it's just me and Aunt Bel now."

My smile widens. That is the *best* thing that could have happened to her.

"Maybe, one day, if you want to, you can live near us." She swallows with effort and blows out a big breath. "My aunt thinks we should take this super slow. And she's right, you know? We should figure out who we are and what we want from life as people, before we do something stupid like get married or whatever." She rolls her eyes. "Like we'd do that. I mean, *you* may be an expert on marriage, but I want to go to art school and —"

I place my fingers over her lips, and a light blush pinkens her cheeks. It will be hard to keep my distance, but Aunt Bel is right. I have to relearn how to be a human, and find a path of my own, before I can be anything more than her friend and, hopefully, her boyfriend. "Anything... you want."

My new, curse-free body is weak with relief that she's not telling me there's no place in her life for me at all, *ever*. I would accept that, if it was her wish. Thankfully, it's not.

I kiss her again and smile up into her dreamy blue eyes. I could get used to this. "You...all I...wanted. I'm... in love...with you, Essie Roane."

"From my darkest depths to the lightest heights." She closes her eyes. "Whatever face you wear—I'm in love with *you*, Dresden. We'll figure out tomorrow together."

acknowledgments

This was one of those books that gets written, but you don't exactly know *how*. One day, you have an idea, and the next (it seems) there is a book. Obviously, it doesn't really work like that. It takes time to write a book, and it's a lot of work—don't think for a minute that it's not a lot of both those things—but sometimes a story takes over like a fever. You're a little unhinged. You're a little obsessed. You write until it's finished and then worry that you're showing everyone a naked picture of yourself. This was one of those books for me. This book is for everyone who falls in love with the villain. This book is for everyone who doesn't fit a mold—on the outside, or the inside, or both. Thank you to all my fellow wanderers.

Some wonderful people helped make this book possible. First, my agent, Beth Miller, who said yes to this book, and to me. Thank you for being in my corner on this wild ride.

A big thanks to Entangled Teen, especially my editor, Liz Pelletier, who I *knew* I could make fall in love with a beekeeper, and to the entire team for bringing this book to life. A special thank-you to Hannah, Shayla, and Melissa for being an amazing support and publicity team.

The loveliness of this cover had nothing to do with me, but rather, the talented designers at Deranged Doctor Designs. I have a preference for green covers, and I love this particular one.

Thank you to sensitivity readers Amanda Clavette and Maria Emil Deal for adding their voices to this book. I am so grateful for your perspectives, and for how they improved Essie's character.

I'm ever grateful to the supportive women of the Maine Romance Writers. You ladies are my rock.

Thank you to my girls, Mariah and Jess, whose friendship and encouragement and feedback mean the world to me, and special thanks to Katy, whose insights and support I appreciate so very much.

Thank you to the extraordinary Pintip Dunn, who I am grateful to call my friend. An hour is ten minutes, when it's spent on the phone with you.

I couldn't have done this without the loving support of my mom and dad, and my brother, Evan. Finally, a big thank you to Pete and Poppy. You inspire and challenge me. You're the reason for it all.

GRAB THE ENTANGLED TEEN RELEASES READERS ARE TALKING ABOUT!

SEVENTH BORN
BY MONICA SANZ

Sera dreams of becoming a detective and finding her family. When the brooding yet handsome Professor Barrington offers to assist her if she becomes his assistant, Sera is thrust into a world where someone is raising the dead and burning seventhborns alive. As Sera and Barrington work together to find the killer, she'll discover that some secrets are best left buried…and fire isn't the only thing that makes a witch burn.

HAVEN
BY MARY LINDSEY

Rain Ryland has always been on the outside, looking in, and he's fine with that. Until he meets Friederike Burkhart. She's not like normal teen girls. And someone wants her dead for it. Freddie warns he'd better stay far away if he wants to stay alive, but for the first time, Rain has something worth fighting for, worth living for. Worth dying for.

BRING ME THEIR HEARTS
BY SARA WOLF

Zera is a Heartless—the immortal, unaging soldier of the witch Nightsinger. With her heart in a jar under Nightsinger's control, she serves the witch unquestioningly. Until Nightsinger asks Zera for a prince's heart in exchange for her own.

No one can challenge Crown Prince Lucien d'Malvane...until the arrival of Lady Zera. She's inelegant, smart-mouthed, carefree, and out for his blood. The prince's honor has him quickly aiming for her throat.

So begins a game of cat and mouse between a girl with nothing to lose and a boy who has it all.

Winner takes the loser's heart.

Literally.

TRUE STORM
BY L.E. STERLING

All is not well in Plague-ravaged Dominion City. The Watchers have come out of hiding, spreading chaos and death throughout the city, and suddenly Lucy finds herself torn between three men with secrets of their own. Betrayal is a cruel lesson, and to survive this deadly game of politics, Lucy is forced into agreeing to a marriage of convenience. But DNA isn't the only thing they want from Lucy...or her sister.

By a Charm and a Curse
By Jaime Questell

Forced to travel through Texas with the enigmatic Carnival Fantastic, Emmaline is completely trapped. Breaking the curse holding the carnival together seems like her only chance at freedom, but with no curse, there's no charm, either—dooming everyone who calls the Carnival Fantastic home. Including the boy she's afraid she's falling for. Everything—including his life—could end with just one kiss.

The November Girl
by Lydia Kang

I'm Anda, and the lake is my mother. I am the November storms that terrify sailors, and with their deaths, I keep the island alive.

Hector has come to Isle Royale to hide. My little island on Lake Superior is shut down for the winter, and there's no one here but me. And now him.

Hector is running from the violence in his life, but violence runs through my veins. I should send him away. But I'm half-human, too, and Hector makes me want to listen to my foolish, half-human heart. And if do, I can't protect him from the storms coming for us.

entangled teen

an imprint of Entangled Publishing LLC